Assumed Engagement

By Kara Louise

ISBN 978-1-4357-3282-7

Published by Heartworks Publication

Printed in the United States of America

Library of Congress Cataloging-in-Publication Data

Kara Louise
Assumed Engagement

Note from the author~

This was the first novel I wrote based on
Jane Austen's *Pride and Prejudice*.
It started out on paper to be only about seven chapters,
but as I began to write, it grew and grew.

When I first posted this story, it was done without any editing.
To put it in book form, I had the excellent help of Mary Ann,
who has helped me now edit all my books.
I thank her immensely. She does a great job!

I owe all my inspiration to Jane Austen,
who gave us her story and characters
that continue to touch the hearts of people today.

As with my other stories, I hope you find this enjoyable.

Chapter 1

This story begins at the conclusion of Chapter 36 in Pride and Prejudice.

Fitzwilliam Darcy paced around his room in a highly agitated state. He was packed and more than ready to leave and wondered of his cousin's tardiness. They had both gone to Hunsford Parsonage to bid their farewells to the Collinses and their guests, but Darcy had not remained to wait on Miss Elizabeth Bennet, who was, they assumed, out on one of her favoured walks. Darcy knew for a fact that she was. He had encountered her earlier and had presented her with a letter, explaining the facts of his dealings with Mr. Wickham and the reasons for his interference with her sister and Mr. Bingley. He departed the parsonage quickly, not wishing to encounter her again. His heart still stung from the fierceness of her words in refusing his proposal. His cousin, Colonel Richard Fitzwilliam, apparently had remained at the parsonage, hoping she would return so he could see her once more before he left.

Darcy remained in his room, steadfastly intent on avoiding his aunt's merciless ranting. His only hope for sanity was to keep himself sequestered in his room until it was time to depart. His plans were to go north with Richard where they both had business. From there, he would go to Pemberley for a short duration before returning to London, where he would be reunited with his sister once again. He ached inside for the return of sanity to his life, his own home and surroundings, and his closest living relative, his sister, Georgiana.

Ever since coming to Kent and to the home of his aunt in Rosings, he had been tormented by the presence of Elizabeth Bennet, whom he had been trying to put out of his mind these past few months. Her unexpected presence there at the home of his aunt's clergyman unnerved him greatly. He found himself conflicted in his heart and mind. His heart had ached for the sight of her, for the light, playfulness of her nature, her fine, attractive eyes, her sparkling reason and wit. His mind had argued with assiduous reason against her station in life, how she was so decidedly beneath him. Then there was her family…

Durnham, Darcy's manservant, and Winston, his driver, had the carriage packed and waiting. He watched from his window, anxiously keeping an eye open for Fitzwilliam. *Where is my blasted cousin?* He wanted nothing but to depart.

He finally spied him coming down the lane and gathered his composure to venture out of his chambers and face him, his aunt, and his cousin, Anne, as he set out to take leave. As Fitzwilliam entered, he could hear his aunt's voice raise two octaves in her distress at them having to depart so soon. Darcy knew that if he waited just a few moments before joining them, his cousin would be more than ready to depart immediately and thus be free from his aunt's invectives.

When he finally took the stairs down to join them, he steeled himself for another onslaught, but quickly came to his cousin's rescue and sent him off to some last minute preparations before leaving. Darcy walked out with his aunt, expressing his gratitude for her gracious hospitality during their visit and assuring her that he would come again as circumstance allowed.

"Oh, my dear nephew, please make it soon and plan to stay longer next time. I know how much you love spending time with Anne and me. Please do not make yourself so scarce around here. You know you are welcome anytime and next time you must bring Georgiana!"

"Yes, Aunt, thank you."

Fitzwilliam finally returned. They both kissed their aunt goodbye, and quickly climbed into Darcy's carriage. The façade of friendliness and a smiling face was beginning to take its toll on Darcy. He settled into his seat and his head turned instantly to the window. He knew this was going to be a long ride and only hoped that his cousin was not in a very talkative mood. He trusted his body posture would indicate to him his desire to be left alone.

As the carriage pulled away, Fitzwilliam sighed. "What a wonderful time we had here, Darcy! I must say that it was surely made a bit livelier by the presence of Miss Elizabeth Bennet. Would you not agree?"

"I cannot say that it was."

Fitzwilliam cocked his head and gazed upon him curiously. *He is in one of his moods again, I fear. This is going to be a very long ride.* "Unfortunately I was not able to bid her farewell this morning."

Darcy had looked away and had not heard what he said. "Excuse me?"

Fitzwilliam shook his head. "Miss Bennet. She never returned from her walk. It is unfortunate we were not able to pay our respects before we left."

Darcy's only response was a "hmmph!"

Fitzwilliam recalled how animatedly Darcy had spoken of Miss Bennet before they arrived in Rosings and how surprised and uncollected he became when he found out she was but next door. Something must have happened in their time here to have brought about this change, but knowing Darcy as well as he did, he knew he would not disclose anything to him unless he really wanted to. There was no sense in even trying to pry it out of him. He would have to wait.

Darcy pulled out a book, hoping that would dissuade Fitzwilliam from any unwanted conversation. But as the carriage drove through the woods past Hunsford, he could not help but look out the window, hoping to get one last glance at Elizabeth. *What was she thinking now that she had read the letter? Are her feelings against me stronger than ever or have they softened?* He shook his head, feelings of remorse filling him as he recalled the scene from yesterday.

As they passed the parsonage, he took a last look and wondered if she had indeed returned. He caught Fitzwilliam's eyes, which held a knowing gleam in them. The look Darcy returned to his cousin gave him every determination *not* to inquire of his thoughts at the moment.

Darcy returned to his book, trying to recall what he had last read in it. *What was the plot?* He looked at the last few pages and finally recollected the narrative. His eyes followed the words down the page, but as he found himself at the top of the following one, he realized he had not comprehended anything from it. He went back to the top of the former page and began again.

Fitzwilliam knew the degree to which Darcy enjoyed reading and how he devoured a book. He was quite amazed at the length of time he was spending on one page. He sat back and watched, contemplating what was unnerving this man!

Darcy felt uneasy under Fitzwilliam's scrutiny. He finally looked up and grumbled, "Richard! Would you be so kind as to refrain from staring! I find it extremely difficult to concentrate on this book with you eyeing me in that manner!"

Fitzwilliam could no longer hold his tongue. "What is this, Darcy? You have appeared quite disturbed all morning! What is weighing on your mind? We have quite a long ride ahead of us and I would be more than willing to lend my ear."

"There is nothing wrong with me that a bit of silence will not cure! Now, if you please, let me get back to my book, and you… you do what you wish, but leave me be." With that, Darcy returned to his book, intent on grasping each word on the page and losing himself to the story before him.

Fitzwilliam smiled. *Oh, to be a man tortured by love*!

The day's travel was interrupted only by a stop in a small town for a quick meal and to freshen up. There had been few attempts at conversation and Fitzwilliam was grateful that as the day drew on, Darcy became slightly more agreeable in returning a discourse. Whatever had been distressing him was slowly dissipating, at least on the surface. His eyes still betrayed the struggle that was going on inside of him.

The sun disappeared from the horizon and Darcy was glad for the darkness that began enclosing them. It soothed his soul, as he felt it was somewhat akin to the darkness inside him. He cast a glance at his cousin and was grateful to find that he had dozed off. He knew how to put on a mask around people with whom he was not acquainted, but found it very difficult to do so around those he knew well, and Fitzwilliam was one he knew and admired greatly. He was convinced, though, that he could tell *no one*, not even his cousin, of his proposal to Elizabeth and her subsequent refusal.

His only concern was that blasted letter he had written to Georgiana just three days prior, eager to tell her of his intent to ask for the hand of his beloved Elizabeth in marriage. He anticipated in his letter to her that he would return to London in a week or two and would impart all the pleasant details to her then. His greatest joy was that she would be getting an admirable, new sister!

He had requested that she keep this a secret at present as things would probably not be finalized yet, not being certain when he would have the opportunity to meet with her father. But even with the assurance that Georgiana would keep silent, he greatly feared that someone might somehow find out. How could he face anyone, knowing he had been slighted; and by a woman who should have been most grateful for an offer of marriage by a man of his means?

On proper reflection, however, he realized that Elizabeth's refusal was the very thing that confirmed in his heart that she was the woman he wanted for his wife. She was not, by any means, persuaded to love, or even accept him, because of his wealth. It was almost due to her indifference to him that he was so attracted to her; in addition there was her beauty, grace, wit…

Oh, it is no use! he thought to himself as a frustrated moan escaped him.

"Pardon me, Darcy. Did you say something?" asked Fitzwilliam, awakening from his light sleep.

"No. I am merely tired and sore. I hope it is not much longer." He shifted in his seat, hoping to appear to his cousin that he was stiff from sitting so long. In reality, it was due to the uncomfortable direction his thoughts had been going.

When they reached their final destination, both men exited the carriage and gratefully stretched their legs. Darcy and Durnham moved towards his room with his trunks, leaving Fitzwilliam to wonder what agonies his cousin was suffering. He doubted that their three days here would enlighten him much, as once Darcy began his business dealings, nothing would distract him. He consoled himself that maybe one day he would know, but now he could only conjecture that it was due to a broken heart.

The three days passed quickly and Darcy was glad for the diversion of work. He had people with whom he had to meet concerning his properties and was also giving instruction and advice to his cousin regarding some business ventures. He found that the challenge and thrill of seeing his business transactions fruitful made his thoughts stray less and less to his days at Rosings and one particular young lady with very fine eyes.

By the end of the three days, he was ready to depart. Fitzwilliam would remain one additional day and then leave for the country to visit his family. Darcy was anxious to get back to Pemberley.

"Well, Darcy," began Fitzwilliam. "It has been most enjoyable and profitable for me to have had this time with you. I am most grateful for your patience with me and your generous instruction."

"It is nothing, Richard. Give my regard to your family when you see them next."

"I will. And you do the same… especially to Georgiana."

"Till we meet again," said Darcy as he pulled himself into the carriage.

As he seated himself, he turned to look at Fitzwilliam. His cousin offered him a very half-hearted smile as the carriage pulled away. *He knew there was something wrong,* he thought. *I am most grateful that he did not press me for details. When I am old and grey and can look back on this and laugh, I might confide in him.*

Darcy leaned his head back and sighed. This would be a difficult journey. The solitude would indeed give him much time to think and ponder. His mind would have little restraint and yet he felt he needed to rein in his thoughts to avoid thinking of *her!* He looked down at his book and felt very little inspiration to pick it up and read. No, he would wait. He opened his satchel and took out some papers from a business transaction he had just finalized. He read them over and found himself soon tiring of them and closed his eyes.

Behind his closed eyes was suddenly a pair of the finest eyes of a beautiful young lady, beholding him and smiling. Suddenly they became dark and angry and she turned from him. Gradually she began to fade away. Could he really let her fade from his thoughts like this? Would he be able to do it? Would he be able to find some other, more suitable woman to be his wife? Certainly there was no other woman in his acquaintance now; he must set out to meet others. But he knew that he would always hold out the comparison to Elizabeth. Any other woman would most certainly fall short; would always be second best.

Darcy let out a deep sigh, his elbow resting on the window and his fist coming up to make a rest for his jaw. Both his jaw and fist tightened as he contemplated getting on with his life without Elizabeth. If only he had listened to his own advice to Bingley in discouraging him from pursuing a relationship with Elizabeth's sister, Jane, and heeded it himself! Why could he not have done that! If he had, he would never have proposed and he would only have had to deal with some momentary disappointment in letting go of his feelings for Elizabeth instead of the horrendous humiliation at being rejected by her.

He had been presumptuous in his thinking that Elizabeth would agree to marry him. He had not courted her in a manner that was proper; at least in any way that was apparent to her. He had so relished their sharp, witty conversations together and had on many occasions simply enjoyed being in her presence. But these feelings of delight had not been reciprocated on her part. He had been a fool! And he had no one to blame but himself.

When the carriage stopped at midday, Darcy was amazed at how quickly the time had passed and realized they were but a few hours from Pemberley. Again, he gratefully stepped out and let his long legs extend to their fullest; then went to an inn to refresh and obtain something to eat.

When he returned, he saw that the sky ahead was getting dark.

Winston, who was a very capable and conscientious driver, looked to his master. "Sir, it looks like a storm up ahead. Do you think we ought to remain here for the night and wait out the bad weather? They can put us up for the night at the inn."

Darcy considered this, but knowing how close they were to Pemberley, advised his driver and valet that he wanted to continue on.

"Right, Sir."

Seated once again in the carriage, Darcy determined that for the remainder of the journey he would have to regulate his thoughts. He had to begin now! He thought of his father and how he often would go to him for advice; how he wished he were still here now to advise him. Would he have been able to confide in him the particulars of this situation? He knew not, but at the moment he wished to hear his words of compassion and wisdom.

Within an hour of their setting out again, raindrops began to splatter around them. Darcy hoped it would only be an insignificant storm, although as he looked out through the window, he saw the dark clouds looming ahead. Soon, flashes of lightning and claps of thunder exploded around them. Darcy knew that the roads would soon be muddy and was grateful for the excellent repair his carriage was in. He regretted, though, his decision to go on ahead, as it was going to be a difficult journey. They were now fairly far into the countryside and there would be no place to stop until they reached Lambton.

He could feel the difference in the ride of the carriage as the roads became more and more difficult to manoeuvre. He lifted up a silent prayer that they would make it through safely. Suddenly there was a tremendous bump and Darcy felt the carriage rock. It went from one side to the other and he let out a shout as his arms reached out to try to balance himself.

A loud cracking sound was heard as the carriage suddenly turned on its side. Darcy felt a stabbing pain in his back and then, as the carriage went off the side of the road and landed on its top, Darcy hit his head and found himself in darkness, quiet, and then… nothing.

Chapter 2

Longbourn

"He proposed?" Jane looked at Elizabeth, her eyes wide with overwhelming astonishment. "Mr. Darcy proposed! I can scarce believe it!" Jane shook her head in disbelief.

Elizabeth was grateful to finally be home from Kent and reunited with her beloved elder sister, Jane, who had just returned from London herself. The first moment they had to themselves that evening in her bedroom, Elizabeth confidentially told her of Mr. Darcy's proposal and her subsequent refusal of it.

"Yes, but remember I did refuse him. I *had* to refuse him," Elizabeth solemnly assured her sister. "He never showed any regard for me. His proposal was hardly a declaration of love. He made it quite clear that he had struggled in vain from the very beginning regarding our family's relative situation and poor connections and that his own better judgment advised him against this alliance. How could I be anything but offended?"

"I cannot believe any man would say such things in a proposal of marriage!" Jane stated bewildered. "What kind of man would do this?"

Elizabeth's large brown eyes looked away as if in deep thought. She arched one eyebrow and she replied slowly, "I believe it would have to be a man who was very sure of being accepted."

"Mr. Darcy *had* to believe you would accept him. He had to have been so sure of himself, that he gave no thought to his words or how he spoke them! Think of it, Lizzy, any woman would not have had the slightest hesitation in accepting him, if but simply for his fortune."

Upon hearing these words Elizabeth suddenly looked down, wringing her hands. Jane quickly added, "Not that I am saying you should have accepted him. But imagine how he must feel! He must be so hurt and humiliated!"

"I would not concern yourself with Mr. Darcy," Elizabeth sighed. "I do not believe he will suffer much by my refusal." She chuckled apprehensively. "It has been over a week. I am sure his regard for me is all but forgotten."

"I simply do not understand. Were you ever persuaded of what his feelings were for you?" Jane asked, shaking her head the whole time, trying to comprehend what her sister had just told her.

"I had not an idea of it. Every conversation we shared frequently resulted in sharp words. We could barely carry on a civil exchange for more than a few sentences. You are as surprised as I am, Jane." Elizabeth smiled at her sister.

Jane then gently took her hand. "It is not that I am surprised he asked you, Lizzy. I am surprised because he seemed to think us all so decidedly beneath him. He always appeared to me to be wishing he were anywhere else but here in Hertfordshire."

"That he did."

"What was he like at Rosings? Did you notice any peculiar regard there?"

"We had our share of strained conversation there, as well. At times he appeared very uncomfortable. When I first saw him, I was of the opinion he was definitely *not* happy to see me. His cousin, Colonel Fitzwilliam, was very open and friendly, but Mr. Darcy seemed very withdrawn and uncomfortable. His coming to me with an offer of marriage was the last thing I would have ever expected from him. But Jane, you must promise not tell a soul of this. You are the only one who knows!"

"Oh Lizzy, you know I would not!"

Elizabeth sighed and looked down at her hands that now gripped Jane's tightly. "Jane, there is one more thing that came out from all of this."

"What would *that* be?" asked Jane anxiously.

"He wrote a letter to me after I had refused him. He presented it to me the next morning." Elizabeth looked up. Jane was staring intently, hanging on each word.

"In it, he told me what really happened in his dealings with Mr. Wickham; how Mr. Wickham had deceived us with his story about him. Jane, it was actually Mr. Wickham who betrayed Mr. Darcy and his family."

"No!" whispered Jane. "You mean Mr. Wickham fabricated his story?"

"Yes, I imagine he did it to suit his own needs; to make us look favourably on him and unfavourably toward Mr. Darcy."

Elizabeth went on to share with her sister the unfortunate circumstances regarding Wickham; in particular, his brazen actions toward Miss Darcy. As she shared this with Jane, she became more and more appalled that her attitude toward Mr. Darcy had been based mainly on the deception of one who had been determined to ruin him. She felt more and more remorseful of her attitude toward him in this area. How could she not have discerned the truth earlier?

Jane's face showed her distress over this news. "I cannot believe that he had fooled us all! Are you quite certain that Mr. Darcy did not misconstrue the events? Perhaps both of them simply have a mutual misunderstanding."

Elizabeth looked at Jane and with a reflective air stated, "There is but such a quantity of merit between them; just enough to make one good sort of man." Elizabeth let out a deep sigh. "I am afraid one has got all the goodness, and the other all the *appearance* of it."

The realization of her words penetrated Jane, but her thoughts took her to Charles. Her expression of astonishment at once turned to heartache. Tears filled her eyes and she looked down quickly. Elizabeth reached out and touched her arm, "What is it?"

"On proper reflection, I must conclude that Mr. Darcy had all the *admiration* and Mr. Bingley had only the *appearance* of it." With that, her breathing became soft sobs.

"Jane, I *know* that is not true! I am convinced that Mr. Bingley has all the regard for you that one can possibly possess." Elizabeth tried in vain to reassure her sister of Charles' true affections.

"Forgive me, Lizzy. I did not mean to…" She could not finish her sentence as she struggled to regulate her tears.

Elizabeth drew her sister into her arms and hugged her tightly. "There is no need to ask forgiveness, dearest Jane. I do not claim to understand any of the events that transpired over these past few months." She was distressed to see the prolonged hurt in her sister and know that it was caused in part by Mr. Darcy's own doing. She felt her stomach knot, as she felt the anger that she had toward him again flare.

Since she had been apprised of the truth in his letter regarding his dealings with Wickham, she struggled with consistency in her feelings toward Mr. Darcy. In *that* area her anger had diminished towards him. But she could not let herself forget the *other* provocation. There was still the issue of his inexcusable interference in Jane's and Bingley's relationship. This distressed her gravely.

Jane leaned over and kissed her sister. "Lizzy, I want you to know that I do respect you for your decision to refuse Mr. Darcy. You did what you felt you must; what you knew you had to do! As much as Mama would have expected you to be grateful and accept such a proposal, I know too well that you could not be persuaded into marriage with such a man!"

"Thank you, Jane. It does make things easier knowing you understand. Please, whatever you do, do not let Mama find out about this. I would never be able to live in the same house with her again if she knew I refused yet *another* proposal; and from a man worth ten thousand a year!"

Jane laughed in the midst of her tears. "That is so true! Would she not be completely undone! Well, it is getting late. Good night, dear sister. I am so glad we are both home again."

"Good night, Jane. I am so glad to be back and have you to share things with again!"

As Elizabeth slipped into bed, she was welcomed by her own sheets, her own pillow. As she laid her head on her pillow and reached back to plump it, she made a determined resolution. She would do whatever she could; do everything in her power, to get Jane back together with Mr. Bingley. Feeling somewhat satisfied by this decision, she drifted off into an uneasy sleep.

~~*

The next day arrived too soon for Elizabeth. She had slept fitfully through the night and now all she wanted was to remain in her cosy bed and sleep the whole day through. The sun crept in through the window, beckoning her with the notion that since it had arisen, so should she. She lay in bed a few minutes longer, looking around her room, savouring the feeling of being home again. Her eyes went to the window and out to the grounds that lay beyond.

She suddenly thought of her walks in the beautiful grounds at Rosings, and how, on more than one occasion, she unexpectedly encountered Mr. Darcy. She had assumed they met by accident, but now she wondered, could he have purposely sought her out? He never truly made any effort at conversation as they continued to walk together, and she often felt his accompanying her had been out of politeness. Now, she could not be certain.

She thought back to how different he was at Rosings than in Hertfordshire. At the latter he had been stiff and formal, arrogant in his countenance, abrupt, and distant. Yet at Rosings he appeared unsettled, disquieted, and uneasy. He did not have the arrogant air about him that he had earlier. When he walked with her out in the grounds, she recalled how he often looked at her with a manner of kindness. But that he was often so quiet, she took his behaviour to be strictly out of forced civility. He *had* been different there, but not enough to give her any reason to believe him enamoured with her.

The beckoning sun finally had its way and she arose. She dressed quickly and joined her family downstairs for breakfast. Not being terribly hungry, she ate only a biscuit and a little fruit. Mrs. Bennet was discussing the need for some items from the milliner's shop in town and Elizabeth, anxious for a diversion, offered to walk into Meryton to pick them up. Jane enthusiastically offered to join her. Fortunately for them, their three younger sisters were otherwise engaged for the morning, so the two would have the sole pleasure of each other's company as they walked into town.

As they set out for Meryton, Elizabeth was again glad for Jane's company. How she had missed her these past weeks! Their conversation echoed much from the night before. Lizzy had to be careful what she said to Jane. She would not tell her of Mr. Darcy's interference in swaying his friend's regard for her. There would be no reason to tell her. So she guarded her words very carefully.

As they walked, Jane turned to her sister with a resigned look on her face.

Elizabeth returned her look with a sigh. "You are not happy, Jane. It pains me to see it."

Jane tilted her head to one side, as if to dismiss as irrational what she was about to say. "It is just that I am afraid I still prefer Mr. Bingley to any other man I have ever met. I do believe that he…" She stopped herself from continuing that thought. "Yet I am resolved to think of him no more. There! I shall be myself again, as if I had never set eyes on him." She looked at Elizabeth and steeled herself for her next words. "I will be perfectly content. Do not concern yourself with me."

Elizabeth heard her sister's words, but knew that within her heart it was a completely different matter. How she ached to make things right by her. Just how she would do it was yet unknown to her. She took her sister by the arm and gave it a reassuring squeeze. They walked the remainder of the way to town in silence.

The milliner's shop in Meryton was gaily decorated with ribbons and lace and hats. Elizabeth walked over to the lace handkerchiefs and picked one up. *This one would look very nice with my initials embroidered on it*, she thought to herself. It had a tatted edge and a cut out heart in each of the four corners. Jane purchased a few items and they stopped by a bakery for some fresh baked goods before slowly strolling back to Longbourn.

As they made their way back to the house, they saw a gentleman leaving on horseback. Neither of them was able to recognize him.

"I wonder who that was," Jane pondered aloud.

"I could not tell. Do you suppose he was delivering a post?" asked Elizabeth. "Shall we go in and find out?"

As they entered the house, there was great commotion, coming mainly from Mrs. Bennet.

"Oh, girls! Look what we just received!" She rushed over to them, putting her arm around Elizabeth and holding out a letter. "This is from a Georgiana Darcy; she is the sister of that fine Mr. Darcy."

Elizabeth looked quizzically at her mother. "What could *she* possibly want?" she asked, astounded with that news.

"She writes to you, Lizzy," her mother began.

"Mama, you read a letter that was addressed to me?" cried Elizabeth.

"I had no choice, as we had to give a reply to the carrier while he waited. We were not certain when you would return. But look, read what she says!"

Dear Miss Elizabeth Bennet,

With much anguish I must inform you that my brother, Fitzwilliam Darcy, was in an accident just outside of Lambton as he returned to Pemberley two days ago. The carriage in which he rode overturned and he sustained some injuries. He is under the care of our doctor here at Pemberley. We have been assured that he had no broken bones, but he has been unconscious since then and of this the doctor is concerned.

I knew that you would want to know, and I hope that I am not asking too much for you to come to Pemberley as soon as possible. Even though he is unconscious, he does occasionally call out your name and I wonder if you may be the only thing that will bring him out of this sleep. Miss Bennet, the doctor has not been overly optimistic concerning my brother's condition. It has been two days since the accident. As each day passes and he still does not regain consciousness, I can see the doctor becomes more gravely concerned.

We have also summoned his good friend, Mr. Charles Bingley, with whom I know you are acquainted. He is on his way here now, as well.

I would be exceedingly grateful if you would come. I have no doubt that you would most likely desire to be here and hope that arrangements can be made to bring you to Pemberley promptly.

Please reply as to whether you will be able to come and when you plan to leave Longbourn. I will arrange the coach from Pemberley to meet you in Lambton.

Thank you.
Yours, &c,
Miss Georgiana Darcy

"See, Lizzy, that fine gentleman, Mr. Darcy, has been calling out your name! You must go to him. Miss Darcy believes that only you can help him! I have sent back the reply that you and Jane will leave tomorrow morning and be in Lambton by the afternoon!"

Elizabeth looked at her mother in disbelief. "But Mama, he is not even conscious, not in his right mind, and calling out my name? I cannot believe it! His sister must be mistaken!" Elizabeth struggled to come up with a way to prevent this. She knew the only reason her mother would have agreed to this was that, in her mind, a man worth 'ten thousand a year' was asking for her daughter and that, even though he was quite ill, he was a very promising prospect as a husband for her.

"Now, Lizzy, you simply must go. I have replied that you would be arriving with Jane. When Mr. Darcy sees how well you tend him and how kind and giving you are, his affections will certainly be engaged toward you. And just think! Mr. Bingley will be there. Jane will be able to see Mr. Bingley again!"

Elizabeth suddenly stopped, realizing what her mother just said. *Jane will be able to see Mr. Bingley again*! A light began to flicker in her dark eyes. "I suppose it *is* a good idea, Mama." Elizabeth looked over at Jane, whose mouth suddenly dropped open. "Come, Jane, I think we must go ready ourselves to leave on the morrow."

Jane rushed to join her, stopping her by taking her arm. She whispered frantically, "Lizzy, I know what you are up to! You cannot do this! I know you are only agreeing to do this because of me!"

Elizabeth put her hand to Jane's mouth to silence her and prodded her to walk with her away from the gathered family. "I do not understand why Miss Darcy wrote me. If she only knew what really happened between Mr. Darcy and me! He is probably suffering nightmares about me and yet she must think he calls my name out of admiration or fondness."

Her thoughts went from Mr. Darcy to Jane and Charles. "Jane, I think this may be just the opportunity to bring you and Mr. Bingley back together; to find out for a certainty what his feelings are for you. I do believe Providence has dealt us a very interesting hand!"

Hope blending with a touch of fear filled Jane's countenance. "But what if Mr. Bingley…"

"If it appears he no longer has regard for you, we will return home at once."

Elizabeth smiled at the situation that had presented itself to them. How ironic it would be to be at Pemberley, in Darcy's own home, that Jane and Charles would be brought back together -- right under his nose!

For Jane's sake, Elizabeth had to appear sure of herself. A grin overspread her face as she said, "Jane, I think Mama has done us an immense favour. Besides, what can we do? She has already sent the reply. It appears that we are going to Pemberley tomorrow!" The two sisters grasped hands and smiled. Jane's heart pounded as it had not done in months. The pounding in Elizabeth's heart suggested something entirely different, yet she was not sure what.

Jane moved to go to her room and ready herself for the journey tomorrow. She turned with a soft smile and said, "You know that Mama is not just expecting a proposal to come out of this for me, Elizabeth, but for you, as well. Would Mama not die if she knew that you had *already* received a marriage proposal from Mr. Darcy?"

"No, I believe she would simply faint. She would, however, die if she knew I had *refused* his proposal!" With that, both girls laughed uncontrollably, spurred on by the nervousness each felt.

Elizabeth went directly to her room and sat on the edge of her bed, contemplating what this would mean for her. It would be quite awkward for her to face Mr. Darcy again. She knew that for a certainty. She had no way of knowing how long Mr. Darcy would remain unconscious. If... when... he awoke, she would definitely offer an apology to him for her misjudgement of his dealings with Mr. Wickham. She would, however, stand up to him again, in defence of her determination to bring Jane and Mr. Bingley together again. She was resolved to do it. She only hoped that they could remain at Pemberley long enough for Jane to determine Charles' true sentiment toward her.

Clothing and accessories enough for a week were packed for the sisters. They did not know how long they would be there. It could be for just one night if things turned out disastrously, yet there was always the possibility that they could stay longer. As she contemplated staying more than a few days, Elizabeth found herself thinking of Mr. Darcy and his injuries. He could be in grave condition, indeed. An apprehensive thought kept resurfacing. What if he never regained consciousness, as Miss Darcy so greatly feared?

She did not know whether the knots in her stomach were a result of concern for his welfare or her fear to face him again. She only knew that the remainder of the day and evening were very discomfiting to her. Her mother continually interjected her opinions on how the two of them should behave when they arrived at Pemberley, what they should say, and how they should sit, stand, and walk. Mrs. Bennet had settled it in her mind that they would both be engaged by the time they returned.

Mary had to express her concern that this was not a very proper thing to do, to allow her two unmarried sisters to go to the home of a single man and to have his single friend there, too. Even though his sister would be there, she was not of the opinion that this was at all wise.

At first, Kitty and Lydia protested that they could not accompany them. Very quickly, however, they realized it would be quite boring there as no officers would be around and Pemberley was at least five miles from any reasonable sized town where they could find some diversion.

Mr. Bennet made himself scarce throughout the day, knowing he would not be able to talk any sense into Mrs. Bennet or control any of his daughters. He knew this excursion would involve both their elder daughters being in the same household with two very eligible men. He trusted the sensibility of Elizabeth and the purity of heart of Jane, but was not overly enthusiastic. He had not been persuaded in favour of either of the men and the way they had treated his daughters, but to his wife, they both held great advantage in being very prospective husbands. To Mrs. Bennet, this was most fortunate!

That evening, he felt it essential to speak with his favourite daughter. "Lizzy, what your mother has, in effect, forced you to do is not the wisest thing she has ever done. I know how much you dislike this Darcy. If he gives you any trouble, if he is at all discourteous to either of you, I want you to return home immediately! Ten thousand a year or not! And as for Jane and her Mr. Bingley, I beg the same for her. I do not want my two daughters returning home beaten down and broken hearted. Do I make myself clear?"

"Yes, Father." Elizabeth reassured him with a gentle, appreciative smile. "Do not worry about us."

Her words to her father were as much words to herself. If only she could stop worrying about what might happen. Was she secure enough in her opinion of Charles' affections for Jane that once he saw her everything would be as it had been months ago? This was, after all, the main reason they were going.

She could not help but wonder also what would happen when she had to face Mr. Darcy again. What if he had recovered by the time they arrived at Pemberley? How would she explain her presence? Her heart thunderously pounded in her chest as she contemplated this. These were situations about which she could only speculate. She could plan and prepare in her mind, but in reality, she knew not how things would turn out! The only thing she knew for a certainty was that tomorrow they would take their leave for Pemberley, the great estate of which she had been asked to be mistress!

Chapter 3

The following morning greeted Elizabeth in much the same way she was feeling - grey and gloomy. Although it was not raining, there was a thick mist in the air that coated everything with a pellicle of heavy dew. The sun began to retreat; it ceased trying to bring any warmth and comfort. A light fog was just beginning to lift as she crawled out of her warm bed. She stretched and took a deep breath trying to lighten the heaviness that was tugging at her.

After a warm, filling breakfast, Elizabeth and Jane watched as the servants loaded their trunks onto the carriage and then turned to bid their family goodbye. James, their coachman, was making a final check to make sure things were secure and ready to go.

The look of grave disquiet in Mr. Bennet's eyes did not escape Elizabeth's notice. He had spoken his mind to her last night and she was comforted by his concern. She often wondered why he never took control of family matters, usually deferring all decisions to his wife, as unwise as they often were. She was grateful that her father felt enough trust and admiration of her to leave her with his deepest thoughts and concerns.

Mrs. Bennet gave last minute instructions to the coachman, to Jane, and to Elizabeth. "Now James, be sure that the girls get on the right hack chaise to Lambton before you leave, and Jane, make sure you stand and sit properly, and Elizabeth, you behave most kindly to that Mr. Darcy. You know that he must be a most agreeable man. Oh, I know you girls will have a wonderful time!"

In her frustration over her mother's inconstancy, Elizabeth was often tempted to remind her how she had from the very beginning held an ill opinion of Mr. Darcy. She knew it would be a useless effort, however. Mrs. Bennet's concern for the material wealth of these "prospective husbands" made her overlook everything else. Elizabeth sighed helplessly as she thought what great lengths her mother would employ to secure husbands for her daughters!

Jane and Elizabeth set out in their coach for the post station in Meryton. There, they quit the Longbourn coach and James saw them on to the carriage that would take them to Lambton. As they settled themselves in, neither spoke. Each girl struggled with her own set of conflicting emotions. Elizabeth grappled in her mind as to what Mr. Darcy would think when he saw her at Pemberley, considering the way she had last treated him. She felt more and more ashamed of her response to his proposal. Yet she was resolute to carry this through and do battle with him, if she must, in order to reunite her sister and Mr. Bingley.

Jane's doubts resurfaced as to whether Charles actually wished to see her. She reasoned in her mind that, after all, it had been about five months since he quit Netherfield. He left without saying goodbye and had made no attempt to contact her, even while she was in London visiting her Aunt and Uncle Gardiner. This was certainly not an indication of someone who held much regard for her. She absentmindedly shook her head, which was noticed by Elizabeth.

"What is it, Jane?" she asked.

"What if Mr. Bingley does not wish to see me. It has been so many months. When he did have the opportunity to pay me a call in London, he did not take it. Maybe we should not be going."

"Jane, have faith. Everything will be all right." Elizabeth wished she could tell her what she knew; that the reason Charles did not pay her a call in London was due to Mr. Darcy's interference and intervention in separating them; that her very presence in Town had been kept from him. As she reassured Jane, she prayed that her intuition in this matter was correct.

To keep herself occupied during the day's travel, Elizabeth drew out the lace handkerchief she had purchased in Meryton. Threading a needle with a dark blue thread, she began to embroider her initials. She made a simple line drawing of an *EB* in one corner, and stitched it in a running stitch. She then added some simple flowers around it, using some pinks, greens and yellows. When she had finished, she was pleased with her work.

Jane kept herself busy reading, although the book could not command her attention as she wished. She found herself gazing out the carriage window watching the scenery go by and wondering what these next days would bring.

"Lizzy," Jane was the first to break the silence that had been their companion for much of the time. "Do you believe in Providence or fate?"

Elizabeth laughed gently. "Should this not be a question for Mary?"

"No, I would prefer your opinion."

"Well, I guess I believe more in Providence. If all things are in the hands of the Almighty One, then fate has no place. I think some people would be of the opinion that some things are fate and some are Providence, but I do not think that could be. Either He has all things in His hands or He does not. Why?"

"I have been considering the events that have brought about our going to Pemberley. Could I even think to attribute it to Providence… or is it fate and things are just happening by chance?"

"Jane, however it turns out, we must accept that it is for our good. We may not always agree with it; it may not be what we want. Remember what Reverend Burbridge says, 'His ways are not our ways.'" Elizabeth hoped that her words would give comfort to Jane no matter what happened at Pemberley with Charles.

Jane suddenly changed the subject. "Lizzy, do you think it possible that Miss Darcy also invited Mr. Bingley to Pemberley because she has an attachment to him? After all, that is what Miss Bingley hinted at in her letter."

"I believe Miss Bingley wrote those things to discourage you. At the most, I believe it was only wishful thinking on her part."

"What do you suppose Miss Darcy is like? Do you suppose she is proud and arrogant like her brother?"

"I do not know. Mr. Wickham had confided in me that she was not amiable, that she was very proud. But then, can we believe any of what he told us, knowing what we now know about him? She must be very naïve, though, to have thought herself in love with such a man."

"It does appear, though, that she has a great love for her brother."

"Yes, of course she does. He is, after all, her only immediate family. Since her father's death he is now both her brother and her father."

The remainder of the ride resulted in much contemplation by both ladies. Neither wanted to talk any more of the anxiety each was feeling. A reassuring smile from Elizabeth occasionally made its way to Jane. Her sister needed all the encouragement she could give her.

They arrived in Lambton just as the sun was setting. They carefully descended from the carriage and found the coachman from Pemberley was already waiting there for them. He introduced himself to the two girls as Winston and directed them to Pemberley's coach. Elizabeth took the opportunity, as they were walking over to it, to inquire about Mr. Darcy.

"He is about the same, Miss. No improvement. It is quite distressing. In the beginning, he cried out in his sleep, tossing and turning a bit. But that has now stopped. The doctor can think of nothing else to do, save pray. I can find no sign of internal injuries, but if he received a bad head injury, he could be this way for a long time or…"

The coachman shrugged and shook his head sombrely, looking down. He did not finish what he was going to say. By his tone of voice Elizabeth was able to finish his thought herself. Suddenly she felt that fear grip inside her again, but this time she knew the source. She feared that Mr. Darcy may never wake up!

"May I inquire as to how the accident happened?" asked Elizabeth.

Winston related the details. "The carriage lost a wheel and overturned just outside Lambton. There had been much of rain. We were almost home… almost safe. As it turned over, his manservant, Durnham, and I jumped from the coach and Durnham suffered a broken ankle. I only received minor bruises and was able to run for help. But when help arrived, Mr. Darcy was unconscious and has not regained consciousness ever since."

"How long ago was that?"

"It has been four days ma'am."

The girls were helped into the coach and Elizabeth suddenly felt gravely concerned. Four days of being unconscious was not a good sign. How was he to eat or drink? She looked out the window and noticed darkness beginning to settle around them.

Jane saw her concern and smiled. "I am quite certain that he will come through this. He is a strong man; has a strong constitution."

Elizabeth smiled back at her weakly. Now it was Jane's turn to reassure her.

As the last remnants of daylight lingered, they found themselves outside the town of Lambton and in beautiful countryside. Elizabeth thought to herself how much fun it would be to explore these woods, the hills and valleys, the streams and trees. She thought of how Mr. Darcy probably knew these woods by heart, having grown up and lived here all his life. "Oh, Lord," she suddenly prayed silently, "Please bring healing to Mr. Darcy. Please let him enjoy these grounds again. Amen."

Soon the darkness settled around them and Elizabeth could no longer enjoy the prospect of the countryside. Without the added distraction of delighting in the view, Elizabeth began to feel nervousness build on top of the fear she had been experiencing since hearing the words of the coachman.

They were almost there. Soon their purpose in coming would present itself. Jane would see Charles. Her only fear was that Mr. Darcy succeeded too well in making him forget her. She leaned her head back against the seat and closed her eyes. She again prayed, this time for Jane and Charles.

Her eyes were still closed when she heard Jane softly say, "Oh my!"

Elizabeth's eyes opened and she joined her sister in their first view of Pemberley. Elizabeth was speechless. She could not see clearly for the dark sky, but could tell from the lights that it was a magnificent estate. Soon the coach came to a halt, and the coachman was at the door opening it for the ladies to assist them down. As they stepped out, Elizabeth was overwhelmed with the majesty of the residence. It was quite stately and she was rather impressed with it. Her eyes took in the full length of the dwelling as they walked toward it.

Her heart pounded as she grasped the truth that this was Mr. Darcy's home. Her hands began to shake and she put the one inside the other to hold them still. Jane looked from one end to the other, and then to Elizabeth.

"Lizzy, have you ever seen anything so grand?" asked Jane ecstatically.

"No, Jane, I have never seen a more happily situated house," her voice trembled as she and Jane walked toward the main entrance. "I like it very much." Her answer had been a whisper, but very intense.

As Winston escorted the ladies to the door, they were greeted by a host of household servants. The housekeeper, Mrs. Reynolds, welcomed them inside as the two sisters now admired the interior. It was decorated in an affluent, practically elegant, but not ostentatious, way.

"Come this way, Miss Elizabeth, Miss Bennet. I will show you to your room. Miss Darcy will meet you in the drawing room at half past the hour. She is in with her brother presently."

The two guests were led up the stairs and down a grand hall. Elizabeth felt a mixture of admiration and awe at the furnishings and decor. She turned her eyes toward every room they passed, at every picture and piece of furniture lining the hallway. She could see that someone, at some time, put much love and thought into this home. That was the feeling it suggested. Even though it was a grand estate, it was also a home, with warmth and love pouring out from its walls.

As they were shown into their room, they were pleased to find it was rather large with two beds, a beautiful mahogany armoire and table, and a dressing chamber off to the side. Several candles had been lit and a fire was burning in the fireplace, giving them much desired warmth. A plate of breads, cheese, and fruit awaited them.

"You may freshen up, have a bite to eat, and then come down to meet Miss

Darcy in the drawing room, which is down the stairs and directly to the left. She will make your acquaintance there in about 20 minutes." With that, Mrs. Reynolds left.

"What do you think?" asked Elizabeth, wondering what thoughts were going through Jane's mind.

"Oh, Lizzy, is it not simply wonderful? Netherfield is very nice, but this is grand!" She saw the pensive look on Elizabeth's face and quickly added, "You are not remorseful of your decision to refuse Mr. Darcy's proposal, now that you have seen Pemberley, are you?"

"Oh, no, Jane," laughed Elizabeth. "I simply find it hard to believe that this is where he lives. In some ways it seems grander than him, in other ways he seems grander than it."

A knock at the door brought in a manservant with their luggage. A maid was right behind, offering to put away their clothes in the dressing chamber. With the maid in the next room, the sisters had to refrain from talking any more about Pemberley. They enjoyed some of the food that had been put out and set about getting themselves ready to meet Miss Darcy.

The time passed quickly and they soon heard a grandfather clock down the hall chime the half hour. "I believe it is time to meet our hostess!" exclaimed Lizzy with a nervous sense of excitement. "Shall we go?"

Just as they were to set out, Elizabeth walked over to the table where some of her toiletries had been placed. She pulled out the handkerchief she had embroidered in the carriage and sprayed a mist of gardenia toilet water on it. Bringing the handkerchief to her nose, she breathed in the fresh scent of it, and then tucked it into the pocket of her dress.

The two ladies walked out into the hall and proceeded down the stairs. As they came to the bottom, they walked into an open room on the left and saw a young girl sitting on a divan. As soon as she saw them, she rose and demurely walked over to them. She curtseyed politely. Her words were very carefully chosen and spoken in a very slow, deliberate manner. "I am so glad that you have come. I am Georgiana Darcy. I believe... one of you is Miss Jane Bennet, and one is Miss Elizabeth Bennet."

Elizabeth laughed nervously. "Thank you, Miss Darcy. I am Elizabeth Bennet. It is good to meet you." She smiled at the young girl, who obviously was making a determined effort to be polite and gracious. She could see the strain of the past few days on her face. "This is my sister, Jane."

"It is my pleasure. I am afraid, Miss Elizabeth, that my brother has improved very little since my letter."

"I am so sorry; we were informed of that from your coachman, Mr. Winston."

"I did not know what to do. I am so glad you could come. I knew that with the two of you being just engaged, I had to inform you."

Elizabeth's eyes widened and she tried to disguise her startled look. *She thinks we are engaged?*

Miss Darcy blushed and looked down. "I know the announcements have not been made. My brother... about two weeks ago... wrote me from Rosings to tell me that he was going to propose. But do not worry; he told me that I must not tell anyone and I have not."

Elizabeth glanced at Jane with a look in her eyes that told her to go along with what she was going to say. "Miss Darcy…"

"Please call me Georgiana."

"Thank you, Georgiana. Then you must call me Elizabeth. I am very grateful for you thoughtfulness in writing me and informing me of his condition. I know that with the shock of what happened, the thought to write was commendable."

"I have only done what I felt I should."

"And so you have. Pray tell, you wrote that Mr. Bingley was also coming. Has he arrived yet?" Elizabeth asked.

"No, he should arrive sometime tomorrow. He had some business he had to attend to in London that took him through today."

Elizabeth looked over at Jane and saw her relax a bit at this news.

"Georgiana, what does the doctor say about your brother's condition?"

Georgiana began shaking and tears filled her eyes. Her voice continued in strained sobs, "He does not know what is to be made of his condition. He says all we can do is wait… and pray." Georgiana trembled as she began to weep.

She looked up and straightened her deportment. "Elizabeth, you are bearing up very well. I know you will be a stronghold for me… as well as my brother."

Elizabeth's heart went out to Georgiana as she appeared to be so fragile and timid. She appeared to have such a difficult time coming up with words to say or she was terribly afraid to say them. She had a tendency to look down at her hands as she spoke, but Elizabeth was glad that she made an effort to look up and meet her gaze, as if receiving strength from it.

Elizabeth took her hand and gave it a squeeze. "I would try not to worry Georgiana. I am sure your brother will improve very soon. Jane and I were just discussing how strong he is. That must account for something!"

"I can only hope so. I trust that your presence here will facilitate that. Would you like to see him now?" she asked.

Elizabeth drew in a deep breath, looked at Jane, and then replied as her eyes turned back to the young girl. "Yes, I do believe now would be as good a time as ever. Would you be so kind as to take us to him?"

"Please follow me. We have him in the infirmary, which is back here to the right."

Elizabeth and Jane followed her and made their way toward the rear of the house. As they came to a closed door, Georgiana lightly knocked and it was opened by a nurse. When Elizabeth walked in, she first noticed a strong medicinal smell, along with a smell of cleansing fluid. She saw the bed on the left and a tumbled head of dark, curly hair resting on the pillow.

Elizabeth walked closer and gasped at what she saw. Here lay Mr. Darcy, very pale and still, dark circles around his eyes. Curls from his hair were matted down against his forehead, probably brought about by the slight fever from which he had been suffering since being brought home. As she came closer, that same fear she experienced earlier returned and gripped her. He looked as if he truly had died, but she quickly looked at his chest and was reassured when she saw it rising and falling very slowly.

Elizabeth looked back at Jane and saw that she had barely walked in the room. Jane's hand went over her mouth and Elizabeth noticed her face grow pale.

"Lizzy, do you mind if I do not come in? I really cannot…" With that she ran from the room.

Elizabeth looked at Georgiana. "Are you all right?"

"Yes. I suppose I have become accustomed to how he looks. But, how are you?"

"I must admit it is a shock. He looks so unlike himself."

"Yes. I wish so much for him to waken so I can see his warm smile and inviting eyes. You can imagine what an excellent brother he is." Georgiana paused and took in some deep breaths. "He is usually the one who is so generous and takes prodigiously good care of me. I cannot imagine what I would do without him." The tears came again to Georgiana and Elizabeth wrapped her arms around her.

Elizabeth found it hard to believe that Georgiana's words were about the man that the whole society of Hertfordshire found proud and arrogant, aloof and uncaring. Could this really be the same man? She had to remind herself, though, that in his society he was most likely all ease and friendliness. It was the likes of her society that caused him to behave so abhorrently.

"If you will excuse me, I will leave you to spend some time alone with him. The nurse will be outside the door if you need her. Please talk to him, Elizabeth. Let him know you are here, by his side. The doctor says we really do not know whether he can hear us… but we can always hope that he can." The words from Georgiana, spoken through her tears, were passionate, imploring Elizabeth to try to get through to him.

"Yes, Georgiana, we can hope."

Miss Darcy left and the nurse stepped outside the door. Elizabeth looked compassionately at Mr. Darcy. How different was his countenance now. In his features there was no more pride and no arrogance. She felt utterly helpless seeing how frail he looked. She came around to the side of the bed and sat down upon a chair that had been placed next to the bed, most likely for Georgiana.

She wrung her hands, wondering what to do; what to say. She could not imagine he would want to hear her voice -- not the voice of the woman who had so harshly lashed out at him and so vehemently refused him. But she felt she had to say something.

"Mr. Darcy, I do not know whether you can hear me. It is… Elizabeth. Elizabeth Bennet." She paused, wondering what more to say. "You are probably wondering what I am doing here. Your sister is apparently under the mistaken impression that we are engaged." She laughed nervously. "She wrote to me telling me of your accident and asking for me to come. So here I am."

Her eyes were drawn to the matted curls against his forehead. Her thoughts went to the day he had come and proposed. These same unruly curls had fallen across his face. How silly that she suddenly thought of that. Finally she drew her hand toward him and with much uneasiness she lifted the curls and pulled them away from his face one by one. The last one, a longer curl stayed within her fingers and she held on to it, rubbing her fingers around it. Her heart pounded as she contemplated this man laying here. She suddenly let go of his lock of hair and pulled back, angry for letting herself be drawn to him in such a way.

"This is a fine state you find yourself in, Sir. Your sister is beside herself with worry; you are all she has. She looks up to you so dearly. If you are in there… somewhere…" She suddenly felt herself at a loss for words.

There was no response from him, his breathing remained constant, no flutter from his eyes. Georgiana had said that maybe he could hear voices. She could not believe he could hear her. She sat there quietly for a moment and finally decided the only thing she could do was pray.

She picked up his hand in hers, covering it with her other hand. "Almighty God, if you hear my prayer, please answer, according to Your perfect will. I pray that you might heal Mr. Darcy. I pray that there would be no lasting ill effects of his injuries, and that he would be up and around soon. Amen."

She found herself staring at his sturdy hand; now limp in hers. She thought of his hand as it had taken hers during their dance at Netherfield. It had been strong and firm. At the time she only associated its strength with his arrogance. Now she felt it was indicative of his very secure character. There on the dance floor she had tried to make out his character. How errant she had been in so many things. She had to admit when he asked her to dance, she ought to have recognized that as a sign of his regard for her. But she had been too adamant in her feelings against him to have even considered it. As her mind was engaged with these thoughts, he moaned and stirred. This caused her to start. She looked at him, but it was followed by silence and stillness.

"I know you are in there, *somewhere,* Mr. Darcy. I know that *somehow* you can pull yourself out of this. You *must* come out of this! You must!"

With that, tears filled her eyes. She put her hand in her pocket and pulled out her newly embroidered handkerchief. As she brought it up to wipe her eyes, she was grateful for the pleasant scent of the gardenia toilet water. "I am sorry, Mr. Darcy, for the very harsh words I lashed out at you at Hunsford; it was very unkind of me to speak to you the way I did. Of both yours and Wickham's character I was deceptively mistaken, please forgive me," and then in a softer, firm voice, "yet do not think that I absolve you of everything I said there! There is still the matter of my sister and Mr. Bingley!"

She rested her head against the edge of the bed and gave in to tears, contributing them to fatigue and stress. After a while, she realized it was getting late, and opened the door to find the nurse waiting there. "I think I must get some rest, now. Will you be with him for the rest of the night?"

"I will stay here a few hours, and then another will come. If he were to awaken, we would want someone to be with him. This is the way it has been since the accident."

"When does the doctor come again?"

"He comes every morning. He is in Lambton, only 15 minutes away by horse, so we can send for him anytime if we need him."

Elizabeth thanked her and then walked to her room. This time, though, she walked through the great house taking no notice of the splendid rooms and halls that surrounded her.

When she had climbed the stairs and entered her room, Jane was grateful to see her, feeling embarrassed for her behaviour earlier. "Lizzy, I am so sorry; I just could not stay in that room for the smells; the way he looked. It is good that you are so strong."

"I heartily understand. I was scarcely prepared for it. But what are we to do about Miss Darcy? She believes that I am engaged to her brother! No wonder she was so insistent that I come. I did not have the heart to correct her this evening. She has this hope in her that he will hear my voice and wake up. We should let her have that hope a while longer; at least until we know something more of his condition."

"I was thinking that perhaps we ought to tell Mr. Bingley about her incorrect assumption when he comes tomorrow. He can help us decide what to do."

"That is a good idea, Jane. He knows Miss Darcy very well and will know how best to handle this."

Jane was prepared for bed, and they talked as Elizabeth readied herself. "Tomorrow, Jane, you shall be united with your Mr. Bingley."

"Lizzy, he is not my Mr. Bingley. But I am rather looking forward to it. I scarce believe I will be able to sleep at all tonight!"

"I am sure you shall, and you shall have very sweet dreams." Elizabeth went over to Jane and kissed her goodnight.

Elizabeth then walked over to the candle and blew it out, leaving the room in darkness, but for the light from the moon that came through the window and the embers that burned softly in the fireplace. She slipped into bed and from there she could see the moon. It was full, but there were dark clouds that obscured it as they occasionally drifted by. She shivered as she thought of the light that had been Mr. Darcy's life, and how it had now been obscured by this accident. How she prayed that this too would pass, as the clouds above passed in front of the moon and moved on; finally giving way to its luminance again.

~~*

Elizabeth slept fitfully through the night, images from the evening resurfacing in her dreams, but more bizarre. Mr. Darcy's lifeless body sometimes appeared like a skeleton, or very white and ghostly. She awakened once, fearful that it was a sign of what was to come. Had she cried out? She looked over at Jane, who did not stir, so she felt most likely she had not, but she feared closing her eyes again and of sleep, knowing that the same images were lying just beyond, waiting to assault her again.

Chapter 4

As morning broke, Georgiana was up early and at her brother's side. There was still no change. She had been hoping that Elizabeth's presence would make a difference, but it had not. He lay still; the only sign of life was the very faint sound of his breathing.

Elizabeth came down and decided to spend a short time with the young girl at Darcy's side. She could not say much. What more could be said; what further encouragement could she give? She was beginning to wonder if it was now too late to still hope for any improvement, but she would not let herself give in to this despair, so as not to worry Miss Darcy.

After sitting with her for a respectable amount of time, Elizabeth left her to visit the dining room. She determined to bring something back for Miss Darcy and when she entered the dining room, she filled a plate with a variety of foods, not knowing what the young girl would be inclined to eat. She poured a cup of hot water and set some tea in it to begin brewing, and then carried it to Miss Darcy herself.

Georgiana spent most of the morning by her brother's side, barely touching any of the food that Elizabeth brought in, although sipping occasionally at the tea. Feeling somewhat weakened by the stress of late, her lack of sleep and appetite, Georgiana crumpled over Darcy's lying form in tears.

The doctor arrived soon after and upon entering, saw Miss Darcy crying upon the bed. He walked over to her and gently patted her back. How difficult it was for him to see her thus! She lifted her head, acknowledged him, and gave a mumbled apology for her lack of composure.

"Please do not apologize to me, Miss Darcy. It is to be expected. You have been under much stress the past few days, getting very little sleep, and your concern for your brother is very great." He looked over at the plate of food in the room. "It appears you have not eaten very much. Am I correct?"

She shook her head.

"I think you must eat something. Go down and get a fresh plate of food and give me some time to examine your brother. Will you do that for me?"

"Yes, thank you, Dr. Brisby. I believe it might do me some good. Let me know as soon as you have finished."

"I will give him a thorough going over. I will also make an attempt to get some liquid down him and give him a good bath. Give me an hour or two."

Georgiana nodded, looked over to her brother, and then back to the doctor with a pleading look. "Thank you. My prayers are with you, Doctor."

Georgiana went down to the dining room and found Elizabeth and Jane visiting in the sitting room. They were grateful to see her; concerned for her well being. Georgiana tried to express a greeting, but words would not come.

Elizabeth noticed immediately that she had been crying, her eyes red and swollen. She instantly went to her side and put her arm about her, escorting her to the dining room. She suddenly felt all the young girl's weight fall upon her as Miss Darcy collapsed in tears again. Elizabeth supported her and brought her to a chair and helped her sit.

"Here, Georgiana. Let me get you something to eat and drink." Elizabeth promptly addressed one of the maids to bring some tea and she began filling a plate with some breads and fruit. "Please try to eat a little bit."

Georgiana looked up with grateful eyes and whispered a genuine, "Thank you."

Jane looked on with great sympathy, amazed at how Elizabeth handled the young girl. She smiled to herself as she saw an attachment growing between the two and was content to let her sister handle the situation. They both sat themselves down with the distraught girl and encouraged her to eat, with futile results.

"I saw the doctor come in. Does he say anything?" asked Elizabeth.

"No, at least... there were no words of... hope. He is examining him now as he has every day. All I can do now is to wait."

"Georgiana," Elizabeth offered, "I find that a walk outside does much to exhilarate me and give me strength. Please try to eat a little more and then, would you join me outside whilst we wait for the doctor to finish?"

"Oh, I do not know if I should leave..." Georgiana picked up some bread and took a few bites and then began sipping at her tea.

Elizabeth was encouraged that at least she was eating something.

"Let me assure you it will do you so much good. Besides, it will make the time go faster while the doctor is in with your brother. Jane, would you care to join us?"

"No, Lizzy, I would prefer to stay close by the house." The look Jane gave Elizabeth implied her impatience to see Charles and her determination to be there as soon as he arrived.

Elizabeth gave her a knowing smile and gently reached for Georgiana's arm. "Shall we go?" she asked, as her brows lifted in encouragement.

"Thank you," Georgiana delicately said.

Elizabeth contemplated this young girl. Last night she had spoken timidly but very satisfactorily about her brother. This morning she was reserved and shy, quite affected apparently, by another day of little hope. Elizabeth felt a very strong sisterly type of affection that she would like to help her through this.

The day had dawned bright and sunny. The clouds had moved on and the air was fresh and clear as they stepped outside. Elizabeth escorted Georgiana, with her arm through hers, as much for strength as for comfort. Elizabeth inhaled sharply as she took in the beautiful prospect around the house; one that she had not seen last night for the darkness. Her heart swelled with admiration for the beauty and natural order of this place, but she felt it would not be wise to dwell on that subject with Georgiana at the moment. So they walked briefly in silence as Elizabeth's eyes looked around taking in the splendour.

Georgiana finally, cautiously, broke the silence. "I do not know how to thank you. My brother, in his letters, spoke highly of you; of your charm, intelligence, and wit. He assured me that I would... that I would truly like you. I must agree with him... that I do."

Elizabeth felt herself blush and was somewhat discomfited by her words of praise. "Thank you, Georgiana. I am quite fond of you, as well."

"Pray forgive me for my stammering. Oftentimes, I feel as though I do not know how to... speak with others... in a way that is expected. My brother is so good, but he is often gone. Miss Annesley, my governess is very competent in teaching me my studies... but," she paused.

"You wished you were not so reserved?"

Georgiana nodded.

Elizabeth quickly thought about how best to approach the subject with this tender girl. "I certainly do not possess all the answers to your dilemma, but let me tell you what I have observed." She took in a deep breath and silently prayed, *"Lord, please give me the right words."*

"I have found, in my observance of people, that being reserved can be for one of two reasons. There are other reasons, of course, but these are the most common. The first is that there is a fear of saying something wrong, a fear of being misunderstood or judged ill by something you say or do. So to prevent that, you hold yourself back. The second is not desiring to impart oneself to others due to one's own feelings of superiority and having no inclination to converse with someone you feel beneath you. I believe the former may be your case."

"I believe I *am* afraid of what people may think. But what can I do about it?" asked Georgiana.

Elizabeth took her hand and looked directly in her eyes, holding her gaze. "Well, you must realize that what you have to say is very important, whether you are simply stating a fact or your deepest feelings about something. I believe, from what I have seen, you are very mature and would not say or do anything improper. But you must gain confidence in yourself and not put so much consequence on what you think others may be thinking."

Upon hearing this, Georgiana looked down and blushed. "Miss Elizabeth, I have done some things recently that I am... very ashamed of. I... let... my brother down unimaginably. What I did was... very wrong and immature. It caused William much grief and consternation. My greatest fear is that I may let him down again."

Elizabeth noticed the change to her formal address and she inwardly berated herself for saying something that would cause Georgiana to recall her inappropriate relationship with Wickham. But she would not let on that she knew of the particulars. "And how did he treat you in this situation. Was he very harsh on you?"

"Oh, no, never! He has always been so loving, so kind and forgiving. I just cannot bear to hurt him again…because of how it makes me feel." Tears began streaming down her face and she buried her face in her hands.

"You dear girl, I am quite certain that you do not have to worry about disappointing your brother. He thinks so highly of you. We all occasionally do things that are wrong, even your brother must have some faults." Elizabeth's mind went back to Netherfield, and her conversation with Mr. Darcy about his faults.

"Oh no, not that I can see. He is so very perfect."

"Georgiana, no one is perfect. And I am sure he does not expect you to be perfect either." Elizabeth tried her best to reassure her.

"He has always had such high standards for himself and he has them for me, as well. But Elizabeth, I do believe you are right. I do keep things to myself, so not to give others the opportunity to think ill of me."

"You said yourself that your brother is loving, kind, and forgiving. You must not fear his disappointment in you for something you might say or do. That would not be his character!" Elizabeth startled herself with her words about him.

"But what do I do? How do I change?"

"First, you must tell yourself that he will not judge you ill, neither will anyone else who is worthy of your concern. He loves you precisely the way you are! Then, to help you with conversations with others, perhaps you could keep a journal?"

Georgiana looked up at her quizzically. "A journal?"

"Yes," began Elizabeth, wondering at her own inspiration. "It would help you to write down things you discover; what you hear about people, or places, or things. Write down your thoughts and feelings. Then when you meet people, whether new acquaintances or old, write down what you learn about them. You can refer to your journal and have ideas on what to talk about when you encounter these people again. You may even ask your brother about certain places or things in advance and then write them down. I have found that writing things down does help me formulate my thoughts better and to remember them better, too."

Georgiana looked at Elizabeth with wide-eyed wonder. She suddenly, unexpectedly, gave her a big hug. A smile on her face gave Elizabeth all the assurance that she would, indeed, give this a try. "This sounds like a very helpful idea."

Elizabeth then added, "Now would be a very good time to start. You must have many feelings about what has been happening with your brother. Writing down your thoughts and feelings is also good therapy.

"Oh Elizabeth, thank you. I look forward to beginning right away!"

Elizabeth smiled and breathed a sigh of relief. She was not certain that this would help her, but at least Georgiana was willing to give it a try and it might help her keep her worries about her brother at bay. They turned to head back toward the house when they saw a barouche carriage coming up the road.

"Oh look," cried Georgiana, "it must be Mr. Bingley! Let us go meet him!"

Georgiana turned and in a stride that was between a skip and a run, she made her way down the path toward the house. Elizabeth turned to join her, grateful for the special time and bond that just transpired between them, but feeling the necessity to carefully, lovingly inform Georgiana of the truth of her and Mr. Darcy. Yet in her heart, she felt it was not yet the right time!

~~*

Jane had been watching out the window and saw the carriage arrive. It pulled up to the house and the door was opened for Charles Bingley. The Pemberley servants rushed outside and met with his coachman and valet and helped him with his belongings, bringing them into the house. Bingley glanced about him, always amazed and impressed with the grounds and house that was Pemberley.

Jane's heart nearly leapt out when she first saw Charles step down. How handsome he still looked; how terrified she felt now that the moment was here.

As he entered the house, he surveyed the scurrying of servants attempting to make his arrival smooth. As he looked beyond them, he noticed a woman standing off to the side. He suddenly stopped, feeling somewhat unstable as he wondered whether his eyes were betraying him. No, he realized it *was* Jane! He could not get his feet to move toward her, he only stood, staring while trying to comprehend the situation.

Each looked upon the other with many unanswered questions. Jane was trying to determine whether the look on his face displayed joy or displeasure in seeing her. Charles was overwhelmed with feelings rising to the surface that had been repressed, but was also wondering what she was doing here!

He finally gained control of his senses and a smile broke through as he took himself immediately to her side.

"Miss Bennet!" he exclaimed. "How good it is… how *good* it is to see you again!" His exuberance was all Jane needed to be finally relieved of all the anxiety she was feeling this whole day. "Excuse me, but is your family well?"

"Yes, thank you. And yours?"

"Splendid!" he murmured. He took her hand and held it, "How long it has been since we have seen each other! It has been, I believe, almost five months!"

"Has it been that long?"

"Yes, I believe it was November twenty-fifth, at the ball at Netherfield!"

The servant bringing in Bingley's luggage walked over and told him they would be putting his things in his usual room. He only nodded, not taking his eyes off Jane. "It *is* good to see you!"

"Mr. Bingley, there is something I need to talk with you about, privately."

He looked concerned, and suddenly realization swept across his face. "Oh, no! It is not Darcy! Has he…?"

"No, he is still the same. But it involves his sister."

"Miss Darcy?"

"Yes."

He stepped aside with her, away from the bustling servants. "What is it?"

"You may wonder what I am doing here."

"To be honest, I was."

"It is really all because of a misunderstanding that we have not yet been able to remedy."

"A misunderstanding?"

"Yes. Apparently Miss Darcy believes that Mr. Darcy and Elizabeth are engaged! She wrote to us of his accident, believing her to be engaged to be married to him and felt she would want to know of his condition and be here with him!"

Charles let out a hearty laugh as he heard this. "You cannot be serious! Mr. Darcy and your sister engaged? How could she have ever come to that assumption?"

Jane looked down to her hands and then back to Charles. "Mr. Darcy *did* make an offer of marriage to Elizabeth when he encountered her while visiting his aunt at Rosings, but she turned him down. He had sent off a letter to Georgiana before he proposed to let her know he was going to ask for her hand. The accident occurred before he was able to inform her of Lizzy's refusal."

Suddenly Charles' face clouded over. "I am afraid I do not understand. This is all too peculiar to me. Why, Darcy was so hard on me about..." He looked at Jane and did not finish his thought. "So Miss Darcy understood her brother to have asked for your sister's hand, but was unaware that she turned him down?"

"Yes. We came here unaware of this misunderstanding and have not let her know because of the hope she put in Elizabeth that she could bring him out of the state he is in. We do not know what to do now, when we should tell her."

"And there is no change in Darcy?"

"No."

"I would suggest we not say anything yet, at least until we know something more of his condition."

"The doctor is in with him now. He should be coming out fairly soon."

With that, Georgiana and Elizabeth appeared at the front door.

"Oh, Mr. Bingley! How good it is to see you!" Georgiana went to him and he reached out his hands to greet her. As he took her hand, he pulled her towards him and gave her a sympathetic hug.

"Miss Darcy, if there is anything I can do to help you and your brother, please advise me."

"Thank you. I am just so grateful you came!"

"Mr. Bingley, it is good to see you," added Elizabeth, smiling warmly.

"And you, Miss Elizabeth. What a pleasant surprise this has been, to discover that you and your sister are here!"

The party went into the sitting room, deciding to wait there until the doctor came out. Elizabeth felt a great burden lift as she watched the interaction between her sister and Charles. They certainly were continuing where they had left off. Georgiana watched the two in delight and with a little confusion, as she had not been aware of the fact that Mr. Bingley had any affection for anyone, let alone Miss Jane Bennet.

When the doctor came out, his only encouraging words were that his patient had not changed for the worse, he was holding his own. He encouraged everyone to continue to speak to him, stimulating his senses, trying to get through to him wherever he was deep inside. He assured Georgiana he would return the next day or at a moment's call.

Charles asked Georgiana if he could go in and see him with her. She took him back to the infirmary while Jane and Elizabeth visited and waited. Elizabeth smiled at her sister. "I do believe he was happy to see you, Jane."

"Do you really? I feel so much more relaxed, having seen him and now that the first meeting is out of the way."

Elizabeth leaned forward and in earnestness said, "Jane, may I suggest something to you? Let him know, without any reservation, how you feel. Do not leave him in any doubt of your feelings."

Jane blushed and said, "You know I am more reticent in that area, but I shall make an effort!"

Charles came out after awhile, obviously shaken by what he saw in there. "He is so altered; I cannot believe he is the same man! Come, Miss Bennet, I feel the need for a walk and some fresh air. Would you care to join me?"

Elizabeth suddenly found herself alone and after a while, felt the need for fresh air. She decided to go for a walk herself and after looking out to see which direction Charles and Jane had set out, she set out in the opposite direction. This time, without Georgiana, she was able to take in the sights and sounds of Pemberley. The lake and stream that ran through the woods around the house boasted crystal blue water. The trees and flowers suggested a natural, yet lovingly tended appearance. She felt as if she could walk for miles around here!

When she finally returned to the house, she found Charles and Jane in the sitting room. She greeted them and then announced that she would be going to her room to freshen up. Upon ascending the stairs, she heard some music coming from somewhere ahead. She had not yet ventured out beyond her and Jane's room, and ventured forth, feeling drawn to the music.

She came to the end of the hall and turned, finding herself facing a magnificent, long hallway. It was lined with portraits on either side, presumably of people on the Darcy side of the family. She stopped and looked at each one, reading their names and dates, trying to determine who each one was. She saw Mrs. Anne Fitzwilliam Darcy and gazed into the kind eyes of the woman looking down at her. Could this be Mr. Darcy's mother? She was very beautiful and Elizabeth thought she would have liked to know her.

Next to her was a painting of Mr. Frederick Evans Darcy. Elizabeth believed for a certainty that this was his father. She could see the resemblance; he had the same dark eyes and dark curly hair.

She next came to the painting of Mr. Fitzwilliam Richard Darcy. She breathed in deeply, seeing on him a broad smile that had only on a rare occasion graced his face in her presence. She thought of the man lying downstairs, comparing him to the one in this picture and then comparing those two completely different men to the one she knew. How puzzling this man was!

Becoming aware of the music again, she walked toward it, glancing from right to left at pictures lining the hall. When she came to the door from which the music was coming, she stopped, seeing that it was Georgiana playing at the pianoforte.

How beautifully she plays! thought Elizabeth, who quietly stayed where she was, so not to disturb her.

When Georgiana finished, Elizabeth exclaimed, "Georgiana, that was simply beautiful!"

The startled and somewhat embarrassed Georgiana quickly looked over and saw her standing in the doorway, watching her. She blushed and said, "Oh, it was nothing. I was just practicing. I find that the music helps me… take my mind off my concerns. This is what gives me strength."

"And it was beautiful. I wish I could play like that!"

Georgiana tilted her head and looked at Elizabeth with a look of reflection in her eyes. "You know," she said softly, "My brother often quietly comes to the door… just as you did… and listens to me play without me knowing. How often he would startle me, as you have just done."

Elizabeth smiled, although with a bit of discomfort, as she answered, "I do not doubt that he enjoys your playing as much as I did."

"He wrote me once of how much he also enjoyed hearing you play. He said he received much pleasure from your playing and singing."

Elizabeth felt herself flush and quickly responded, "I am sure he exaggerated. I play very ill, indeed."

"My brother rarely exaggerates, Elizabeth. I should like to hear you play. Do you mind?"

Before Elizabeth could answer, Mrs. Reynolds came in and apologized for interrupting. "Miss Darcy, something has arisen that we need to discuss. The nurse has been called away to help Dr. Brisby with a difficult labour in town. Apparently it is beyond the ability of the midwife, and his other two nurses are unavailable. If we have to, we know where we can send for her if anything arises, but we must keep someone with Mr. Darcy throughout the night until she is able to return."

"Thank you, Mrs. Reynolds." Georgiana looked at Elizabeth for support.

Elizabeth reassured her with, "We will be down immediately and discuss how this is to be done. Come, Georgiana."

They met downstairs and planned out two-hour intervals to stay with Mr. Darcy until a nurse returned. Even Mr. Durnham, Mr. Darcy's valet availed himself of some time. He had been principally staying in his quarters nursing his broken ankle, but now felt he could venture out on his crutches and help at this time.

Everyone but Jane, who still felt inadequate to place herself inside that room for any length of time, offered to sit with him. Elizabeth was to replace Georgiana from the eleven o'clock hour to one in the morning. She was to be replaced by Durnham, then Winston, and then Bingley after that.

The threesome visited in the sitting room, while Georgiana spent most of the evening in her brother's room. Elizabeth visited the Pemberley library and spent a good amount of time looking through the vast collection of books there. If she could have spent a year here, she would have barely touched the surface in reading the books she desired to.

She picked one up and brought it back to the sitting room to read. She noticed

Jane and Charles were still very attentive to each other and Elizabeth smiled as she saw more regard on Jane's part than she had in the past. She was obviously taking Elizabeth's advice to heart.

Elizabeth was soon involved in the book she was reading and was surprised at how quickly the time had passed when Georgiana came out and asked her if she could relieve her. Elizabeth could see the drawn look of fatigue on her face and encouraged her to get herself right to bed and try to get a good night's sleep. "Please do not worry about your brother tonight; he is in good hands."

Georgiana smiled and wished everyone a good night.

Elizabeth picked up her book and set out for her two-hour sit with Mr. Darcy.

At first, she was content to just read silently from her book until she recalled the words of the doctor. *Try to stimulate his senses.* She decided to read aloud to him. She thought that would be easier than to try to carry on a one-sided conversation with him. This would be the next best thing.

Elizabeth began reading. Occasionally she would glance over at him as she read and make some silly comment about the book, ask him whether he was enjoying the story or was he bored with it, or suggesting that perhaps he had already read it before himself.

After a while, he began to stir a bit. She noticed his breathing became more laboured. She put the book down and watched him. She saw that his face had become more flushed, he was perspiring heavily. She put her hand to his forehead. He was burning up! Since the accident he had been running a mild fever, but this appeared to be very high. She looked at the clock on the wall and saw that it was ten minutes before one o'clock. Durnham should be coming soon. She would have him find someone to go for the doctor as soon as he came in.

Elizabeth went over to the sink that was in a room adjoining the infirmary and filled a basin with water. She found some cloths and brought them over to the side of the bed where she dipped one into the water and wrung out as much water as she could. Taking the cool, damp cloth, she applied it to his forehead, face and neck. She knew that she needed to cool his body down from the outside, to try to lower the fever that was ravaging him on the inside. Concern gripped her, not knowing what brought on this sudden rise in temperature. She repeated this procedure over and over again.

Finally Durnham hobbled in on his crutches and Elizabeth quickly apprised him of the situation. "Please send someone to find the doctor and tell him that Mr. Darcy has a very high fever. If you are able, please return soon and help me with him."

"Should I summon Miss Darcy?"

"I do not want to wake Georgiana yet, as she needs her sleep. Let us wait a bit before we do that."

"I will fetch Winston, and then be back right away!" Elizabeth was grateful that he was able to use his crutches with ease.

She felt herself trembling as she applied the cloths, wondering if it was lowering his fever at all. Occasionally he thrashed about, startling Elizabeth with each violent movement. He began to moan, unintelligible sounds, but at least they were sounds. In her heart she hoped that this meant he was coming back to them, but she also knew it could just be the result of delirium from the high fever. His nightshirt was becoming soaked with the tremendous amount of perspiration.

"Please, Mr. Darcy, fight. Fight this. I know you can!"

She soon felt herself perspiring from all her hard efforts and pulled out her handkerchief from her pocket. She drew it across her face and forehead, breathing in the fragrance of the gardenia scent. It helped give her new strength. She set it down on his bed by the pillow as she continued to minister to him.

Elizabeth knew that she had to get him out of his nightshirt and begin applying the cool cloths to his chest and arms. She tried to remain composed as she reached for the shirt that was clinging to his chest. As she reached for the top button, her fingers intermingled with the curly hair on his chest, and she nervously pulled them back. Shaking, she forced herself to reach out for the button again and struggled to keep her mind focused on the simple task of unbuttoning a button. Finally she took a deep breath, and despite her blush, accomplished her task. The first button was undone.

The next two buttons were just as difficult, but Elizabeth determined to accomplish it without so much a flinch. As she pulled back his shirt, she let out a gasp as she gazed down at his masculine chest. She watched his chest rise and fall, and with each breath she took in a breath of her own, as if to encourage him to continue breathing and to help ease the laboured effort each breath required.

Durnham returned within five minutes and informed her that Winston was now on his way to find the doctor. He asked what he could do to help.

"Take some cloths and dip them in the water. Wring them of all the excess water and then apply it to his face and neck, chest and arms."

With an even greater struggle now, she dipped the cloth back in the water and applied it to his chest and arms. Durnham looked up and obviously noticed the strain on her face. "Are you sure, Miss, that we should not get anyone else to help? You look a little unstable yourself."

"No, I am quite well," she lied.

They spent about a half hour dipping, wringing, and applying the cloths to Darcy. His thrashing diminished slightly and Elizabeth put her hand again to his forehead and was relieved to find that his fever had diminished.

Elizabeth relaxed a bit, standing at his side. How she wished the doctor would come, but at least she felt that he was now out of immediate danger. She closed her eyes for a moment; feeling the effects of exhaustion.

When she opened them, she found herself gazing with much incredulity at Darcy. His eyes were fluttering. She stood transfixed as she watched him slowly, but deliberately, open his eyes. His eyes were glazed, looking at her, through her, she could not determine whether there had been any recognition in them. During these moments her heart literally stopped. She wanted to jump, shout, scream, but nothing came.

But just as suddenly, his eyes closed.

"Mr. Darcy! Come back. I know you are in there! Durnham, did you see that? He opened his eyes!"

"I did Miss Elizabeth. I think he may be well on his way back to us!"

"Mr. Durnham, please stay here. I think I must get Georgiana now!"

Elizabeth ran through the house. It was now close to three o'clock; she had spent almost four hours with him. She knew Georgiana needed more sleep, but felt she had to give her this encouraging news. She climbed the stairs two at a time, came to Georgiana's room and knocked excitedly at the door.

"Georgiana, come quick! We believe your brother may be waking up!"

Chapter 5

*T*he first thing that Darcy became aware of was how hot he was. He felt as though he was burning up! He did not know where he was, but wherever it was, it was as hot as a fiery furnace. He tried to get away from the heat that flooded his body, but he could not escape. He tried to move, but his body would not obey any commands.

He suddenly felt himself being drawn... he did not know to where. All he needed to do -- wanted to do -- was give in and his torment would cease. Or did he just want to give up? It would be easier, he felt, to resign himself to those forces that were at work against his body; to let himself be taken to... where? He was not sure.

His mind was hazy, not even allowing him to grasp who he was. He only knew he was somewhere in the depths of this body, and although he had no particulars, he felt that he had nothing waiting for him at the other side. He knew that to pull himself back up in that direction would require more of an intense struggle. Was there anything for him there? Was it worth the fight or should he just give in? All he knew was that he wanted relief from this heat.

Suddenly he was aware of something cool being wiped across his head, face, and neck. What a contrast this cool touch was to the burning sensation that racked his body! It was a very gentle touch, bringing much needed relief. He wanted to cry out for it to continue. He did not want it to stop! It soothed him to his innermost being.

He did not understand why he could not command his body to move, or his voice to speak out, or his eyes to open. The cooling touch continued and he felt strengthened in his ever weakened bones and muscles. They still would not submit to his wishes, however.

He then became aware of voices. His mind faltered and could not discern what was being said. He recognized that the voices were hushed, somewhat intense. He knew words were being spoken, but he was unable to comprehend them. He struggled to understand, but to no avail. One voice was low and abrupt, the other voice gentle and soothing. He felt drawn to the gentle voice, feeling strengthened merely by the sound of it. Was he being strengthened enough, however, to fight what was so forcefully trying to pull him down?

Unexpectedly, there was something else. It was very faint, but what was it? A scent -- some kind of flower. He tried to move his face toward it, but any attempt was futile; the scent was still off in the distance. For some reason he associated the scent with the gentle voice. He made an effort to take in a deep breath. Yes! He was able to inhale more deeply, but knew not from where it came.

The coolness being applied to his face and neck suddenly moved to his chest and arms. He felt it begin to win the war against the heat in his body. It seemed to pull him closer to the voice; further away from the dark depths in which he had been dwelling. Suddenly he was able to recognize some words, "fever... strength... Darcy."

"Darcy!" That was who he was! But Darcy who? How he wished he could think! Why was everything such an effort? Darcy... William... Fitzwilliam! That was it! That was who he was! Fitzwilliam Richard Darcy! Then there was that voice again; the cool touch, and that faint scent which seemed to linger around him.

If only he could see what was going on. If only he could discern who these people were, where he was, and why he was this way. Still nothing seemed to obey his command, except an occasional deep breath as he searched for that gardenia! That is what it is! A gardenia scent!

Now if his mind only helped him recall how to open his eyes, move his hand, open his mouth to speak. He knew he had to keep trying. As hard as he concentrated, he wondered if perhaps this was just a dream. Maybe he had died. Was this what it was like to be dead? No. He forced himself to rivet his attention on the array of senses he was experiencing. To him, they confirmed this was real and not a dream... and definitely not death. He felt continually strengthened by them.

As he fought against the continual pull to let himself be drawn back into the abyss, he became aware of something new. He found the muscles that controlled his eyelids. He put every ounce of strength into opening them. They fluttered and finally he succeeded in getting them open. When he opened them, it was to a vision more enchanting than anything he could imagine. Was she an angel? Her eyes... so fine.

He only had the strength to keep them open for a moment, and uncontrollably they closed on him. But he knew now that he had won the battle. There was no longer any force pulling him down. He would come out of this struggle.

This vision -- it was familiar -- yet not. He knew she was the source of the voice, the touch, and the scent. He was quite certain that he knew her. His mind would not yet let him remember presently, but he was confident it would come to him. With this knowledge and assurance, he rested and fell into a real sleep, as he had not slept in five days.

~~*

"Georgiana, come quick! I think your brother is waking up!"

When Georgiana realized what Elizabeth was saying, she quickly jumped out of bed and put on a robe.

"Heavens! Can it be true? What happened?" she asked ecstatically as she made her way to the door.

"He opened his eyes! He actually opened his eyes!" Elizabeth related.
"Is he now awake?" she asked.
"No, but I believe he is in a real sleep; not unconscious as he was."

They rushed back to the room and found him sleeping. There was a look of peace on his face that had not been present before. Elizabeth and Durnham informed Georgiana of their evening spent bringing down his fever. She was at first upset that they did not waken her earlier, but was later glad to have been spared the distress it most likely would have caused her.

They all waited in his room standing around him; Bingley finally joining them as he woke up from the commotion. Winston finally returned with the doctor, who was encouraged by what happened and gave much praise to Elizabeth and Durnham for their help in bringing down his fever. He had been prevented from coming any sooner, as he had not been able to leave his patient in town until now.

Their eyes were all on Darcy, anxious for another sign of life. The doctor checked his breathing, his temperature, and his heartbeat, announcing that they were all strong and improved. After examining him, he felt it was safe to leave him. He gave strict instructions that when he awakened, he was not to be allowed to overexert himself. He would continue to need plenty of rest.

"Let him eat and drink what he wants, however just a little at first," the doctor advised them. "Keep him as calm and relaxed as possible."

He then informed Georgiana that he was required to leave, but would return later in the day. When he left the house the sun was coming up over the horizon.

Elizabeth suddenly felt all the weight of fatigue upon her, having been up all night, and announced that she would try and get a little sleep. Everyone else felt similarly and decided to retire except Georgiana, who remained by her brother's side. She would not chance missing any developing improvement in him.

Georgiana eventually fell asleep, as well, with her head coming to rest on the edge of her brother's bed, but she slept lightly.

The servants were just beginning to move about and begin preparations for a new day when Georgiana was awakened by some rustling. She lifted her head promptly and looked toward her brother. He was stirring a little. Her heart quickened as she gently called out his name. "Fitzwilliam...William. Can you hear me? Can you open your eyes?"

She watched in awe as his eyes flickered and opened. Initially, it seemed they were not able to focus, but she was greatly encouraged. "Oh, William, you are back! Can you hear me?"

He nodded weakly. Georgiana threw herself across him and hugged him, breaking down in joyful tears. "I have been so worried about you! I was so afraid you would never come back to us!"

Darcy tried to lift his head to look at his sister, but she was merely a blur. He was barely able to lift it for lack of strength, and he became very dizzy as he did so. He was still not able to find the muscles that would allow him to speak. All he could do was moan.

To Georgiana, his waking was wonderful indeed! She wanted to inform everyone that he had awakened, but she did not want to leave his side. She would wait until someone came by and give them the grand news.

Suddenly a mumbled voice came from his lips. "Wha... happened?"

"You were in an accident. Do you not remember? Your carriage rolled over. You have been unconscious for five days!" She went on to acquaint him with the details of the mishap. His eyes often looked clouded over and confused. He found it difficult to concentrate, and his mind was not fully working. It was a struggle for him to follow her lengthy story.

He closed his eyes and focused all his effort on moving his hand over to Georgiana's and placed it upon hers. He wanted to squeeze it in reassurance, but had to settle for letting it rest on hers. He took in some deep breaths to give him some strength before he added, "Durnham, Winston?"

"They are both well. They were able to jump from the carriage before it rolled. Mr. Winston only sustained some minor bruises; Mr. Durnham, however, broke his ankle."

Darcy shook his head slightly. He began grasping more and more that his sister said, but had questions he could not find the wherewithal to formulate. Georgiana sensed that he wanted to know more, but did not know what more to tell him.

She sat with him in silence for a while, filled with utter joy in having him back. She held his hand even tighter, as if trying to pass some of her strength on to him. She wanted to tell him so much, but knew she should do so a little at a time.

Finally she said, "You gave us quite a scare last night. Your fever was terribly high. Normally we have had either the doctor or his nurse at your side, but last night we had neither due to a medical urgency in Lambton. Fortunately, Miss Bennet was by your side and she was instrumental in helping lower your temperature."

Darcy opened his eyes and looked at Georgiana bewildered. Darcy suddenly had a moment's recollection of a hazy dream. *Was it from last night? The heat, the voices, a face. Had that been Elizabeth? What would she be doing here? No, she could not be here.* When they had last parted it had not been on good terms at all! She had turned down his proposal and had most decidedly made her case against him. His mind must still not be lucid. He must have misunderstood her.

"Who...?"

"Miss Bennet... Miss Elizabeth Bennet. She and Mr. Durnham both were with you most of last night..." She stopped as she saw Darcy's eyes darken, as if he was trying to comprehend something. "What is it?"

He looked up at Georgiana, trying to sort out what she was saying. Finally with every attempt to draw from his reserve of strength he asked, "What is... *she* doing here?"

The look on his face caused Georgiana to withdraw sharply from him. Her hands began to shake and she pulled them from his. Elizabeth had told her, 'You do not have to worry about disappointing your brother.' Why then, was she now feeling such great apprehension? The look on his face imparted something that very much alarmed her.

Georgiana guardedly continued, "After your accident... I immediately wrote to Miss Bennet. I thought she ought to know."

"Miss Bennet? Why…?"

The tone of his voice caused a feeling of great dread to come upon the young girl. Georgiana felt anxieties arise in her that she had not experienced in well over a year. She could not determine the reason behind it, but she felt almost faint.

Georgiana moistened her mouth which was now very dry. "I felt she needed to know because the two of you are engaged."

Darcy abruptly turned his head away from Georgiana. His words came out slow, deliberate, and with great effort. "Miss Bennet and I are *not* engaged!"

Georgiana's hands went to her mouth in shock. She could neither move nor could she utter a sound. She looked down, unable to meet the stern gaze of her brother, but knew, from the tone of his voice that he was very angry.

She began shaking and was only able to utter a meek, "I do not understand. You wrote to me…"

"Unfortunately, I did." This was taking more strength than he had, but he had to finish. He took a few more breaths and summoned what little strength he had left. "She refused my offer of marriage!"

A sudden look of alarm spread across Georgiana's face. She brought her hands to her face and he heard a smothered, "No!" as she pulled farther away from him. "That cannot be! Why did she not tell me? I do not understand!"

Georgiana, gasping and dissolving in sobs, turned and fled from the room, almost colliding with Durnham as she ran out the door. Darcy watched in horror as his beloved sister, who had been so grieved over his condition and so grateful for his recovery, was now in a state of anguish and utter shock.

Durnham rushed in and asked if anything was the matter.

"Get one of the maids and have her see to Miss Darcy; make sure she is all right. Then come back immediately. I have some questions."

His heart pounded, both from the exertion of these last few minutes and his confused emotions. *Why had Elizabeth come? Why was she here?* What was he missing? He could not get his mind to come up with any logical answers. *Think, man!* Even if Georgiana had a misunderstanding about whether or not they were engaged, Elizabeth certainly did not. He shook his head, trying to sort things out; his brain refused to cooperate.

He brought his hand to his forehead and rubbed it. This was no good! He turned his head to the side, and suddenly caught a scent that drew him back to recollections of last night. The heat, the cold, the voices, *the scent*! His hand slowly reached back as if searching for something, behind his head, under the pillow. He felt something and pulled it out.

It was an embroidered handkerchief. He looked at the colourful embroidery that occupied one corner and his heart stopped as he noticed the initials, *EB*. He brought it to his nose and breathed in the gardenia scent. He recalled the vision of the woman in the night, the fine eyes. As the vague memories became clearer, he now knew they were of Elizabeth.

He began to dwell on the fact that Elizabeth had been walking the halls of Pemberley these last few days. She had eaten in his dining room; sat in his sitting room. Had she taken her early morning walks out in the grounds of Pemberley? How many times in the previous months had he imagined her thus, and now, while he had been completely oblivious, she had been there. *But why?*

He had more questions than answers and was anxious for Durnham to return. As he heard him hurry back down the hall, Darcy stuffed the handkerchief back under the pillow.

"I have sent Mrs. Reynolds to look after Miss Darcy, Sir."

"Thank you." Darcy took a deep breath. "Durnham, was Miss Bennet standing over here last night?" he asked pointing to the left side of the bed.

"Miss *Elizabeth* Bennet was. She spent most of the time with you last night doing all she could to bring down your fever. I came in to assist, but she did most of the work. She certainly seemed to know what to do!"

Darcy tried to think of what else to ask, but he was not sure that Durnham would have any answers. He need not have worried, though, because Durnham immediately continued, "She has been most helpful to Miss Darcy. She is certainly strong. She came right in and was not at all dismayed at your appearance when she first saw you. You looked quite a fright! Almost looked dead! Poor Miss *Jane* Bennet, as well as Mr. Bingley, struggled with composure at seeing you!"

Darcy's eyes slowly turned to Durnham. "Miss Jane Bennet *and* Bingley are both here?" Durnham nodded.

Realization suddenly hit Darcy. He took a deep breath as he finally was able to formulate a reason for Elizabeth's presence here. She must have come, in response to Georgiana's letter, to reunite her sister with Bingley. He was not sure how it all came about, but was confident that had to be part of the reason.

Darcy suddenly began issuing orders to Durnham. "Draw me a bath and get my clothes! I must get up and get dressed!"

Chapter 6

Durnham looked at the fire in Darcy's eyes and felt now, for a certainty, that his master would fully recover. He could not grant his request, however. "I am sorry, Sir, but I must refuse, at least on the latter. The doctor said for you to take things slowly, not to do too much at first. I will draw your bath, granted you need one; however, I will not have you going to all the trouble of dressing. You are still dreadfully unwell. I will get you clean night clothes and your robe, but that will have to suffice!"

"Are you defying me?" asked Darcy incredulously.

"I am only abiding by the orders of the doctor, Sir. Getting up and dressed would not be the wisest thing for you right now. You need to conserve your energy."

"Durnham, there are some things I need to discuss with a few people and I cannot do it... dressed like this!"

"And why not, Sir? Everyone in this household has seen you in your night clothes, and *less!*"

Darcy abruptly turned to him and asked, "What do you mean *and less*?"

"Last night Miss Elizabeth had to remove your shirt to wipe down your chest with cool cloths." He inwardly smiled, knowing the mortification Darcy must be feeling. "Now, Sir, let me draw your bath. I will summon Winston to help me move you and also get a plate of food and drink for you." He bowed and turned to leave.

Darcy was agitated, but knew he could do nothing without his valet's help. "Fine, let us get to it!"

When Durnham set off to draw the bath water, Darcy decided to try to sit up. Once again he felt dizziness overtake him and had to lie back down. He would have to do this in small increments. He did not want to recline in a bed all day. If he was to talk with Elizabeth, he wanted to be sitting upright in a chair. He preferred to do it in his dress clothes, but obviously he had to settle for his nightclothes and robe. He shook his head in much consternation.

When Durnham returned, Winston accompanied him. They came to the side of the bed, and supporting Darcy's back, slowly lifted him. He closed his eyes as another wave of dizziness swept over him. Once in a sitting position, he put up his hand for Durnham to stop. He sat there for a while as he waited and hoped that he would not faint. Finally he indicated to Durnham to continue.

His valet helped him swing his feet over the side of the bed. Darcy felt the muscles of his legs scream out to him as he moved them for the first time in five days. He stretched and wiggled his toes, trying to work out the lethargic muscles.

"Now, Mr. Darcy, put your arm around Winston and let him carry as much of your weight as possible. I will not be much help with my broken ankle. But I shall be ready to catch you if you start to fall."

The men went helped Darcy walk to the bath chamber and as he stepped into the bath. As he settled in, he relaxed and felt as if he could fall asleep sitting right there. They did their best to wash his hair and then lathered him with soap. With that finished, Durnham prepared his face for shaving. As Darcy leaned his head back, he closed his eyes and was soon fast asleep again.

"I have a feeling that our friend here is going to be worn out by the end of the day!" Winston said to Durnham. "You know he will never let himself get all the rest he needs!"

When Durnham finished, they let Darcy sleep as long as they could. They knew it would do him good. After a while they gently shook him, and at length Darcy began to stir. He looked around him; feeling a little disoriented, but finally was able to recall all that had transpired that morning.

Both men helped him out of the bath and dressed him in clean nightclothes and his robe. They escorted him back to the infirmary, where they sat him down in the chair that was next to his bed.

"Sir, it would be best if you sit here for a moment to gain more strength before we take you to your study. Try to eat a little bit and have something to drink."

"Thank you. I think I will. Will you check on my sister for me?"

Winston agreed to do that as Durnham went back to clean up the bath chamber. Darcy was exhausted, but did not want to let the others know. He sat in the chair, picking at some of the food that was put out for him when he suddenly remembered the handkerchief. He stretched out to reach under the pillow and drew it out, bringing it up to his face. Yes, it still carried the fragrance of gardenia. He quickly, surreptitiously, slipped it into the pocket of his robe.

When Winston returned, he informed Darcy that Georgiana had locked herself in her room and was seeing no one. At this news, Darcy felt an even greater resolve to leave this room. He was more determined than ever to see Elizabeth. Since he had discovered she was there, that had become forefront on his mind. He wanted answers from her. He *needed* answers from her. He did not know if he wanted more to shout at her for deceiving his sister or to tell her again how much he loved her, as the memory of the face from last night came again before him. He knew he had to see her.

When Durnham and Winston returned to his side, he asked them to take him to his study. As the two men helped him through the great house, Darcy tried his best to walk as much as he could on his own strength. They came to the study and placed him in a large overstuffed chair off to the side of his desk, lifting his feet and placing them upon a footstool.

"Please ask Miss Elizabeth to come see me." He looked over at the two men

and added, "Then find Bingley. I want to talk to him, after I have seen her."
They nodded and set out to carry out his request.

When left to himself, Darcy wondered what he would say when she came in; how he would respond to seeing her again! His mind was in turmoil, wondering if she deceived Georgiana out of a vindictive spirit in anger against him or simply a selfish one in trying to reunite her sister and Bingley. He could not believe she would be so malicious, but why had she been so uncaring in how she treated his sister?

Winston went out to search for Bingley, but was told that he had most abruptly gone outside with Miss Jane Bennet when news spread of Darcy's awakening. Upon searching the grounds closest to the house, he could not be found.

Elizabeth had just come downstairs when Durnham found her.

"Miss Bennet," he bowed. "Mr. Darcy wishes to see you in his study."

Elizabeth's jaw dropped and her eyes widened in disbelief. "Mr. Darcy has awakened, then?" She suddenly felt discomposure quickly spread throughout her body.

"Yes. He is expecting you."

Elizabeth was not prepared for this. When she left him last night he had not fully awakened. Obviously he had discovered she was there. *What must he think of my being here?* she wondered.

Knocking lightly at the door, she heard his voice weakly command her to come in. She timidly stepped inside looking at first toward the desk, but then moving her eyes over to where he sat in the chair. He still looked pale and weak, but he sat upright. She noticed now how fresh and clean he looked; how the curls on his head were still wet from being washed and the locks were glimmering and bouncing in the light, unlike the other night when they had been matted to his forehead.

When she met his gaze, however, she saw a steely determination that caused her to draw back.

"Mr. Darcy," she politely said and curtseyed. "I am so glad to have heard you are recovering. We have been quite concerned."

"Hmmm, yes. Thank you, Miss Bennet. Please excuse me for not rising." He noticed she seemed tired, there was very little light in her eyes and they were dark. She seemed uneasy, but he still found her very engaging.

There was an awkward silence that Elizabeth broke. "I am sure you must be wondering what I am doing here." She smiled nervously, gearing herself for the explanation she had planned to give him.

"No, Miss Bennet. I perfectly comprehend your reason for being here." His voice became harsh despite his obvious struggle to maintain his strength. "It is fairly obvious that you came here with your sister with the intention of reuniting her with Bingley; throwing her back in his favour!"

"Excuse me, Sir. I do not believe she was ever *out* of his favour!"

"But you agree that you came here for the sole purpose of manipulating the situation between the two of them!"

"Manipulate! Mr. Darcy, if anyone did any manipulating, it was you! You manipulated Mr. Bingley's affection to steer him unwillingly away from my sister! Coming here only provided them the opportunity to meet again. What you did to separate them was unwarranted and unjust! I do not believe that you could have been more wrong about the feelings two people have for each other!"

He looked at her; his eyes boring through her. "Quite the contrary, Miss Bennet, I assure you. I believe there was another time when I was *more* wrong!"

Elizabeth looked at him, feeling as if he had twisted a knife in her back and then she looked down. She felt as though the world was spinning around her.

When she finally looked back at him, she met his gaze. She wondered why every meeting with this man resulted in argument. Where was the man for whom Georgiana had been so full of praise? Where was the man who was so generous and thoughtful? Where was the smile that beckoned down at her from his portrait, but always seemed hidden from her somewhere deep inside?

Unexpectedly he became civil again and asked, "Now that you are here at Pemberley, how do you like it?"

His sudden change of manner surprised her. "I like it very much, Sir. It is a grand place that I am sure anyone would find to their liking."

He accepted her response and asked, "And Georgiana, you have gotten to know her well?"

"Um, yes," Elizabeth suddenly gulped. *Where was Georgiana?* Why had she not seen her since she had gotten up? Why was she not at her brother's side, even now? "She is a very sweet girl. I have enjoyed her company."

Darcy noticed Elizabeth's fine eyes suddenly dart about, filling with dread. "Have you?" he asked sarcastically.

Darcy shifted in his chair, looking past Elizabeth, and then looked back at her. "I have been quite unaware of what has happened here these last few days, as you well know. But may I ask you why you let my sister believe that we were engaged the whole time you have been here and did not tell her the truth?"

Elizabeth gasped and her hands flew to her mouth. Her eyes widened with a fear that was too great to disguise.

"Sir, where is Georgiana now?"

"Apparently she has locked herself in her room and will not allow anyone in to see her."

He looked at Elizabeth intently, waiting for a response, but she seemed stunned, unable to say anything.

He continued, "When I told her that we were *not* engaged, as apparently she had been led to believe; that you had refused my offer of marriage, she fled the room in great distress!"

Elizabeth could bear it no longer. She muttered a very anguished, "Excuse me," and rushed out of the room. The last Darcy heard was, "I must go talk with her!"

Darcy crumbled in his chair. He put his head back and felt great distress. In one morning he had the two most exceptional women in his life run out of his room completely distraught. He knew not what to make of it. In one way, he owed Elizabeth his life, feeling it was her very presence that helped pull him back out of that dark chasm in which he found himself last night. Yet how could she have behaved this way toward his beloved sister?

He stuffed his hands in his pocket and suddenly felt the handkerchief. He pulled it out and put it again to his face, savouring the gentle scent. He felt confused, anxious, irritated; he did not know what all else. Not knowing why, his only response was to call for his valet, "Durnham, come in here!"

Durnham came in immediately and Darcy was at a loss for words. He needed to bark some command at him, but knew not what he wanted. He greatly desired for him to fix things, make him stronger, make him think clearer. "Bring me some coffee!" was all he was able to say. "And make it strong!"

As Elizabeth ran out of the room towards the staircase, she encountered Jane and Charles.

Charles approached her with a wide grin on his face. "Oh Miss Elizabeth, we have the most wonderful news!"

Elizabeth nodded and said, "Yes, it *is* good news that Mr. Darcy has finally awakened. He is in his study."

"Oh yes, that! But *we* also have some good news! I am going to go in and inform Darcy right away. Your sister shall tell you!"

Charles walked away and Elizabeth smiled at her sister, who was also beaming. "He proposed, Lizzy. Charles and I are to be married!"

Elizabeth wrapped her arms about her sister in a big hug. "I am so happy for you Jane! This could not have come at a better time!"

"Why do you say that?" she asked.

"Because in that study is a man who is very angry with me and upstairs is his sister who probably will never trust me again." Tears ran down Elizabeth's cheeks. "I fear we shall probably have to leave Pemberley, at the latest tomorrow."

Jane saw that her sister was visibly upset and took her hand. "Elizabeth, what happened?"

Through her tears, she quickly relayed what had happened; how devastated Miss Darcy became when she discovered the truth about Elizabeth and her brother.

"I was just on my way to her room now to try to talk with her. But I fear that it would be best if we leave Pemberley. We should probably begin to get our things in order and make arrangements to return to Longbourn as soon as possible."

Elizabeth leaned over and kissed her sister on her cheek, and whispered, "I am so happy for you!" She then pulled away and said, "I must go now to see Georgiana."

Elizabeth took the stairs quickly, praying for the right words to say. She came to Georgiana's door and lightly knocked. "Georgiana, it is Elizabeth, please may I talk with you?"

There was no answer. "Please, Georgiana, I wish to talk with you; may I please come in?"

Slowly the door opened, and Elizabeth was taken aback at the condition of the young girl. Her face was flushed and her hair dishevelled. She was shaking and unable to mutter anything intelligible. She was so completely distraught that

Elizabeth felt all she could do was put her arms around her and take her in her arms.

Elizabeth held the girl gently, taking her back over to her bed, and they sat down. Neither was able to say anything as they both allowed their tears to fall. Eventually Elizabeth gathered herself and whispered, "I am so sorry, Georgiana. You must allow me to explain."

Elizabeth felt the girl tense and try to pull away. "Please, you must believe me when I say that I did not mean to hurt you by not telling you about your brother and me. I did not know how to tell you and you believed so strongly that my being here would help him recover. I could not break the news to you until we were more confident of his recovery."

Elizabeth drew herself from the girl and looked at her. "Look at me, Georgiana. I would never intentionally hurt you."

Through sobs, Georgiana rasped, "I do not understand."

"I cannot excuse myself for what I did, but I at least want you to know why."

Georgiana looked at her. Elizabeth did not even know where to begin, but she had to begin somewhere. "When you wrote to me, telling me of your brother's accident, I was not aware that you believed us engaged. What you did was based on what you believed to be true from your brother's letter. You had no reason to doubt that I had accepted his offer. You acted in a compassionate, thoughtful way, desiring to inform me of his condition."

Georgiana shook her head. "No, I acted impulsively; it was immature. I have let my brother down again."

"Please do not believe that, Georgiana! You were thinking of him! He cannot think ill of you for this!"

"My brother is so angry with me, I cannot bear this again!"

"Trust me. He is not angry with you. If he is angry with anyone, it is me."

"But Eliz... Miss Bennet, I still do not understand." She looked at her with great anguish in her face. "I just do not understand."

Elizabeth did not know how else to explain her actions to the young girl. She felt inconsolable that her actions led to Georgiana's present state. How she wished she could turn back the clock and make things right. "I would do anything to change the decision I made not to tell you. Please forgive me."

Georgiana looked at her through her tear-filled eyes. "But I do not understand... *why* did you refuse my brother's offer of marriage?"

Elizabeth looked down and took in a deep breath. Of course this young girl would not understand! What was she to say? Elizabeth took one of Georgiana's hands in both of hers. "There were several reasons. The first was actually a misunderstanding between the two of us that has since been cleared up. At the time I felt he had acted unjustly. The other reason is because he did something that I found very difficult to forgive."

Georgiana looked at her questioningly. "What was it he did?"

Elizabeth answered in a very soft voice. "He purposefully tried to separate Jane from Mr. Bingley when he began to suspect that his friend was close to proposing. He then persuaded him to abandon any thought of marriage to her by claiming she held no regard for him, when indeed she did."

Georgiana looked at her in astonishment. "I cannot believe my brother would do such a thing! Why, anyone can see how happy Jane and Charles are together! Are you quite certain he did that?"

"Yes. He admitted it to me himself. I felt I could not marry a man who would hurt my sister in such a way; have so little regard for her." She brought her face close to Georgiana's. "When you wrote to me, I agreed to come, along with Jane, so they could see each other again. If Mr. Bingley did indeed still have affections for her, this would give them another chance to find out. And do you know what has happened? He made an offer just this morning and Jane accepted! If you had not written that letter to us, this may never have occurred!"

Elizabeth tried to smile, hoping that this would soothe Georgiana. Her crying stopped, but her breathing was still interspersed with spasms of deep, short breaths.

Elizabeth reached into her pocket for her handkerchief to wipe Georgiana's eyes. She was surprised when she could not find it. *I must go look for it later*, she thought to herself.

Georgiana eventually calmed down a bit and Elizabeth breathed a sigh of relief. "Georgiana, I think you must go down and talk this through with your brother. I know he harbours no ill feelings towards you." *Only towards me!*

"Will you accompany me?" she asked.

"No, I am afraid I must get my things in order in preparation to leave."

"You are not leaving?"

"Yes, I think we must," answered Elizabeth. "I think it would be best. Take some time to freshen up and then go down there and talk with him. Besides," she smiled, "He is too weak to do anything too terrible!"

Elizabeth left Georgiana, feeling confident that she had been able to set things right with her. She knew, however, that to set things right with Mr. Darcy, it would take a major miracle.

~~*

After Elizabeth had rushed from the study, Darcy put his head back against the chair feeling emotionally and physically drained. He did not have the strength to reason what had taken place or why. He did not know if the anger he felt now was directed against himself or Elizabeth.

He wished to be able to think more clearly, but all he felt capable of doing this moment was to close his eyes and fall asleep. Much to his chagrin, the door burst open and Bingley marched in.

"Darcy," greeted Bingley with a wide grin, "Welcome back to the land of the living!"

"Bingley," nodded Darcy as he steeled himself for Bingley's exuberant personality. He was certainly not in any sort of frame of mind for it.

"You had us genuinely worried! How good it is that you are yourself again!"

"Not quite myself, I assure you."

"Uh, yes, well…" Bingley looked down, seemingly at a loss for words. Darcy waited a bit, surprised by this uncharacteristic silence. Bingley began wringing his hands together and looked several times as if he was going to say something, but then stopped. Darcy took advantage of this time to try to settle down, catch his breath, and focus his mind.

Bingley finally found the words he was looking for. "Darcy, I have something to tell you, and I do not want you to be upset. The doctor advised us not to upset you. So I am telling you in advance to remain calm."

Darcy looked up at him suspiciously.

Bingley took a deep breath. "Just a little while ago… I asked Miss Jane Bennet for her hand in marriage. And she accepted!" He gave him a nervous smile, and stepped back, as if anticipating some extreme response from his friend.

Instead, Darcy remained very cool. "Congratulations, Bingley. I am happy for you."

Bingley looked at him in amazement. "You are? Well, thank you, Darcy. I appreciate your congratulations and want to assure you that I am very happy too! But you look tired; I will not keep you any longer. I just wished to inform you of that and to let you know how glad I am you have come back to us!"

"Thank you, Bingley. I appreciate that."

With that, Bingley quickly backed out of the room and rejoined Jane, who informed him of the things Elizabeth shared; that they would most likely be departing in the morning.

Darcy closed his eyes and as sleep became increasingly hard to refuse, he slipped his hand back into his pocket and grasped the embroidered handkerchief, holding on to it as if it were some sort of lifeline to his complete recovery and sanity.

Chapter 7

Georgiana rinsed her face and straightened her hair and clothes to ready herself to go to the study. She could do nothing about her red eyes, but felt that Elizabeth was right. She needed to go talk things through with her brother.

She was anxious to get back to him; to stay by his side and look after him. She was still not convinced, however, that he was not angry with her. When she came to his study, the door was slightly ajar and she pushed it open.

Darcy was still in his chair, his head back and his eyes staring vacantly at the ceiling. He held a cup of coffee with one hand and had his other hand in the pocket of his robe. When he heard her step in, he looked up and smiled.

"Come in, Georgie." He had not called her that special term of endearment for a long time. She had lately wondered whether he thought that she was too grown up to be called that anymore. But by his using it again, it reassured her and did what it was intended to do -- endear her to him.

She approached him and knelt on the floor at his feet, laying her head against his knee. "I am sorry for running out on you earlier." Her eyes began to well up with tears again, and Darcy reached down and put his arms around her.

"No, please forgive me." He stroked her head and gently said, "I am afraid I am not quite myself and was more concerned earlier about trying to understand what you were saying than I was concerned for your feelings. I am afraid I was severely abrupt."

"I did not mean to distress you, especially in your condition. I should never have interfered in your personal situation by inviting Miss Elizabeth to Pemberley."

Darcy took a deep breath and let it out slowly. "Georgiana, there was no way for you to have known what happened after I wrote you that letter. If anyone is at fault, it is I, for writing too prematurely. I had an arrogant presumption that I would be accepted by her. I was wrong."

Georgiana looked with great wonder at the expression on his face, seeing great pain. She knew it hurt deeply to have to discuss this. There was more to this situation between him and Elizabeth than either of them was willing to share, but because she felt he was still so physically weak and this line of conversation was taxing on him, she decided to let the subject drop... for a while at least. She was content to stay at his side while he rested and she pondered what could be done to remedy this state of affairs. She had a curious conviction that her brother and Elizabeth belonged together.

~~*

Elizabeth returned to her room to begin packing. She had a diversity of feelings about leaving Pemberley. She regretted leaving Georgiana, but wanted to be out of Mr. Darcy's presence as soon as possible. She knew from this last encounter and what had happened previously between them that his regard for her certainly must have dwindled to nothing. How he must congratulate himself that she had not accepted him and that he was not bound to her in any way. Yet knowing he felt this way did not sit well with her.

She knew Pemberley's servants would be willing to pack for her, but she chose to do it herself. At the moment, she wanted the solitude of her room and its refuge. As she proceeded to gather her things, she realized her hands were shaking. If she had known how these few days would have turned out, she never would have agreed to come. Yet how could she regret the friendship that had developed between her and Georgiana? And she certainly could not regret Jane's and Charles' engagement.

She went to the dressing table and picked up her personal items and put them in her small bag. She picked up her bottle of toilet water and carefully tucked it inside, guarding that it would not turn over and spill. The sight of it reminded her that she needed to go looking for her handkerchief. Where had she last used it? At the moment she could not remember.

After lingering as long as she could in the room, Elizabeth decided to venture out and join Jane so they could make plans to leave on the morrow. She opened the door and was grateful no one was around. She carefully walked down the stairs, keeping an eye open for her sister. With each step she took down the staircase, her heart beat a little faster, knowing she was drawing closer to Mr. Darcy.

When she came to the bottom of the stairs, her gaze went directly towards the study, as if to make sure he was not about to walk through those doors. The door was slightly closed and she wondered if Georgiana had gone in to talk with him.

She walked over to the sitting room and found Jane and Bingley talking. Jane stood up quickly and reached out her hands to Elizabeth. "We saw Georgiana walk to the study. Did your talk with her assuage her distress?"

"I hope so. I cannot believe the mess I have made of things!"

"Miss Elizabeth," chimed in Bingley. "We all had a part in the decision to delay telling Georgiana the truth for a time. It was not solely your fault. I am as much to blame as you."

Elizabeth smiled. "We may all have made the decision, Mr. Bingley, but I fear that based on my history with Mr. Darcy, he is placing most of the fault, if not all, on me."

"Yes, your history with Darcy... That is something that has me completely baffled!" Bingley admitted. "When your sister told me of his proposal to you, I must confess I was completely astonished. In all that time we spent together, he never let on to me how he felt! In fact, he... well, I was surprised."

"I must admit I was completely caught by surprise, as well. But that is in the past, and I think it would be prudent if I be gone from here as soon as it can be arranged."

"Lizzy, surely he can be made to understand," Jane suggested.

"Possibly, someday. But until then, I think it would be best if we leave. I have begun packing and I was just about to inform Mrs. Reynolds or Winston so further arrangements can be made for our departure first thing in the morning."

"Oh how I do wish you would stay!" Bingley entreated. "But I know it probably is best. Your family is most likely anxious for you to return home. I shall look forward to my returning to Netherfield within the week and visiting Longbourn to talk to your father about my offer of marriage!" He looked at Jane and grinned and she returned one back to him.

Elizabeth remembered the reason she had come down and said, "I think I shall go see about our plans for our departure tomorrow. If you will excuse me."

She left them and walked toward the dining room and kitchen area, where she thought she would find Mrs. Reynolds. When she was not there, she inquired from the kitchen staff and they informed her she was outside.

Elizabeth went out to look for her, and as she did, her heart was gripped with a strong pang of regret. As she looked around, she realized how much she would miss this place. How she had enjoyed the few walks through these fine grounds that she had stolen; how almost every window in the house afforded a splendid view; and the house itself Elizabeth considered very fine.

Instead of finding Mrs. Reynolds, she encountered Winston. She informed him of their desire to leave first thing in the morning and he assured her that it would be no difficulty; that the carriage would be available to take them to Lambton. From there he would make arrangements for them to hire a carriage that would take them home. He then let her know how much he regretted their leaving and hoped that they would return someday soon.

As Elizabeth walked back, she shook her head. Perhaps her sister might grace these grounds again, being married to Mr. Darcy's good friend, but she most likely would not. With that thought, she decided to take one last walk. It would be a few hours yet before the sun set and as she had nothing to do in the house, felt a walk would be the best thing for her.

As she walked down one path, she recalled her first amble out here with Georgiana and how they had shared a special connection. She recollected how she had been drawn to the young, shy girl, and how humbled she was that Georgiana seemed to trust her and open up to her.

She walked mindlessly, taking paths that had beckoned to her earlier. When she saw that the sun was about to set, she turned back toward the house. Upon approaching it, her eyes glanced to the window of the study. She felt a peculiar regret about having to leave; particularly leaving things the way they were with Mr. Darcy. She settled that she would go to him before she left and apologize. He did not have to accept it, but for her own peace of mind she would do it.

Climbing the steps to the house, a chill enveloped her as the sun dipped below the horizon. She entered the warm house and was greeted with the smell of supper cooking. Walking into the sitting room and then the dining room, she found them both empty. Inquiring when the meal would be served, she was told that Miss Darcy would be eating with her brother in the study and that she, Miss Bennet, and Mr. Bingley could come to the dining room at any time.

She thanked them and left to find her sister. Remembering, however, that she had her handkerchief when she was in the infirmary the night before, she decided to first check to see if it was still there.

When she went in to the infirmary, all the linens had been stripped from the bed and the room cleaned. She looked under the bed but knew that with such a thorough cleaning, it would most likely be gone. As she took leave of the room, she encountered one of the servants and mentioned her handkerchief.

"I am the one who cleaned this room, Miss, and I am sorry, but I did not see a handkerchief."

"Thank you," Elizabeth said with a little disappointment. "I am not quite certain where I left it, but I do recall having it in here last night. If you do find it after I have left, could you give it to Miss Darcy to send to me or bring with her when she comes for Charles' and Jane's wedding? It has my initials on it, *EB,* and a few embroidered flowers."

"I will certainly watch for it, Miss Bennet."

"Thank you." *Well, it is only a handkerchief,* she thought to herself. *I can always embroider another one.*

From there she went to her room where she found Jane with one of the maids who was packing her things. She sat down with her.

Jane saw her and said, "Lizzy, we were concerned you were gone so long. Is everything well with you?"

"Yes, Jane. This place has such fine grounds. I wanted to take one last walk before I left. I do not think I shall ever again see such a splendid place as this." She breathed in a deep sigh and recalled that the meal was ready. "Oh, I was told we could come down anytime to the dining room for supper. Are you hungry?"

"Yes, I believe I am!"

"Good. Let us send for Mr. Bingley. Do you suppose he will want to join us?" Elizabeth teased her sister.

"Oh, Lizzy, I would certainly hope so!"

When they stepped out of the room, Bingley was already at the base of the stairs, awaiting them. Elizabeth marvelled at how the two of them beamed whenever they saw each other. Both wore wide smiles on their faces. She was sure it could not have been more than a few minutes since they had last seen each other. She shook her head in amazement, wondering how they would behave when they would see each other again after a full week's separation.

During supper, Jane and Charles spoke almost exclusively with each other. Elizabeth joined in their conversation occasionally, but was content to eat quietly. She often looked toward the door, wondering whether Georgiana would come out from her brother's room and join them. She had not seen her since their visit earlier and was very anxious to know how she was faring.

As they were about to finish, Georgiana finally walked in. Elizabeth was relieved to see that her countenance had indeed improved greatly. She walked first over to Jane and Charles.

"May I congratulate you on your upcoming wedding? Both Elizabeth and my brother informed me you are to be married! I am so very pleased that you became engaged right here at Pemberley!"

"Thank you, Miss Darcy" they both replied.

She then walked over to Elizabeth. "Miss Elizabeth, before you leave, I want to tell you how much your visit meant to me. I do look forward to seeing you again when we visit Hertfordshire for the wedding."

Elizabeth took Georgiana's hands in hers. There was so much she wanted to say; so much she wanted to convey. "Georgiana, I have genuinely enjoyed my visit with you also." She gave her hands a squeeze. "And believe me; I am truly sorry for any hurt I caused you by not imparting the truth about your brother and myself to you. I never meant to hurt you."

"Do not concern yourself, Miss Elizabeth. I am just grateful that my brother is greatly improved, and for that, I have much to thank you for."

"No," Elizabeth laughed, "I am sure it was mostly his strong constitution that was fighting for him."

Georgiana excused herself to go back to her brother in the study, as he was directly to be taken to his own room. Winston and Durnham stayed at his side as they ushered him past the dining room. Bingley and Jane went out to greet him and had some dialogue with him while Elizabeth remained where she was. Her absence was very noticeable.

She decided to retire early that night, knowing they would be rising early in preparation to leave. It had been a long day and she was fatigued. How good it would feel to sink into bed and drift off to sleep. When Jane finally came in a bit later, Elizabeth was so sound asleep; she did not even wake up.

~~*

The next morning a maid came and tapped lightly at the door to waken the two sisters. It was still fairly dark outside and the air was cool. It took all of Elizabeth's strength to pull the covers off and begin getting ready. When they both had finished dressing, they packed all the miscellaneous items that had been needed for the morning. Before they left the room, they gave one last glance around, making sure nothing was left. Elizabeth hoped she would find her handkerchief, but it was still not to be found.

The smell of tea and sweet rolls greeted them. Quite a few servants were up and scurrying about. As Elizabeth and Jane enjoyed their last breakfast at Pemberley, footsteps were heard out in the hall. Elizabeth looked over and caught an informally dressed Darcy pass by. He was walking on his own, but Durnham was at his side. He looked in the doorway just as she looked out. Their eyes locked in a gaze that Elizabeth could not turn from. She shuddered as she remembered her decision to go to him and ask for forgiveness before she left. He did not come in to the dining room so she assumed he was going down to the study again.

She knew what she had to do, but waited a few minutes for him to get settled. Durnham came in and poured a cup of coffee and prepared a plate of food for him. "Excuse me, Mr. Durnham. Do you think Mr. Darcy would be willing to see me right now?"

He smiled and assured her now would be a most convenient time. She followed him back to the room and he stood aside to allow her to walk in before him. When Darcy looked up and saw Elizabeth, it gave him a start, having expected it to be Durnham. He looked a little sheepish, as he quickly looked down and placed something from his hand into his trouser pocket. He took the cup of coffee from Durnham, who then excused himself.

"Good morning, Miss Bennet. I hope you and your sister are well."

"We are. Thank you. And you?"

"I feel greatly improved this morning. Thank you. I understand you are to leave this morning. I hope you found your stay at Pemberley hospitable."

"It was Sir, very much so." She paused to gather her thoughts. He was being civil; that helped. She could not determine what he was thinking or feeling by the look on his face. When she had walked in and he saw her, he looked startled; a little ruffled. She knew her being there must cause him much uneasiness.

"I wanted to speak with you before I left to tell you how sorry I am for the misunderstanding and subsequent hurt that my silence caused your sister. Please forgive me."

"That is very gracious of you Miss Bennet. I do forgive you. She apparently has a very high regard for you that has not been altered by this."

"Thank you."

Darcy continued to look upon her, trying to discern her feelings toward him. Elizabeth struggled with trying to meet his gaze. She finally looked away, feeling herself at a loss for words.

An awkward silence hung in the air, until Elizabeth finally responded, "Well, goodbye, Sir. May God grant you a complete and speedy recovery."

"Thank you. May you and your sister have a safe trip home." *How trite that sounded!* How much more he wanted to say, but the disconcerted look on her face said it all to him. She wanted nothing more than to be out of his presence.

She nodded and found that all she could utter was a soft, "Thank you; goodbye, then." She curtseyed and exited the room.

Darcy's heart had been pounding all the while she stood before him, his hand holding tightly onto the handkerchief that was still in his pocket. He almost pulled it out to give it back to her, but selfishly changed his mind. As she walked out, he let out the breath he had been unwittingly holding and dropped his head back. He pulled out the handkerchief and without thinking, put it to his face. He noticed that the scent of gardenia was fading; that he had to inhale more deeply now to catch any scent. He wondered whether his love and admiration for Elizabeth would eventually fade too, just as this scent had.

Georgiana finally came down and was visiting with Charles and Jane in the dining room when Elizabeth returned. The young girl excused herself for a moment to go to her brother, and Elizabeth walked toward the door to go outside as their things were being loaded on to the carriage. Charles accompanied Jane into the study as well so she could say goodbye to Darcy.

Georgiana returned directly and stood next to Elizabeth. "I shall miss you, Elizabeth. I have enjoyed my time here with you. Please forgive me if I made you at all uncomfortable by my assumption of your engagement with my brother. I know that it must have put you in a very awkward situation."

"Georgiana, please do not concern yourself. Much good came out of what you did. I greatly enjoyed my stay here and making your acquaintance."

"I look forward to our visit to Hertfordshire. I should very much like to meet your family and see where you live," the young girl softly said.

"I look forward to that too, Georgiana." She took her hand and squeezed it.

When Charles and Jane came back out, all goodbyes were said. Elizabeth could see the anguish in Charles' eyes in Jane having to leave. He and Georgiana stood back as the two girls approached the carriage. Suddenly Georgiana ran forward to Elizabeth, giving her a big hug and burying her head against her shoulder. "Thank you for everything, Elizabeth!" Tears ran down her face.

Elizabeth wrapped her arms around her, and then pulled away, looking into her eyes. "Georgiana, you did much yourself. Now, do not let those tears spoil your pretty face. If I only had my handkerchief, I would wipe each of those tears away, but unfortunately I have misplaced it somewhere."

"I shall inquire whether anyone has found it," Georgiana offered.

Elizabeth smiled at the girl. As she turned to go, she caught sight of the window to the study. She saw a slight movement in the reflection that drew her attention, but for the glare of the sun could not ascertain what it was.

~~*

Being left alone in the study, Darcy pulled himself up and slowly walked over to window. How often he had gone to a window and looked out at nothing, as a means of escape from what was inside -- both inside of him and inside his surroundings. Now he looked out at someone leaving who had so captivated his heart that he was unsure what to do about it. He had been angry with her yesterday; at the hurt she had caused his sister. He watched, though, as Georgiana ran over to her and hugged her and how Elizabeth had returned the hug in a very fervent way. It gripped the depths of his emotions as he realized she had not just captured his heart, but his sister's as well.

He watched as Elizabeth's eyes glanced up at the study window. His eyes remained fixed on her although he drew back from the window. He knew not whether she saw him; he should not be watching her like this. He continued to watch her, however, as she stepped into the carriage, followed by her sister, and soon they were whisked away. He felt transfixed and unable to move, watching the carriage until it was completely out of sight. He stood there for a few more minutes until he heard Bingley's boisterous entrance into the room.

"Darcy, you are a hypocritical cad!"

Darcy looked at him with a resignation that, for some reason, his friend was none too happy with him.

"Now that you have regained some strength, maybe you have regained some of your sense enough to enlighten me as to what has been going on!"

"You are referring to…?"

"You and Miss Elizabeth Bennet! Now you need not fear, I did not say anything to either one about how unrelenting you were in trying to persuade me against Miss Bennet because, according to your own words, the Bennet family was completely unsuitable. Now, however, I would like to know exactly why you were so set against the two of us, all the while you had designs on her sister!"

Darcy looked at him with much contemplation. Yes, he was right to be confused; to be upset. Darcy had assiduously tried to keep him and Miss Bennet apart. Then he had turned right around and asked for her sister's hand in marriage.

"Bingley, I did it for a number of reasons. Most of those reasons were for my benefit though; only one, I believe, was for your benefit."

"Explain. I am listening."

Darcy narrowed his eyes in thought. "When I told you that Miss Jane Bennet showed very little regard for you, I felt she saw you solely as a prospective husband for reasons of monetary advantage only. You know her mother and how set she was to marry her daughters off to any man of considerable means. No offence intended, Bingley, but I truly felt she had no love for you -- that I could see -- and I felt it would be a mistake for you to marry her if she did not have the same affections for you as you did for her. Obviously I was most wrong and I apologize for it."

"You actually admit you were wrong and apologize?"

Darcy nodded.

"Apology accepted. Now what about those other reasons -- for *your* benefit?"

Darcy's jaw tightened. "I was referring to her inferior connections and her family's appalling manners. These reasons were given not so much for your benefit, but for mine. I had developed strong feelings of attachment for Miss Elizabeth, but could not, *would* not, allow myself to pursue her because of those very things. Every time I brought up those issues with you, I was trying to convince myself of the validity -- the necessity -- of heeding that argument. I was determined to do whatever it took to keep you and Miss Bennet, apart for I knew that if you married her, it would throw me constantly in Miss Elizabeth's presence and I would be powerless to keep my resolve."

"Your resolve?"

"I determined she would not be the most suitable wife for me, as I required someone from a more superior station in life with admirable family connections to be mistress of Pemberley. I resolved to have nothing more to do with her."

"Then you encountered her at Rosings."

"Yes, quite unexpectedly. It literally caught me off guard. I found myself waking each morning and plotting ways to see her. I could not shake the very thought of her from my mind, until finally, I determined to make my feelings known to her and I asked her to be my wife."

"Yes, and quite an interesting approach for a proposal, so I hear!"

Darcy sighed and brought his hand up to rub his forehead. "I was most detestable in my approach, yes. I had never proposed to anyone before. I arrogantly presumed that she would consent. I felt she needed to know how much of a struggle it had been for me to come to that decision. It was stupid, granted! I dwelled more on my conflict than on my love for her."

"So what do you plan to do now, man?" Bingley asked.

"What do you mean?"

"You have approximately two months before our wedding. That is when you will see her again. I suggest you fashion some plan between now and then to put yourself back in her favour."

Darcy looked at him, recalling Elizabeth's exact words to him regarding Charles and Jane. "Bingley, I was never in her favour and I am quite certain she has no intention of being persuaded to love me by any sort of plan of mine."

"Darcy, I have never known you to give up so easily."

"I am only being realistic."

"In the matter of love, sometimes it helps *not* to be realistic!"

Darcy shook his head at the help his friend was trying to give him. "Thank you Bingley. I shall give it some thought. But that is all I promise."

"Good! Now, I shall leave in the morning to go to London, and then later in the week to Netherfield to talk with her father. I shall notify you what the wedding date shall be. That is, of course, if he gives his consent."

"If you get any resistance from Mr. Bennet, just go straight to Mrs. Bennet," Darcy said with a sarcastic tone.

"Darcy, that is cruel. You see, this is where your fault lies. You are so hasty to be critical of someone, just because they are not like you. You must learn to see more than just the outside of a person."

"And you have been able to get to the heart of Mrs. Bennet?"

"Well, let us just say that I am willing to try."

"And let us just say that I am willing to avoid her whenever possible."

Bingley laughed and shook his head at his friend. "Darcy, sometimes you can be so boorish! Pray, if you ever wish to win Miss Elizabeth's heart, you might want to start by accepting her mother!" He laughed and shook his head. "Well, I need to be off now to get myself ready to leave tomorrow. I shall come back before I leave to say goodbye. You probably could use some more rest."

"Thank you Bingley. Until then."

~~*

As the Pemberley carriage turned down the long entrance that led away from the great house, Elizabeth gave one last, hasty glimpse back. Feelings of remorse threatened to consume her and she knew she could not give in to such feelings. After transferring to a carriage in Lambton that would take them to Longbourn, Elizabeth settled in for a full day's journey.

Elizabeth turned to Jane. She would need her sister's help in keeping her mind engaged on things other than Pemberley and its occupants. "Jane, I have not yet heard about Mr. Bingley's proposal. Would you be so kind as to share all the delightful details with me?" She gave Jane a mischievous smile and leaned in to her with wide eyes.

Jane smiled. "I would be more than happy to oblige you. That morning, the two of us were in the dining room having a little breakfast. I believe you were still asleep after being up most of the night. All of a sudden word started spreading that Mr. Darcy had awakened. We were both very excited and relieved, asking the servants what they knew. Suddenly Charles stood up and told me to come with him. I anticipated us going straight to Mr. Darcy's room to see him ourselves, but instead he escorted me outside.

"He told me he wanted to walk down to the lake. We had been there before and he had told me that had always been his favourite place to walk to whenever he came to Pemberley. When we got there, we sat down on a bench and talked for a bit.

"Then suddenly he turned to me, grasping both my hands in his, and told me how much he loved me, how much he had missed me these past few months, and asked if I would consent to being his wife."

"Could you believe it, Jane?"

"I thought I was dreaming, but I felt too happy for it to be a dream."

Elizabeth looked at Jane and smiled, quite amazed. Bingley, it seemed to her, may have been prompted to ask for her sister's hand upon hearing of Mr. Darcy's recovery. She wondered if it may have been due to his being afraid of seeing him before securing her hand. Was he afraid of being talked out of it again? It angered her to think Mr. Darcy could have such a hold on him. But she was grateful he proposed despite his friend. No matter what influence Mr. Darcy had over him before, at least Bingley took a step in the right direction.

"Jane, I am so happy for you. Now we must prepare ourselves for Mother's reaction. Do we dare tell her as soon as we get home, or do you suppose we should remain silent for a while and make her wait?"

"I think Mother will not even let us get out of the carriage before she asks if either of us has secured a proposal!"

"I think you may be right. Shall we each try and guess how long it takes her to broach the subject?" Both girls laughed at this.

The ride home took all day. When the carriage finally delivered them to their front door at Longbourn, all five members of their family greeted them, wanting to know what happened, how Mr. Darcy fared, and what Pemberley was like. But it was their mother's questions that finally came to the point.

"Jane, was that fine, young man Mr. Bingley there? Did the two of you get reacquainted? Do I hear wedding bells ringing in the future?"

Jane blushed, and her mother then would not relent. "Oh, it is to be, is it not? I just knew it! Mr. Bingley proposed?"

Jane finally nodded an affirmative, and the volume of her mother's voice resounded in all their ears. "This is the most wonderful news! Our Jane is to be married! I cannot wait to tell my sister, and the Lucases, and..."

"Mrs. Bennet," interjected her husband. "I do not believe you will need to tell anyone anything, as I am sure all of Hertfordshire has just now heard you announce it. Now, let us go inside before all the well wishers arrive."

Mr. Bennet walked over to his eldest daughter and told her how happy he was. She told him that Mr. Bingley would be coming in a few days to talk with him and get his consent and they would discuss arrangements then.

He then joined Elizabeth and looked in her eyes. "And tell me, Lizzy. How did things fare for you?"

"Well, Mr. Darcy did recover. For that we are all grateful."

"And once he recovered, how did he treat you?"

"He treated me as kindly as I deserved and expected to be treated."

No, she would not go into details about the misunderstanding; how he felt she had wronged his sister. She did not believe that he was angry with her anymore, but was quite certain he would never renew his offer of marriage to her!

Chapter 8

The next morning, an informally dressed Darcy walked by himself down to the dining room to partake in the morning repast with his sister and Bingley. He felt somewhat stronger, but was still under strict orders from Dr. Brisby not to overtax himself.

The three shared a hot breakfast together and then Bingley announced he would have to take leave of them. When Bingley stood up to leave, Darcy asked Georgiana if he could have a moment alone with him. She nodded politely and left the room.

"Bingley, I know that you will soon be often in Miss Bennet's company. And I know that the two eldest Miss Bennets are very close. I would ask a simple request of you. Please do not attempt to plant any notions in Miss Bennet's head about myself and her sister. I know she would only share it with Miss Elizabeth and I will not have her feeling ill at ease around me when I come for your wedding. I dare say she has had her share of awkwardness around me as it is. I would not want her to be troubled thinking I may come and renew my address to her."

"Can I not put in some good words for you, my friend? That should not hurt!"

Darcy shook his head.

"You shall have my word on it, then. And now, I must be off. How good it was to be here, Darcy. I am most grateful that you are on your way to a full recovery! And I must now thank your sister for her part in this past week." With that he winked at Darcy, who answered his friend's gesture with a sigh.

Georgiana slowly walked out to the entryway with Bingley as Darcy followed. He watched them talking and laughing and could only imagine Bingley's enthusiastic praise for how things turned out and how Georgiana should be credited for it all.

After final farewells, Bingley's carriage drove off and Darcy took in a deep breath as he returned to the study. He knew he could sit in there alone; read, rest, attend to some business, or simply let his mind wander. This would do for now. In a few days he looked forward to getting out and walking the grounds and eventually getting his life back to normal. But then, what would be normal?

He knew what he would like normal to be. But no, he shook his head. That was not to be. Bingley had told him to come up with a plan to win Elizabeth's heart. But he could not do that -- he was not that clever. He was convinced that she would see right through him if he tried.

After Bingley departed, the presence, or was it the absence, of Elizabeth hung over Darcy and Georgiana, neither wanting to admit to the other how much they had been affected by her being at Pemberley. Darcy was sullen, blaming it on lingering weakness. He became more determined to gain back his full strength and looked forward to Dr. Brisby coming again, giving him a clean bill of health.

He noticed that his sister kept to herself, carrying around with her some book in which she often wrote. He wanted to ask her what it was, but assumed it was something Miss Annesley asked her to do. Miss Annesley had been asked to come directly to Pemberley to continue Georgiana's studies after Darcy's recovery. He wished to remain at their country estate until he was completely recovered and his sister did not want to leave his side.

Georgiana spent much of each day, when not in studies with Miss Annesley, pondering what she should do about her brother. She was hesitant to mention Elizabeth's name. She was not certain whether he still suffered the stinging blow of her refusal, the pain of seeing her again at Pemberley, just plain love, or a combination of the three. She thought, though, that he behaved quite oddly at times. Georgiana would often catch him looking at something when she came upon him in a room and he would abruptly slip it away into one of his pockets.

She knew he was preoccupied with something, but was not able to determine if his thoughts were agreeable or not. She could not imagine how he felt when Elizabeth turned him down. Georgiana could easily sympathize with him, as she had been deeply disappointed when, after getting to know Elizabeth and finding her much to her liking, learned she was not going to marry her brother.

In those few days she spent with her, Georgiana had determined that Elizabeth was truly the most kind-hearted and amiable woman she knew. She was very different from any other woman her brother had ever shown an interest in and a vivid contrast to the many women who had shown an interest in him. And there had been many! How she would have loved having her as a sister. The thought that this was not to be truly crushed her spirit.

Yes, she believed she knew somewhat how he felt. What she did not feel, however, was the anger and humiliation that he must also have felt when she refused him.

At length, Darcy gained the strength to venture outside. He kept his walks short, simply walking the perimeter of the house. He would return fatigued, but strengthened by them. He felt the pulsating warmth of the sun pierce him through and drew even more vigour from it. When he returned to the house, he would sit in one of the rooms that had sunlight pouring in and would pull a chair into the sun's beam and rest.

A few days after the Bennet ladies and Bingley left, Darcy and his sister sat together in the dining room after a meal. Durnham came in and announced that he and Mrs. Reynolds were going into town to pick up a few things, and asked if he required anything. Darcy picked up a piece of paper and wrote down a few items. "See if you can get these for me."

Durnham looked at the list and then looked back at Darcy, quizzically. He pointed to one of the items on the list and Darcy commented, "You see what it is. See if you can get it!" With that, Durnham set off to go into town. Georgiana noticed her brother's flustered look and slight blushing of his cheeks, but did not think it was her concern to inquire about it.

Two days later, Georgiana was drawn to the front of the house by some noise. She went to the window and found several under gardeners working feverishly to remove some shrubs by the front entrance that lined the marble staircase leading to the front door. She stepped outside and was somewhat surprised that they were removing perfectly good shrubbery and were replacing them with something else. She was so taken by this, that when she stepped back to turn the other direction, she found herself colliding with one of the young under gardeners.

"Oh, excuse me, I am so sorry!" exclaimed Georgiana.

"No, it was my fault Miss Darcy," expressed a flustered young man. "I should have been watching where I was going."

Georgiana smiled and then looked again. "Mr. Bostwick, is that you?" asked a startled Georgiana.

"None other," replied the young man. "It is a pleasure to see you."

"Thank you." Georgiana remembered playing with this young man as a boy when his father, who was the head gardener, brought him along with him. David Bostwick had to have been just thirteen the last time she saw him.

She was embarrassed now, not really knowing how to talk with a young man a few years her senior. "It must be quite a few years... since I have seen you."

"Indeed it has been quite a few years since we have talked. You are often in London and my studies have kept my away a great deal. However I have seen you on occasion from afar when I have come to help my father. I do try to help him out when I am in town and have the chance."

"I am sorry that I have not noticed you before."

"I perfectly understand. You probably would not have recognized me from a distance anyway." He struggled to know what else to say, wanting to keep her engaged in conversation, but feeling he was probably overstepping his bounds. He finally added, "I understand your brother is improving nicely. We are all grateful to hear that."

"Yes, thank you." She suddenly remembered her surprise when she had first come out and asked, "Mr. Bostwick, what is this that you are all doing?"

"We are removing all these hollyhock bushes and are replacing them with those gardenia bushes."

"But those hollyhocks look perfectly fine to me. Why would you do that?"

"We are all wondering the same. Mr. Darcy asked us to do it."

"He did? He has always left the landscape and gardening decisions to your father. Why the interest now?"

"We really do not know. But he is the master, so we do what he says. The hollyhocks are perfectly good so we are going to transplant them elsewhere."

Georgiana smiled at him, and thanked him for the information. He watched her leave with a pinch of admiration in his eyes for the pretty young woman into whom she had grown.

When Georgiana entered the house, she whispered, "That is all so strange."

Durnham walked past and heard her utterance. "What is so strange, Miss Darcy?"

"Mr. Durnham, my brother has ordered gardenias to replace the hollyhocks at the entrance to the house."

"Gardenias you say?" He looked surprised.

She nodded.

"Hmmm. That is very interesting."

"What is?"

"That it is gardenias. He asked me the other day to pick up some gardenia scented toilet water while I was in town. I assumed he was buying it as a gift for someone. But you know, just today, I found the bottle stuck in the back of his armoire and it had been opened. Obviously, he is not planning to give that bottle to anyone. Now if you ask me, *that* is unusual!"

Georgiana shook her head in wonder at his sudden interest in gardenias.

As a revelation came to her, her eyes widened. She had often noticed that Elizabeth had a fresh, floral scent about her that she believed was gardenias! The very possibility made her smile. Her brother was a romantic at heart and he most likely did not even know it! Her heart lifted and she knew now that she had to go to her brother and urge him to talk about Elizabeth.

Georgiana had hardly played the pianoforte for her enjoyment since her brother had the accident. Miss Annesley would oblige her to play a certain amount of time each day for practice, but she had not played solely for her own satisfaction since that time when Elizabeth came upon her. Today however, she felt inspired to play the pianoforte. On her way to the music room, she passed her brother in the study. She knocked on the door and peeked in to say hello. She did not tell him what she was doing, but when she left, she purposely did not close the door all the way. She went to the music room, sat down, and began playing, a song that flowed from the joy in her heart.

Somehow she knew when he appeared in the doorway. She knew not if it was a sound she heard, a reflection of movement somewhere, or possibly a scent, but she knew he was there, listening. When she finished, she asked without turning around, "Did you enjoy it?"

"I did. You know I always enjoy your playing. It was good to hear you play so passionately; it has been a while." He noticed the smile on her face that caused her whole countenance to light up and it encouraged his heart. He had not seen her thus all week.

Georgiana played a few more songs for him, as he sat in one of the chairs listening with his eyes closed. She noticed that he absentmindedly went to his pocket and drew something out. There it was!

Abruptly she stopped and he opened his eyes to find her staring at him. "What is that in your hand, Fitzwilliam?"

She was quite surprised to see a look of embarrassment cross his features. "Nothing. Just a handkerchief," he replied as he stuffed it back into his pocket.

A handkerchief! A smile came to Georgiana's face. It did not escape Darcy's notice. "What are you smiling about, young lady?"

"Oh, it is nothing." *Just like your handkerchief is nothing!*

"Now, Georgiana, you will answer my question. What is that book you have been constantly carrying around with you?"

"Oh, this?" Georgiana picked up a plain, bound book. "This is my journal."

"A journal?" asked Darcy. "What are you doing with a journal? Is this something in which Miss Annesley is having you write?"

"No, Fitzwilliam. Miss Elizabeth suggested I begin writing in one."

She noticed that she had his full attention and went on. "She gave me the idea of writing down my thoughts and feelings; anything I come to learn about people or things. She said writing things down is good therapy and helps you remember things more. In so doing, I can draw from them later when I am in a position to converse with someone."

"Miss Elizabeth told you that, did she?" He tried to appear calm and indifferent, but knew the beating of his heart was making every attempt to betray him. "And what else did Miss Elizabeth say?" he asked.

She looked at him and wondered whether to broach this next subject with him. Finally, she said, "She also told me why she turned down your proposal."

Darcy squirmed in his chair. "She did? And what did she say?"

"She said that there was some sort of misunderstanding between the two of you, which she added, had since been cleared up. But she went on to say that your actions in trying to separate her sister and Mr. Bingley played a large part in her decision. Did you really do that?"

"Yes, and I have already admitted to Bingley that I was wrong. I also informed Miss Elizabeth that my actions were based on what I perceived to be at the time, very little regard for Bingley on Miss Bennet's part..." He added in an undertone, "...however wrong it was."

"I cannot believe you would do such a thing!"

"What else did she say her reasons were?"

"That was all. Just the misunderstanding and your interference with her sister."

He looked at her, surprised. "She was being very kind, then."

"Why do you say that?"

"Because her main reason for refusing me was due to my arrogance!"

Georgiana looked at him in shock. "Your arrogance? I cannot believe it."

"Unfortunately, my arrogance was displayed not only for her, but for everyone in Hertfordshire while I was there. I found myself to be very uncomfortable with the neighbourhood, their ways, their manners. I found it easier to stand off to the side in silence than to befriend these people."

Georgiana listened to his confession with wide-eyed astonishment. "This sounds so unlike you, William."

He continued as if he had not heard Georgiana's words; as if he had to finish his thought. "Then, my arrogance was made very evident to her in the address of my proposal. I am ashamed at what I said. I made certain she was acutely aware of how much of a struggle it was for me to come to terms with her inferior connections and station in life."

Georgiana sat aghast, her mouth opened in disbelief. "I scarce can believe it! You actually said that in a proposal of marriage?"

"Yes." Darcy looked at his sister and shook his head. "She has every reason to think ill of me."

"William, when you said you stood off in silence, did you feel reserved in her company of friends?"

"I suppose you might call it reserve, why?"

"Miss Bennet told me that a person may be reserved because of one of two reasons. She said there may be other reasons, but these are the most common. She opened to the front page of her book and read, "Either there is a fear of saying something wrong; a fear of being misunderstood or judged ill by something you say or do. To prevent that, you hold yourself back. The second reason is wishing not to impart yourself to others due to one's own feelings of superiority, and having no inclination to converse with someone you feel beneath you. She rightly determined that I am reserved due to the first one."

With that she closed her book. "William, I believe your reserve comes from the latter. I think you must have actually thought yourself superior to those people in Hertfordshire. Did you?"

"I do not know how I felt! I was just uncomfortable. I do not have the ability to talk easily with strangers."

"You cannot or you will not?"

He looked at his younger sister and realized she perceived far too much of his true character. He began to feel uncomfortable with his sister's insight and did not want to admit to himself that he was, indeed, proud and arrogant.

"The truth hurts, does it not?" Georgiana asked gently.

"You are telling me that all my life I have striven to be generous, giving, and considerate of others, but basically, I am a proud, arrogant fool!"

"No, William, not all the time, just in certain situations."

"And is that what *you* think?"

"I have not seen it for myself, as I usually see you only in situations in which you are comfortable. But upon hearing this, it does sound like it. William, do you want to do something about it?" she asked him. "Is there a reason that will make you want to change?"

"I think you know the answer to that, but I do not think it will help." Darcy said with a look of anguish in his eyes.

"Well there is no harm in trying. I have an idea that we will begin to work on tomorrow. Now, what was that you had in your hand?"

He looked at her as if he did not understand her question.

"That *nothing* that you were holding... Is it perchance Miss Elizabeth's handkerchief?"

Darcy's face gave away the truth. He had the look of a guilty man found out, as he drew out the handkerchief and showed it to Georgiana. There in the bottom corner were the initials *EB*. She took it from him and held it to her face. When she inhaled, she could smell the very strong scent of gardenia!

Chapter 9

The first few days after Jane and Elizabeth returned to Longbourn, the Bennet household remained in a state of turmoil, being led in the forefront by their mother. She had begun, even before Mr. Bingley had arrived to secure consent, to make plans for her eldest daughter's wedding.

From the time they had stepped inside after returning home, everyone at once prodded Jane for all the details. She was very gracious in answering them all, but Elizabeth could readily see she was becoming quite wearied from all the questions. Mrs. Bennet, it seemed, had no intention of letting the subject drop. As happy as Jane was to talk about Mr. Bingley, the proposal, and the upcoming wedding, there were other things she wanted to hear about from the family.

Mr. Bennet stood off to the side; appalled at the unrelenting commotion his wife created, but savouring the joy his daughter's engagement wrought. He had been uneasy while his daughters had been at Pemberley, but now he could rest easy. It had turned out well, although he would never admit that to his wife.

As mayhem coursed throughout the house and continued the next day, Mr. Bennet took longer periods of refuge in his library. There was no calming his wife and he wondered how he would survive these next few months.

News spread throughout Hertfordshire of Mr. Bingley's and Jane's engagement and then of his impending return to Netherfield. The house, which had been closed since November, was opened, aired out, and supplies brought in to make it favourable for its occupants.

But news also began spreading throughout the area of a different sort, which pained the youngest ladies at Longbourn. This particular news was that the whole militia, which had been stationed at Meryton, was preparing to depart. They would all be leaving for Brighton by the week's end.

Kitty and Lydia seemed the hardest hit by this news. Suddenly the merriment and joy in planning a wedding became a drudgery and chore. They could think of nothing but losing all those fine, well-dressed officers. The balls would not be as festive; Jane's wedding would even lose some of its appeal without the officers in their red coats.

It was the day following that news that Bingley arrived at Netherfield and promptly rode over to Longbourn. The Bennet family had been having a discussion around their dining room table about the dreary prospect of the militia leaving. Lydia was positively unyielding in her whining to be allowed to go to Brighton. Could they go as a family; could she go on her own? There must be some way! Kitty also voiced her opinion, making certain it was known that she wished to go as well.

Mr. Bennet was in the middle of a lengthy argument against such a thing when it was announced that Mr. Bingley had arrived. Gasps came from all over, a breathy one from Jane accompanied by a blush, an exuberant one from Mrs. Bennet, and a cheerful, encouraging one from Elizabeth. Elizabeth took Jane's hand and squeezed it tightly as Mrs. Bennet began ordering everyone around, not doing a bit of good.

Mr. Bennet stood up and announced that he would go to him and that everyone else ought to remain where they were and stay calm! As he walked out, his heart beat a little more rapidly as he realized one of his greatest desires for any of his daughters was about to come to pass. He was soon to give consent to a marriage that was perfectly acceptable to both himself and his daughter. She would enter into a very beneficial marriage, but one that was based on love.

The Bennet ladies remained in the dining room. Jane's heart pounded wildly. In reality, she had no reason for any concern, as Mr. Bennet had made it perfectly clear that he approved heartily of Bingley and would never refuse him. It was merely the waiting that was so difficult.

Kitty and Lydia greatly desired to continue to plead their case to Mrs. Bennet about going to Brighton, but she would not have it, as much as she would like to do the same. Her mind now was focused on the wedding and she could think of nothing else. This left the two younger sisters very downcast and seeing very little hope for a pleasant summer.

The minutes ticked away, as they all waited anxiously. Mrs. Bennet began fanning herself, feeling flushed all over. "Oh, what could be taking them so long? How long does it take to give one's consent?" she asked mercilessly. "He will have me most vexed if he does anything to…" She was interrupted by the sound of the library door opening and laughter, as Mr. Bennet and Mr. Bingley walked toward the dining room. "Girls, sit up; smile, Jane, smile."

Jane found it very hard to smile with her mother pestering her so. Her heart beat so erratically she felt as if she would faint. But a gentle smile did ease its way on to her face when she saw Charles' beaming grin.

Jane timidly approached him as he held out his arm to her and the smile on his face reached all the way to his bright blue eyes. She blushed as every eye was upon her when she took his arm and he nodded to her, as if to say, it is all accomplished, we are officially engaged!

Mr. Bennet broke the reverie of the group and announced, "Well, it appears we shall be having a wedding, come July… if that is agreeable with everyone!"

The air suddenly exploded with cries of delight and praises along with offers of congratulations. Jane continued to smile through her tears of joy, her hold on Charles tightening, as if she needed him to keep her upright. Elizabeth came over to the couple and, with genuine love and delight, expressed her favour. Jane released her hold from Bingley's arm as Elizabeth reached to hug her and she wrapped both arms around her sister in return.

Mrs. Bennet joyfully embraced her soon to be son-in-law and began exclaiming how thrilled she was. She submitted to him that she was certain he would be most happy in his decision to marry their daughter and would never regret it. She was sure they would be the happiest of couples.

Elizabeth and Jane discreetly rolled their eyes as their mother carried on. Bingley simply smiled.

"Mama," broke in Elizabeth, "Shall we allow Jane and Mr. Bingley some time together?"

Bingley spoke up quickly, "I should enjoy it, if it is acceptable to Miss Bennet, if we could go outside for a walk. I should like that very much." He looked at Jane, raising his eyebrows to question if this suited her.

"Yes, that would be most agreeable to me."

Elizabeth watched as the two walked out; Jane's hand securely within Charles' arm. Her heart was content knowing how very happy; how very much in love they were. She sighed, letting the breath out slowly. She had always believed that it would indeed be Jane who would marry well, as she was five times prettier than any of the other Bennet sisters. Now she was engaged to a man who not only was very well off, but one she loved as well. Elizabeth could not be happier for her.

Later, when Jane returned from their walk, Bingley had taken leave. As soon as she entered the house, Mrs. Bennet began planning and plotting details of the wedding. She wanted to begin immediately and it was set that they would travel to Meryton tomorrow to pick out the fabric for the wedding dress and make arrangements immediately to have it made.

The following day, Elizabeth, Jane, and Mrs. Bennet went into town to the millinery shop to seek out the finest fabrics for the wedding dress. Mrs. Bennet could not refrain from telling everyone she met that day the good news about her daughter marrying Mr. Bingley of Netherfield, although most had already heard.

When Jane's fabrics had been chosen, Elizabeth walked outside whilst her sister and mother made some final decisions and measurements were taken for her dress. As she stood outside the shop, she was startled to see Wickham coming toward her with two other officers. It was too late for her to return to the shop. He was the last person she wanted to see and she hoped he would not stop to talk.

When he noticed her, an overall uneasiness spread across his face. He stopped and bowed to her, telling the two other men to continue on and he would soon join them. He looked down at her, then away. "Miss Bennet, I understand you had the fortunate opportunity to spend a few days in the home of my youth."

"Why, yes. My sister Jane and I did go to Pemberley."

"Oh yes. I understand your sister is to be married. I wish her the best."

"Thank you." Elizabeth wished he would just move on. She found his close presence very disturbing.

"Pray, did you find Pemberley to your satisfaction?"

"Yes, it was quite grand."

"I heard of Mr. Darcy's accident and that he fortunately pulled through. Were you there when he recovered?"

"Yes, we were."

"And Miss Darcy -- was she there?"

"Yes, and I found her to be a charming young girl. I believe I was told by someone once that she was proud, like her brother, but instead I found her to be sweet and somewhat shy."

Wickham nervously smiled, knowing she was recalling his description of her. "Well I suppose she has grown up since I last saw her."

"Yes, I suppose she has."

"I am glad to hear that." He shuffled his feet and wondered what, if anything, she knew about his past with Georgiana. He abruptly turned to Elizabeth and said, "Well, Miss Bennet, you must have heard that our regiment is soon to leave for Brighton. I will take leave of you now, as I have much to do to get ready. It was a pleasure getting to know you and your family."

With that, he bowed and Elizabeth forced a smile. *Yes, leave, Mr. Wickham, be gone to Brighton and leave us all alone!* she thought to herself.

When they returned to Longbourn, they encountered a household full of exasperation. Lydia had received an invitation from Mrs. Forster to accompany her and her husband to Brighton. Kitty was all out of sorts because she was not included in the invitation and did not understand why she should not be able to go as well. They were both terribly vexed because Mr. Bennet was not inclined to allow either girl to go.

When Jane, Elizabeth, and Mrs. Bennet stepped inside, Lydia assaulted her mother with the burning request to be allowed to go. "Please, I must go! What else shall I do if I can't go? I have been invited by Mrs. Forster as her particular friend! Please!"

Mrs. Bennet could see no reason not to give in when Mr. Bennet adamantly gave his refusal. "I will not have one of my daughters running off with a group of officers, when my eldest daughter is about to be married. Lydia you will stay here and tell the Forsters that you must decline!"

With that he stormed off. Mrs. Bennet looked at Lydia and whispered, "I do not see anything wrong with you telling the Forsters that you are unable to join them presently, but some time in August, if the invitation is still extended, you may then accept their gracious invitation. The wedding will be over by then and all should be fine."

Lydia was only temporarily relieved, but she was grateful to have at least a little hope of going. Kitty was still very much in distress about being slighted by the Forsters and Mary was appalled that either was even considering going, let alone her mother giving permission. Elizabeth and Jane excused themselves from this spirited conversation and sought solace with each other outside.

They walked to a bench underneath some trees and sat down upon it. Jane was grateful for the solitude, feeling somewhat anxious from all that just went on inside the house and the heightened nerves of her mother, who was trying to pinpoint every detail of the wedding down in just one day.

"Oh, Lizzy, I did not know a wedding would become so burdensome. I do not know how I shall get along with Mama if she continues like this for the next two months. She makes every decision so difficult and wants every detail planned her way!"

"I am so sorry, Jane. Maybe after a few days, she will settle down." Elizabeth sighed, knowing how quiet and unassuming Jane was. She was sure if Jane ever expressed an opinion, her mother would either not hear it or heed it. "Allow me to talk to Mother if you feel she is doing something you do not want. Let me know and I will see what I can do."

"Thank you."

A twinkle in her eye and a smirk on her face suddenly appeared. "But do not forget that we owe this all to her. If it had not been for her and her scheme, *you*," pointing to Jane's nose repeatedly, "would not be engaged."

Jane smiled.

"But swear to me, Jane; promise me, you will never, ever give her credit to her face. We would never hear the end of it."

"As much as I hate to admit it, we do owe this all to her. But we will not encourage her thoughtless actions by thanking her. We must thank Providence for this."

Elizabeth laughed. "Yes, let us be sure to give credit where it is due, to the Lord Himself, and maybe a little credit goes to Mr. Bingley. Do you know when he is going to call on you again?"

"I believe he is to come tomorrow. He will then return to London to meet with his sisters and Mr. Hurst. He has not seen them since we became engaged. I hope they approve."

"Jane, you do not need to get their consent to marry." *Fortunately!* she added to herself. *Miss Bingley would never give it!*

Changing the subject, Elizabeth asked her sister about the walk she and Charles had after they left the house the day prior. Elizabeth was curious as to what they talked about.

"Oh, Lizzy. We had such a wonderful walk. We talked of many things, our dreams, our hopes, and even how many children we would like to have!"

Elizabeth laughed, "I hope you both came up with the same number!"

"He does like children, Lizzy." Jane blushed. "We talked of the wedding." She turned to Elizabeth and took her hands in hers. "I, of course, want you to stand up with me at the wedding."

"Jane, you know I would be honoured."

"Charles is going to ask Mr. Darcy."

Elizabeth felt a catch in her throat as she heard his name mentioned, but was able to smile. "I assumed so, Jane. Now do not worry, I promise that I shall be on my best behaviour with him on the day of your wedding!"

"I was not worried about the wedding day, Lizzy." Jane looked down. "He is such a good friend of Charles, I do hope that you and he can get on well even beyond that, as I expect him to be a frequent guest once we are married."

Elizabeth looked down. She had not really thought about that. All she had allowed herself to think of since she left Pemberley was that she would see him again at the wedding and that somehow she would get through. To be reminded that she would likely be thrown into his presence often after the wedding was a bit more disconcerting.

"Charles has much praise for Mr. Darcy. I cannot help but to think well of him myself."

"He obviously has some very good traits. I have been witness to them myself. But I have also seen a part of him that disturbs me immensely. I cannot forget how he basically shunned our friends and acquaintances here in Hertfordshire. He clearly admitted to me in no uncertain terms that he struggles with those he considers inferior to him.

"But tell me, do you think, that having been to Pemberley and seen its grandeur; you would refuse him still if he asked today for your hand?"

Elizabeth gazed at her, a surprised look upon her face, as she reflected on her sister's question. "I must admit that while I was at Pemberley I felt quite flattered that such a man, the master of such a grand estate, would have asked for my hand. I think any woman would have been flattered. I had no idea the splendour of his home. But Jane, if I were to agree to marry a man solely on what he owned and not on whom he was, I would be a fool. Do you not agree?"

"Yes, if that was solely the reason."

"I admit I have pondered what may have happened if I had agreed to marry him. Would he have whisked me away to Pemberley, dressed me all up in fancy clothes, and made me forget my friends and family, never to see them again?"

"Surely he would not do that."

"How do we know? He certainly never made any effort to acquaint himself with us. As far as I know, he would not wish to associate with them again, or let me, either. Why should I not think that he would want nothing to do with all those I have grown up with and come to love?"

"Certainly you are being too harsh on him. But Lizzy, you have not answered my question. Would you still refuse him today?"

Elizabeth turned to her sister with a sly smile. "I think if he were to come alone and ask for my hand today, I would turn him down."

"If he came alone?"

"Yes. But if he brought his sister along and she entreated me to marry him so I would be her sister, I might find it difficult to remain steadfast in my refusal."

Jane laughed. "You and Miss Darcy certainly seemed to get along well."

"Yes, and I miss her. Please do not get the wrong impression of what I just said. I do not want to try to replace you as my favourite sister. I just sensed that she did not have anyone like I have in you; someone to be her confidant, to share her thoughts and feelings with, and help her through the difficult things in life."

"She would most certainly have that in you, Lizzy."

"And I so enjoyed her! We never met Miss Annesley and I often wonder what she is like. Is she, as her companion, someone in whom Miss Darcy can truly confide? I am confident that she is very capable in what she does, but I fear there might be something that is missing in their relationship, something that is missing in Georgiana's life -- something like an older sister or kindred friend. As much as she reveres her brother, even he cannot replace that need for a woman in her life with whom to share things."

"She does admire him a great deal."

Elizabeth recalled the things his sister said about him; her great praise for him. "Yes, I am certain that she believes him to be the best brother in the world. And the high opinion of him goes beyond his just being a good brother. Praise for him came from others in the household. I would surmise that their good opinion of him most likely comes from seeing him only in certain situations.

"What do you mean, Lizzy?"

"They only see him in the environs of their own social status. They have their town home in London and their great estate at Pemberley. I would think that all of their acquaintances are reasonably equal to them in respect to wealth and class, both in the city and in the country. I do not imagine Georgiana has seen him as he deals -- or struggles -- with those he considers beneath him. How would she know how he acts? No, Jane, I believe she only knows her brother as she sees him in the comforts of their own wealthy, superior world."

~~*

That night, Elizabeth crawled into bed. Her day with Jane had been so favourable. She was especially happy for her, but her mind went back to her question, "Would you agree to marry him if he asked you again, today?" She had told Jane no, if he came alone. But she wondered if that was really true.

She had told Jane that she had been flattered by his proposal after seeing Pemberley. But it was more than feeling flattered. It had prompted a warm appreciation for him that reached to the depths of her. It was a most gratifying feeling knowing that the master of that great estate had singled her out. She knew it was not a prudent basis for regard, but she could not help it.

Rolling on to her stomach, Elizabeth propped her chin upon her crossed arms. She began to dwell on this man; his stately, handsome appearance; how she often caught him glancing at her; and how his wayward curls fell down across his forehead. Her mind suddenly recalled him, as he lay in bed, unresponsive. She remembered being drawn to those curls, lifting them away from his face, opening his nightshirt to his well-sculptured chest and wiping it down with the wet cloths, suddenly aware that she had felt strangely attracted to him then.

She shook her head and rolled back over; wondering what ever prompted her to think such thoughts! She had allowed herself to think of him based strictly on what was on the outside, not on what was on the inside. This kind of irrational thinking would not do!

She had to be honest and admit to herself, however, that if he asked her again, as unlikely as that was, she was not sure she would have the resolve to refuse. She felt she would accept. However, she knew that she could not share that with Jane. Jane would be inclined to tell Mr. Bingley, who would then tell Mr. Darcy. This would cause even more awkwardness at the wedding and she did not want that. No, she would have to keep those feelings to herself.

Chapter 10

Darcy and Georgiana attended church the following Sunday. As they walked to the small white building, they were greeted warmly by the reverend and other parishioners. Many expressed praise to God and great delight in hearing about the recovery of this man of infinite patronage in the church and seeing him much improved. Many commented that it had been far too long since they had seen him.

The reverend, a young man in his early twenties, gave Darcy a firm shake of his hand. "Mr. Darcy, we are delighted that you are able to join us on this Lord's Day. We have all have been praying for your recovery."

"Thank you, Reverend Kenton."

The reverend greeted Georgiana, and then she and her brother walked down the centre aisle of the church, with her arm in his. It gave her great pleasure to be here with him. The church she attended in London with Miss Annesley was very large, and she often felt lost in it. But here she felt connected -- to the people, to the reverend, to the very words of his messages. They walked over to their pew, which now bore a plaque in memory of their mother and father.

Darcy sat down, looking straight ahead. He knew that the eyes of the congregation were upon him. He felt prominently conspicuous, for he knew that everyone was aware of his accident and subsequent unconsciousness. He also knew that it had been quite some time since he had graced a church with his presence.

The service began and Reverend Kenton had the congregation rise and open their hymnbooks to a hymn. Georgiana joined in the singing as if she had sung the song often. Darcy felt uncomfortable, not being familiar with it, so he did not even make an attempt. He was certain that everyone noticed he was not singing.

When the reverend greeted the congregation, he mentioned the recovery of Mr. Fitzwilliam Darcy, and how honoured they were to have him in their midst this very day. There was a general rise of voices and those people who had not seen him come in craned their necks to get a glimpse of him. This added to his already burgeoning discomfort.

All heads bowed as the reverend led in prayer. Darcy looked down, but did not close his eyes. There were few people here that Darcy would consider a close acquaintance. There were some who were employed at Pemberley in some sort of servitude, whether it be in the kitchen, the stables or on the grounds. The Reynolds and Winstons were here, but most of the others he knew only slightly. The remaining people were common townsfolk from Lambton or other nearby villages.

The congregation recited the Lord's Prayer, and then the reverend began his sermon. Darcy found it difficult to keep his thoughts engaged on his message. He often looked down at this sister who was completely riveted to the reverend's words. He smiled at her as he pondered how grown-up she suddenly appeared.

Suddenly the words of the reverend hit a resounding chord within him. "Listen to what the gospel of Matthew says about giving ourselves to others: "When he was come down from the mountain, great multitudes followed him. And behold, a leper came and worshipped him saying, 'Lord, if Thou wilt, Thou canst make me clean.' And Jesus put forth His hand, and touched him, saying 'I will. Be thou clean.' And immediately his leprosy was cleansed."

Darcy knew not why he was now giving the reverend his attention, but he was. "Our Lord Jesus reached out to this man who was a leper. In these times, if you were a leper, you were considered an outcast of the society; you even had to live outside the city and shout, 'Unclean!' if someone approached. There were strict guidelines as to how close someone could come to you. No one could touch you. You were, in a sense, isolated, alone, condemned.

"But here was the Lord, having compassion on him, wanting to heal him. All he had to do was say the word and he would be healed. But he did not. He reached out and touched him. He touched a man who had not been touched by another person in probably some time. Rather than just take the easy way out to help him and just say the words, he gave of Himself. He reached out and personally touched him."

With that, he closed his Bible and looked up. "How many times do we take the easy way out when we try to help someone? Do we just send some money, send some food, or worse, send someone else to take care of it? Do we think that by giving *things* we are doing all we can? We have our Lord as our example. He gave Himself, wholly and unreservedly to people. We need to do the same.

"I am not saying that to give charitably is wrong. Sometimes a need is met best by a monetary gift or a meal or clothing. But what I am saying is that *things* should never become a substitute for *you.*"

Darcy felt the words pierce him. He gave a slight glance at his sister and wondered whether she had hinted to the reverend to speak on this subject. No, she was too shy to do something like that. But he felt like he was speaking directly to him! In his mind he began arguing with God as to why he was a most giving and charitable man, even though it was mainly in the form of monetary gifts. He often gave bonuses at the holidays and extra assistance when needed by his staff. He sent very nice gifts for weddings, new babies. He contributed substantially when he became aware of a need. He gave to most any worthy cause! *He* was guilty of taking the easy way out!

"As we close in prayer today, ask God to help you look for ways to give of yourself in ways you never have before. Let us pray."

Darcy's heart was pounding. What was this he was feeling? Providential conviction? Or was it just coincidence? He found it increasingly difficult to breathe. Was God trying to get through to him, or was he just acute to this subject because of Elizabeth's and Georgiana's recent sketch of his character?

At the amen, the organist began playing and the congregation stood to leave. Darcy wished to depart directly, but he had a suspicion that Georgiana made other plans. He found himself hoping that no one would approach him and mention his accident. It was an unsettling feeling knowing everyone here knew of it. It made him feel very weak and vulnerable.

As they walked out, he was amazed at the people Georgiana knew and addressed. Most people politely acknowledged Darcy but did not approach him. As they came to the parish doors, the reverend reached out his hand to Darcy. "Again, I am very glad you were able to join us today. May God give you continued grace and strength." He squeezed Darcy's hand and smiled.

"Thank you, Reverend."

When Darcy turned, he noticed Georgiana speaking with several of the parishioners. He stood off to one side, waiting for her to finish. Before she returned, however, he saw the Reynolds family. He walked over to Mr. and Mrs. Reynolds and was grateful for their company whilst waiting for his sister.

When Georgiana finished her conversation and returned to him, they both bid farewell to the Reynolds and walked to their carriage. As they stepped in, Darcy inquired, "So, going to church was how you planned to change me?"

She looked at him and smiled. "Oh, no, that was just the beginning. We are going back to Pemberley, have something to eat, let you rest a bit, and then we will be going to visit the Franks and the Wilcox family."

Darcy looked at her in disbelief. "What?"

"You heard what I said. I talked with each of them after church and inquired whether we could stop by. I made sure they knew we were going home first to eat so they would not feel obligated to serve us a meal."

"Georgiana, is that the Franks as in Robert Frank, our stable hand?"

"Yes, the very one."

"And who are the Wilcoxes?"

Jon Wilcox is one of our under gardeners. He is recently married and lives in his parents' home, although it is fairly small. He is hoping some day to have a home of his own.

As she told him this, she pulled out her journal and began writing. "What are you writing?" Darcy asked his sister.

She looked up at him and smiled, "Just some thoughts that I do not want to forget from today's sermon."

"What are they?"

"William, this is my journal, and my thoughts. Presently I do not wish to share them with you."

He folded his arms in frustration and dropped his head back against the seat. He turned his eyes, however, and looked in admiration at this young girl who was turning into a charming lady. Yet growing within him was an anxiety about this afternoon and what it would require of him.

When they arrived at Pemberley, they ate a simple meal that had been prepared by the nominal staff that worked on Sundays. When the meal was completed, Georgiana encouraged her brother to get a little rest before they set out again. Darcy was eager for some solitude and retreated to his study. As he stretched out into his overstuffed chair and put his feet on the ottoman, he wondered what he was getting into with these visits Georgiana had arranged.

His mind went back to a week ago, when he was sitting in this very chair -- as he was right now -- and Miss Elizabeth Bennet walked in. His heart pounded as he recalled that morning. He put his hands in his pockets, searching for the handkerchief. It was not there. He must have left it back in his room. But he did not need it to smell the gardenia fragrance. He looked at the end table and saw the fresh cut flowers that had been put there - gardenias. How fragrant they were!

Suddenly a memory from the past flashed before him. It was of his mother taking a young Fitzwilliam Darcy to visit some of their less fortunate neighbours and she often brought them fresh cut flowers. He looked at the gardenias. His eyes widened as he remembered a scent from the past. Could gardenia have been the fragrance she wore? He shook his head as if trying to recall. Was it the same fragrance, or had he been so captivated this past week by the scent that he now only thought it was one and the same?

He thought back to after his mother died and how he often went into his parent's room when his father was away and smelled her clothes. He felt very safe and secure when he could smell his mother, almost as though she was right there with him. But then one day all her clothes were gone. He went into their room, opened the closet, and it was empty! He remembered the pain that gripped him, almost more than when she actually died.

After that, he would try to recall that scent, looking for anything with it on it. He could never admit this to his father, who tried to be so strong. Darcy felt his father would believe it to be a failing on his part. After a while, as memories of his mother sadly began to fade, so did the memory of that scent.

He brought his hand to his forehead, pushing back the unruly locks that had cascaded down. Is that what brought him back from his state of unconsciousness, the scent that reminded him of his mother? When he had begun awaken, he was not aware that Elizabeth was there. Even when he saw her, he did not really recognize her. That was the last thought on his mind when he fell asleep.

It was but a short time later that he awoke and found Georgiana at his side.

"I did not wish to awaken you. It is time for us to leave. Do you think you can manage the outing?" She noticed the faraway look in his eyes, and thought he may have done too much already this morning and needed more rest. "If you not, I can certainly go with Miss Annesley."

"No, I am quite rested now. But I need first to go to my room."

He slowly took the stairs to his room and went to the nightstand next to his bed, opening the drawer. He lifted a book that was neatly placed in the drawer, and lifted Elizabeth's handkerchief from underneath it. He brought it to his face and inhaled. The scent was fading again, so he opened his armoire and reached to the back behind a stack of folded shirts, pulling out the bottle of toilet water. He shook a few drops onto the handkerchief and slipped it into his pocket.

As they pulled away from Pemberley in the carriage, Darcy looked at

Georgiana. "Did you know that your mother and I used to go on visits such as this?"

"No," replied a surprised Georgiana.

"She called them our *caring calls*. I was fairly young at the time; I would often find an excuse to go outside and play while she stayed in and visited. She stopped doing it just before you were born, and I do not think she ever was able to continue doing it, having a young child to take care of, and then her illness..." Darcy took a deep breath and sighed. He looked over at Georgiana and she had a dazed look on her face. He noticed tears welled in her eyes, and he pulled her close and gave her a hug.

"I never knew that about her. Tell me more about my mother."

"She was very kind and giving. As the reverend said today, she gave of herself. She was there for people." Darcy stroked his sister's hair as she sat spellbound by his words. "She was beautiful; she loved you and our father very much. When she died, I believe a part of Father died. He was never quite the same."

"Oh to have that kind of love in a marriage," Georgiana sighed softly.

"Hmmm. Yes." Darcy felt his heart stir, leaving him pensive for a moment. Finally he continued, "I know you were quite young when she died, but you were very special to her. I often regretted that you have not had her in your life, especially now as you are grown into such a lady. I know that she would be someone who would be able to give you such wisdom and guidance, unlike I ever could."

"William, you have been a wonderful brother. I could not ask for a better one."

"You are too kind."

Georgiana smiled.

The carriage approached Lambton and pulled down a narrow lane. Darcy could tell that the road was in need of repair as the carriage rocked from side to side as it traversed the myriad of ruts. He looked out the window at the row of houses that were situated very close together, with barely a small yard in the front.

The carriage pulled up in front of a small house with window boxes in the front that had been painted blue. There were flower bushes in them but no flowers were in bloom. As they removed themselves from the carriage, Darcy was assaulted by a loose dog. He abruptly shooed the dog away and wiped down his clothes. Georgiana laughed.

"This is where the Wilcox family lives. Jon and his wife live here along with his parents and a younger brother and sister. His father is a local blacksmith."

"And you say he is one of our under gardeners?"

"That is correct. He usually works the outskirts of the grounds."

They exited the carriage and walked up to a very small house. They knocked on the door and were ushered in by a young teenage boy. He called for his mother who quickly came to welcome them. She ushered them into the sitting room and sent the young boy off to find his brother, Jon.

As Darcy looked around, he felt confoundedly stifled by the closeness of the walls. He noticed a pungent odour that began to assail his nostrils. As they waited for Jon, Mr. Wilcox joined his wife, and a daughter came in. Jon and his wife entered last. There was barely room in the sitting room for all eight of them, and Darcy wondered why they did not go into a larger room, there were so many of them in this confined space. He could hear his sister saying something, but Darcy was not able to concentrate.

He recalled as a child coming to these small houses and not being able to remain inside for very long for the same reason. As a child he needed to get outside into the open air, and right now that was all he could think of. Suddenly he was aware that he was being addressed, and struggled to focus on what Mr. Wilcox was saying.

In a desperate measure to keep his composure, he slipped his hand into his pocket. He knew he could not pull out the handkerchief with Elizabeth's embroidered initials and flowers on it, so he rubbed his fingers around the handkerchief, and then released it, pulling out his hand. He brought it to his face and gently rubbed his jaw, letting the gardenia scent on his fingers reach his nostrils. As he breathed in the scent, he immediately felt calm and less anxious. He looked at Mr. Wilcox who just finished what he was saying.

"… and hope he is a good worker."

"Uh, yes, he is a very good worker." But Darcy did not recall ever having seen his son.

He looked over at Georgiana who was so at ease with these people. She readily showed an interest in their lives. Darcy could only think about getting back outside. He knew his first visit was going to be considered a failure. He reasoned, however, that certain people had a gift for this kind of thing; Georgiana did, and he did not.

When they left, he thanked them for their hospitality and wished them God's blessings.

From there they walked across the road to the Franks. At least Darcy knew Robert Frank, as his trusted head stable hand. He had worked at Pemberley for about six years, and the two shared occasional conversation. The house looked a little larger than the Wilcoxes, so he hoped that he would not have the same reaction there.

They approached the door and knocked. A petite middle aged woman came to the door and greeted them. Georgiana introduced Mrs. Ellen Frank to her brother. She welcomed them in, apologizing for the simple accommodations and untidiness that the children had caused. She ushered them into the sitting area and politely offered Darcy and Georgiana a seat. Darcy was relieved that the rooms were larger and did not close in around him as the others had.

"My husband is outside in the back. If you will excuse me, I shall call him."

Darcy heard some children playing loudly out back, but noticed a small child sitting on the floor watching them timidly. She looked to be about four. Darcy thought he would venture over and try to talk with the child. He stood up from the chair and walked over, crouching down as he came to her. She quickly looked back down at the blocks with which she was playing.

"What have you got there, young lady?"

Just then Mrs. Frank walked back in. She noticed that Darcy was attempting to talk to their youngest daughter who was not paying him any heed. "I am sorry, Mr. Darcy, but our daughter, Eleanor, is deaf. She cannot hear you."

Darcy's jaw dropped, not knowing what to say. He looked at Georgiana and then back at Mrs. Frank. "I am so sorry, Mrs. Frank, I did not realize."

"That is understandable, Mr. Darcy. Mr. Frank will be right in."

Mr. Frank entered presently and the two greeted each other warmly. Darcy was still reeling from his earlier blunder. Mrs. Frank carried in a tray of sweet breads and offered them to the pair. Georgiana thanked her and chose one for herself. Darcy declined, as his stomach was now churning. He did not think he would be able to eat a thing. He did, however, accept some tea, which helped soothe his agitated nerves.

The conversation in the household was confined mostly to Georgiana with Mrs. Frank, and Darcy with Mr. Frank. He talked to him about the things he wanted to do in the stables to improve things and Darcy agreed to think on it. His mind, however, kept going back to little Eleanor. He looked over at her and saw how content she was to play with her blocks. *Did she know she was different? How did they communicate with her?* And most of all, why did he not know about her?

When they finally left the house, Darcy was physically and emotionally drained. He climbed into the carriage after helping Georgiana in and put his head back against the seat. Georgiana felt it would not be wise to say anything at present. She was tempted to pull out her journal and begin writing, but she refrained. She knew how he must be feeling. He had been so uncomfortable, yet he had so wanted to prove himself to her. She was sure that he felt a failure.

When he finally lifted his head and met Georgiana's gaze, he asked her, "Why did I not know about the Frank's deaf daughter?" He had a pained look in his eyes.

She looked down. "I do not know. It is possible that at one time Mr. Frank informed you about her and you promptly forgot because it was not pertinent to you, or he may have assumed you would not be interested and so never bothered to tell you."

He looked at her with much anguish. "I suppose I have discovered today of what my real character is made. My pride and arrogance does raise its dragon head when I am in the company of those I feel are inferior to me."

She looked at him and smiled, shaking her head. "I am not convinced it is from pride and arrogance. At least not all of it."

He looked at her questioningly.

"I have seen you in situations with people from our own society." She paused to gather her words. "I have seen your disdain among those who exhibit their prosperity and position for the benefit of making themselves look good to others. I believe that is improper pride. I have never seen you put those things in the forefront to gain an unfair advantage over someone, or to even impress them."

"Then if it is not pride, what is it?"

"I believe our parents taught you the proper perspective of being a Darcy; what it means in terms of your responsibility to the name and the wealth it carries. But I also believe you were never given the chance, however Mother did try, to develop an understanding of people different than us, whether it was because of some perceived inferiority or something else. I think it may be largely due to a lack of knowledge about these people."

Darcy was taken aback at this, as he considered himself very well educated. Even since his college education he did extensive reading, but he must admit he never read a book on how to relate to people different than yourself.

She continued hesitantly, "I believe pride comes into play when you instantly put people into a class depending on how they look, how they are dressed, where they live. You tend to look too much at the externals, judging a person by what is on the outside, not by what is on the inside."

Darcy was not sure how much more he could hear from Georgiana. But he was convinced every word of it was true. "Go on."

"These people are just like us when it comes down to it. They have the same hopes and dreams as we do, the same fears, they fall in love, they experience heartbreak, illness, death. William, if you took away all that we had, Pemberley, our London home, our clothes, you would find we are the same as them. Granted they have not had the same privileges and upbringing in terms of education, manners, and behaviour, but we are basically all the same."

"And how did you come to learn such graciousness among these people?"

"Miss Annesley. We have made a point to go on visits almost every Sunday, whether we have been in London or Pemberley. She feels it is a very important part of any education."

"And obviously one that was neglected in mine."

"Not neglected completely, as you said mother took you on visits. Unfortunately, they ceased when she died." A smile lit Georgiana's face. "I think you have some room for improvement, my dear brother, but we have time. Next week we shall try again, and then in one month's time, if you have greatly improved, we shall move on to another challenge."

Darcy looked at her with some apprehension. "And what, pray tell, will that be?"

"Oh, no. I shall not tell you now. I do not want to have you worrying about it for a month." With that she contentedly turned away.

~~*

When they arrived home, Darcy went straight to his study. He closed the door and went to his desk, pulling out the chair and making himself comfortable. He was tired but there was something he knew he must do. He opened the large desk drawer and looked around for something.

"Ahh, here is one." He pulled out a financial ledger, one in which nothing had yet been written. He opened it to the first page, picked up a pen and dipped it in his inkwell. In large bold letters on the first page he wrote with his flawless penmanship, "The Journal of Fitzwilliam Richard Darcy."

He looked at it with a satisfied nod of his head. He then turned the page and smoothed it down with his hand. At the top of the page he wrote the date and returned the pen to the inkwell. He brought his hand to clasp his chin as he considered what next to write..

Picking up the pen again, he wrote the following:

Entry 1 ~ Matthew 8:1-3 Healing of the leper -Give of YOURSELF!

Entry 2 ~ The Franks - Robert, (head stable hand) wife, three children, one deaf daughter 4 years old. Check on recent developments in working with deaf children.

Entry 3. The Wilcox family - Jon, under gardener, lives at home with wife and his family in small 2 bedroom house. What can I do to help?

He closed the book and slid it over to the side of his desk, where, he knew, he would refer to it again.

Chapter 11

Darcy spent the next week catching up on his business affairs and preparing for a short journey to Cambridge. He had strict orders from Georgiana not to overtax himself and to make every effort to return by the end of the week. She wanted him rested for Sunday and another afternoon of visits following church. He assured her that he would only be gone three days and not to be anxious about him.

He was grateful that he felt increasingly strengthened. He went out for walks each day and felt that he was ready now for a short trip. He was anxious to get some things accomplished that had been neglected and he looked forward to get started.

When he was set to leave early in the morning, he sought out Georgiana to say goodbye. He pulled her close and squeezed her with a very fervent hug. She feigned a groan, as if he were squeezing her too tight. He pulled away and looked at her.

"You be a good girl, now, and I shall see you shortly." He kissed the top of her head.

"Goodbye William. Please take care of yourself. I should hate to have you recovering this weekend from fatigue when I have plans."

He smiled and grabbed her chin with his thumb and fingers. "You and your plans. I think you must stay awake all night plotting and scheming ways to rid me of all my faults."

Georgiana smiled at him, remembering how she had always considered him perfect; without fault. She still felt he had more goodness and integrity than anyone she knew. But she had taken on what she considered her mission to help him become aware of -- and improve -- those little faults that led to certain misconceptions held by others of him. Particularly held by one pretty lady.

When Darcy settled in the carriage, he turned to wave goodbye. Georgiana lifted her hand and waved back as she watched it pull away. She had spent more time with him these last few weeks than she had in a long time. These next few days the house would be quiet without him. She watched as the carriage went down the wide parkway and then turned down the road that led to the south grounds of the house. She sighed, suddenly feeling very alone. She knew that Miss Annesley would have her go through her studies throughout the mornings.

At least that would keep her occupied.

When the morning gave way to afternoon, Georgiana finished her lessons, spent some time practicing on the pianoforte, and suddenly did not know what to do. She wished she had Elizabeth there to talk to. She missed having someone like her in whom to confide and decided to write her a letter. She went into her room and drew out some stationary and her pen and ink. Sitting down at her desk, she began composing her first letter to Elizabeth since she had left.

Dear Miss Bennet,

I wanted to write and express to you again my deepest gratitude for all you did for my brother and me whilst you were at Pemberley. I know that right now you are shaking your head and insisting that you did not do anything out of the ordinary, but I assure you that you did. For me, you were a tremendous support and strength. You cared, you talked, and you listened. I could not have asked for anyone better suited to meet my needs during that critical time. I know that your coming here was due to a misunderstanding, but I cannot help but think that it was providential.

I feel as though I have grown tremendously since that day we walked out on the grounds. I took your advice and began putting down my thoughts in a journal, and have found it most helpful. Miss Annesley is back with me now and she greatly approves of your idea. I am sorry you were not able to meet her. She is a very sweet lady and I know she would have thought highly of you.

Our plans are to stay on at Pemberley at least through summer, leaving only when we come for the wedding. We will probably come a few days early. I so look forward to renewing our acquaintance then. I never had the pleasure of hearing you play and sing while you were here, so please promise me that you will oblige me while we are there.

My brother has almost fully recovered. He is just now departed for Cambridge on business, and it is already quite lonely here without him. I cannot tell you, Elizabeth, how much I have enjoyed spending all these days with him. He has been so kind and attentive. I do not know what I would do without him. I know that business shall eventually take him away more frequently, and I shall not see him as often, so I try to enjoy every moment I have with him now.

I do hope Jane and Mr. Bingley are doing well and that plans for their wedding are coming along nicely. How glad we both are that they are to be married! We both are of the same mind that they shall be very happy.

Again, as I said when you left, I look forward to seeing where you live and meeting your family.

Give my regards to Jane and Mr. Bingley. And Elizabeth, to you I pray God's blessings.
Yours, Georgiana

Georgiana reread the letter and nodded. She was pleased with it and placed it in an envelope, sealing it with wax. She only hoped that the few good words she put in for her brother would have some positive effect on Elizabeth's esteem of him. She hoped she had not overdone the praise. She brought the missive downstairs and placed it on the sideboard just inside the dining room, where Mrs. Reynolds would arrange to have it delivered on the morrow.

There were still a few more hours of daylight left, so Georgiana decided to take a short walk. When she stepped out, the first thing she noticed were the gardenia bushes. It made her smile, knowing the reason they were there. She walked down the steps and bent down to smell them. How fragrant these beautiful flowers were!

When she stood, she turned and found herself staring into the face of under gardener David Bostwick. "Oh, please excuse me Mr. Bostwick." She tried to step off to the side, but his words brought her to a halt.

"Excuse *me*. It seems as though we are always bumping into each other. I see you enjoy the fragrance of the gardenias."

"Yes, they do smell so sweet."

"My father tells me that years ago your mother loved gardenias, as well. She had some planted around the grounds. But after she died there was one winter that was so severe they did not survive. They were never replaced. My father wondered if that was the reason your brother asked to plant some of them here by the front door."

Georgiana listened in awe, as she appreciated any bit of information about her mother. "Mr. Bostwick, I did not know that about my mother… about her liking gardenias. I am not certain whether my brother was aware of that or not… at least he has never told me that about her. I sincerely appreciate you informing me of that. Do you remember much about my mother?"

"Oh, yes. I can remember her bringing out cookies and milk for my brother and me when we would come with my father as he worked. Do you remember my eldest brother Samuel?"

She nodded.

"He is to be married in a few weeks."

"Yes, I know. I believe my brother and I will be attending the wedding ceremony."

He looked back at her surprised. "Mr. Darcy will attend the wedding? I am sure he would not be able to spare the time. Certainly he must have more important things to do."

Her eyes sparkled with her smile. "Oh, he is planning to come; he will be there." She smiled as she thought to herself, *It will be our practice for the wedding in Hertfordshire to see how he handles all the local country folk that will be in attendance!* "Mr. Bostwick, what else do you remember of my mother?"

"She always smelled so good. Maybe it was gardenia scent also."

Georgiana smiled and wondered if this could be true, as well.

"I hope I am not keeping you from something, Miss Darcy. Were you on your way somewhere?"

"Oh, no. I thought I would come out and walk about the house for a bit."

"Do you mind if I join you? I could tell you a few other stories about your mother, if you wish."

Georgiana felt her heart skip as she looked at this young man who had once been an occasional playmate of hers. "I… uh…would enjoy that."

As the two of them walked, Georgiana listened as he told her how her mother would occasionally visit their home and that his mother had a very great admiration for her. As Georgiana heard this, she felt a wonderful connection with her mother, and wondered if her desire to reach out to those less fortunate was a gift from her.

Mr. Bostwick then began talking of the work that was being done in the different gardens and Georgiana enjoyed his running commentary on the landscaping that he had worked on. She was too nervous to return a discourse, and did not even know how to begin to carry on a conversation with him. When she was very young, he had simply been a playmate, but now that all changed. And she knew that change dictated how she was to respond to him and treat him, especially regarding the difference in their wealth and consequence.

When they came back around to the front, he bowed politely and expressed his appreciation of their time together. She had a very difficult time looking up to meet his deep blue eyes that looked down on her. Something inside her stirred, but she dared not wonder what it was. He was just an under gardener. Everything inside her told her she must remember that.

"Thank you for escorting me, Mr. Bostwick. I am most grateful for the light you have shed on my mother." She quickly curtseyed and rushed back up the steps, her heart faltering and her face feeling very flushed. When she came in the door, she closed it and leaned back against it, feeling quite light headed.

Mrs. Reynolds came by and asked her if she was well.

"Yes, Mrs. Reynolds, I am just… breathless." She prayed that her flushed face would not betray what she was feeling. "I was out walking."

Georgiana looked at the older woman who had been working with the family since before she had been born. "Mrs. Reynolds, I understand my mother used to wear a certain fragrance. Do you recall what it was?"

"Oh, yes, Miss Darcy. Her favourite scent was gardenia, just like Miss Elizabeth Bennet wore. In fact, when Miss Elizabeth walked in that first evening, I could not help but think of your mother. It is amazing how strong the memory of a scent can be. I think it must have stirred some sort of memory in your brother, too, as he has suddenly brought back the gardenia bushes that we lost so many years ago in the bad winter."

"Yes, so it seems," Georgiana said thoughtfully. "Thank you, Mrs. Reynolds."

She wondered whether her brother had been drawn to that scent the first time he met Elizabeth. She knew it would have to be more than just a scent to keep his interest, but the thought of it was quite engaging.

Georgiana thanked her and decided she would do some reading in the sitting room. She found a book that she had recently begun and made herself comfortable in a chair. Mrs. Reynolds came in after a bit and announced that her cousin, Colonel Richard Fitzwilliam, had arrived and was waiting for her in the entry. She hurriedly went out to greet him.

She had written two letters to the Fitzwilliam family; the first detailing the accident and the second informing them of his recovery. She had not heard from them, and assumed they had been away from home.

She rushed downstairs, anxious to see her cousin who was almost as close to her as her brother. He and Darcy had taken responsibility for her when her father died, becoming co-guardians of her. As much as she still felt quite ashamed that Richard knew of her relationship with Mr. Wickham and the threatening impropriety of it, he had always displayed a gracious, forgiving spirit toward her. She had never once felt condemned or looked down upon by him.

She found him in the entry and walked over to him, giving him a hug.

"Why Georgiana, how are you? It is good to see you!"

"I had begun to wonder what happened to you. We had not heard from you or your family since I wrote the letters."

"Our family was in the north on holiday. We just returned to find three letters awaiting us; two from you informing us of Darcy's accident and recovery, and one from Darcy asking if I could possibly journey here when he went out on business this week. Rather than write a reply, I came immediately. Unfortunately my family was unable to join me. Has he already left?"

"Yes, he left early this morning. He should return in three days."

"How unfortunate that I missed him today. Well, my cousin, you must tell me all about this accident of Darcy's. Quite a story, from what little I hear, and to think it happened immediately after we had been together."

"Let us go into the dining room and we shall have some tea and something to eat while I tell you." Over tea and cake, Georgiana gave a brief summary of the details that she had not written in his letter. She told of their concern for him, how day to day he showed little sign of improving, and then how finally one morning he awoke.

"I would never have doubted that he would awaken. He is too stubborn." With that her cousin laughed.

Fitzwilliam stood and walked over to the sideboard to refill his cup with some tea, when he noticed a letter lying there addressed to Miss Elizabeth Bennet. He picked it up and looked at it curiously.

"Georgiana, this is a letter to Miss Elizabeth Bennet." He looked at Georgiana, lifting one eyebrow toward her. "I did not know that you were acquainted with her."

"Yes." And then suddenly with realization, Georgiana added, "Oh, you must have met her while at Rosings when you were there with my brother. I had forgotten that you had been there with him. But I actually did not meet her until she came here when my brother was ill."

Fitzwilliam drew his head back in surprise. "She came *here?*"

Georgiana blushed as she recalled the circumstances surrounding her coming, but felt she needed to explain it to him. "I confess that I incorrectly assumed that Miss Elizabeth and my brother were engaged and wrote her, asking her to come when he was in such grave condition."

Fitzwilliam shook his head, drawing his hand to his chin pondering her words. Leaning toward Georgiana, he asked, "Engaged?"

"He wrote me a few days before he proposed, letting me know he was going to ask for her hand. Because of the accident he was never able to write back to me that she refused."

Fitzwilliam made a concerted effort to process this very surprising and unexpected information, but found himself unable to respond with words. After a few moments of silence, he let out a boisterous "Ha ha! So that explains his notably agitated behaviour when we left Rosings!"

Georgiana's face reddened in alarm. "Richard, you were not aware of this?"

"Oh, no, but I knew something was wrong with him and I suspected it had to do with Miss Bennet. I am just surprised that he actually proposed to her. I had no idea he had such strong regard for her. But then you say she refused him?"

Georgiana nodded, now wondering if her brother would be upset at her for letting their cousin know.

"Is this not ironic?" Fitzwilliam met Georgiana's concerned eyes, and quickly reassured her, "Do not worry your little heart Georgie, I will not let on to anyone else about this misfortunate incident of his. I am sure he would not want that bit of information spread about the country."

"But why do you say is ironic?"

Fitzwilliam laughed. "He has always had it so easy, always getting anything he wanted. I used to wish he had an older brother just to make life a little more difficult for him. Being a second son, he would have had to work a little harder to get what he wanted. In a way I resented him for it, as much as I loved him." He raised his eyebrows at Georgiana and said in a sympathetic voice, "But now, when there was something he really wanted, he actually could not get it. I am quite amazed!"

He sipped on his tea, and then looked back at Georgiana. "But you said she came. Why would she have come?"

"She actually came with her sister, Jane, with the hope of reuniting her with Mr. Bingley. I sent for him, as well. I now understand my brother had earlier done some underhanded persuasion to disincline Mr. Bingley toward her sister when they actually were both very much in love."

Fitzwilliam put his cup of tea down, and looked down, breathing in deeply. "Heavens, no!"

"What is the matter?"

"Well, I suppose part of Miss Bennet refusing him is *my* fault."

"Your fault? Why?"

"I met Miss Bennet on a walk on the grounds of Rosings Park the day before we left. We began talking of Bingley, and I conveyed to her the fact that your brother was very self-congratulatory about his separating him from a young lady who would have made him a very imprudent wife because of her connections. I had no idea I was talking about her sister."

"What did she do? What did she say?"

"As I recall, she claimed she had a headache and we returned directly. She did not come with the rest of her party to Rosings later that afternoon, and Darcy promptly disappeared. When he returned later, his behaviour was erratic and I could tell he was disturbed. He must have gone to propose to her that afternoon, fresh after I talked to her. Little did I know by that innocent conversation with her, I was sealing his fate!"

"I would not take too much blame, Cousin. There were other reasons -- other than that one -- that strongly affected her decision to refuse him. But it is all very complicated. I am not sure I understand it myself."

Fitzwilliam and Georgiana spent the rest of the afternoon visiting with each other. He thoroughly enjoyed hearing about Darcy's misfortunes, and only wished he had been at Pemberley when his cousin awoke and found Miss Bennet there. Georgiana always enjoyed her cousin's company. He had a ceaseless supply of laughter, laughing enough for her and her brother together. But the degree to which he enjoyed her brother's misfortune began concern her.

That evening as they were settled in the sitting room, Fitzwilliam made a boisterous confession to Georgiana. "Georgie, you have certainly made my day! I have not had a more enjoyable time talking to you about your brother!"

"Please be kind to him, Richard. I fear that if you are hard on him, he shall be angry with me for revealing it."

"Do not worry my Georgiana. I shall only tease him a fraction of the amount I usually do, being considerate of his broken heart and recent illness, of course." With that he laughed.

"That does not ease my mind at all, Cousin. Besides, he is making an effort to change his ways. He and I visited a few of our hired hands this past Sunday. We have plans to do it again this Sunday and hopefully the week after."

"Visits, you say? Did he actually step inside their homes?"

Georgiana proudly nodded.

Fitzwilliam let out a hearty laugh. "Oh, I can scarce imagine Darcy visiting the homes of those of lesser consequence. I dare say that does stretch one's imagination trying to fathom it."

Still chuckling from this last bit of information, he rose and said he would be retiring, and looked forward to more conversation on the morrow.

Georgiana informed him, "I will be spending the morning with Miss Annesley, but the afternoon should be free. I would like to hear about your family tomorrow, Cousin."

"Oh, but that would be so boring! But I shall oblige you. Good night, Georgiana."

~~*

The next afternoon, Georgiana heard all about their holiday and how his family was doing. She was quite aware, however, that he was still keen on hearing more about Darcy, as he kept bringing it up. She finally resolved that she would say no more to him, afraid that what she already said was too much.

By the third day, he had given up trying to get her to talk more about the incident between Darcy and the lovely Miss Elizabeth Bennet. Georgiana spent the afternoon listening for the sound of the carriage, and finally, just before the evening meal, they heard it pull up. They both stood, in anticipation of welcoming back Darcy.

Darcy stepped out of the carriage to see Georgiana and Fitzwilliam coming out to him. He extended his hand in a firm handshake to his cousin, expressed his gratefulness that he had been able to come. He walked over to Georgiana and greeted her with a fervent hug.

Darcy had always been able to anticipate his cousin's thoughts and actions by simply looking upon his face. The look on Fitzwilliam's face now gave Darcy much concern. There was a mischievous and knowing look in his eyes and a smirk on his face that had no end.

The three entered the house and Darcy asked, "When did you arrive, Fitzwilliam?"

"The afternoon you left. I am sorry I missed you. I did not take the time to write. I felt coming immediately would be quicker than a letter, as we had been gone for some time and just returned home."

"And have you and Georgiana had a nice visit?"

"Oh, yes, a very informative one too." Darcy met his glance, noticing his raised eyebrow and the smirk, which had now turned into a sarcastic grin.

"All right, Fitzwilliam. You look like you are just itching to torment me about something. Let us get it over with."

"Ah hah! It has been quite the highlight of my life just to hear the incredible story of the Don Juan Darcy and the elusive Miss Bennet. It has been my night time story for the past two evenings, putting me to sleep very nicely. I believe Georgiana has another instalment this evening.

Georgiana looked down and blushed, wishing he would not go on like this.

"Go ahead; get it out of your system, Fitz."

"Darcy you are too serious! You take yourself too seriously. I do not doubt that learning to laugh a little more -- learning to laugh at yourself even a little -- would greatly improve your disposition."

"Fitzwilliam, I do not need you to point out all my faults."

"All your faults? I have not even begun!"

"When you have finished, let me know. I have some business I want to discuss with you. I shall be in my study when you are ready."

His cousin had always been this way, prodding him and teasing him, when Darcy absolutely hated to be teased. Yet the two had an inseparable bond. It may have been because of the difference in temperaments that they were so close, each filling the void in the one that the other had. Darcy shook his head in amused exasperation.

Georgiana regretted more and more the fact that she had let their cousin know all the details about her brother and Miss Bennet. She knew that once Richard began his relentless teasing, it would not cease. A look of remorse swept across her face that Darcy did not miss. As he turned to go into his study, he reached over to Georgiana and pulled her close. He looked down and smiled, and tousled her hair, to reassure her that he was not displeased with her.

As Darcy left for his study, Georgiana pulled her cousin back. "Richard, may I talk with you? I cannot help but agree with you about my brother's solemn disposition. In fact, I believe we are both of like dispositions in this area. I wish he would laugh more, but I know not how to begin to bring about such a change in him.

"Georgiana, why are you suddenly trying to alter your brother?"

She looked down and blushed. "It is just something I feel inclined to do. But tell me, why do you suppose he is so serious? I do recall when I was a child that he was a cheerful, spirited boy."

Richard's face softened. "Georgiana, when your mother died, Darcy took it very hard. His father was very strong in how he dealt with it, and Darcy felt he must be strong also, holding all his feelings inside. I believe he was hurting terribly and had no one to help him through his grief. Then when your father died, that added to the grief he had never dealt with."

Georgiana's eyes welled up with tears. "And I suppose having to take on the responsibility of raising a young girl contributed to it even more."

Her cousin put his arm around her. "Georgiana, please do not blame yourself for Darcy's temperament. He is who he is because of himself. If he wants to change, he will change. He can make an effort. I have seen him lively enough in situations that I am assured he has it within him. As a rule he just chooses not to show it."

Fitzwilliam lifted her chin to look up at him. "And Georgiana, I do believe you, also, have it within you. You are a charming girl, with an engaging smile and a gentle laugh that could prove to be quite contagious to your brother. I trust that the more he sees you laugh, the more he will begin to laugh. And maybe, just maybe, we can get him to laugh at himself!"

Chapter 12

Ever since Bingley had returned from London, Elizabeth found herself longing for Jane's companionship. Her sister spent a great deal of time with him and his sister at Netherfield. Elizabeth was grateful that Jane had the disposition to smile sweetly at Caroline's disdainful manners, but as Elizabeth did not have the graciousness to do the same, she stayed away as much as possible.

Her time apart from Jane, however, gave her ample time to work on the needlework sampler that she was stitching for engaged couple.

She picked up the sampler, looking at the work she had finished. It was about three-quarters completed, and she was pleased with the neatness and precision of her stitches. She thought to herself, *This is Jane's life - neat, precise, orderly.* The sampler contained a verse from the Bible, "Delight thyself in the Lord and He shall give thee the desires of thine heart." She felt it was so appropriate for the two. Yes, they certainly had been given the desires of their heart.

The words of the verse were enclosed in a burgundy heart made of laborious french knots. Flowers of many types and colours were woven inside and outside the heart coming off of green stems. At the bottom of the sampler she would embroider their names and the date of their wedding.

She turned it over to the back to tie off a colour of thread. She laughed as she looked at the sampler from the back and thought to herself, *This is my life! Disorderly... loose threads hanging... not leading anywhere... all tangled together.* At this point in her life she was not sure what the desire of her heart was. But if the thoughts that had been assailing her lately had been any indication, the *who* of her desire was someone who most likely had no intention of ever renewing his address to her.

With little prospect of anything that might cheer her these past few days, she became intent on finishing the sampler. So preoccupied was she with her work and her thoughts, that she barely noticed the entrance of Kate, one of the Bennet maids.

"A letter for you just arrived, Miss Elizabeth, from Miss Georgiana Darcy."

Elizabeth excitedly reached for the letter. "Thank you, Kate." She quickly opened it and began reading. She smiled as she could imagine the young girl actually speaking the words that were written on the page. As Elizabeth read how grateful Georgiana was for all she had done, she began shaking her head in mock protest. Then she laughed aloud as Georgiana went on in the letter to say she was sure that Elizabeth was at that very moment shaking her head in objection. *She knows me too well!* thought Elizabeth.

She reread the portions about Darcy. As she read each sentence about him, she was drawn back to those few days when she was in his midst. She reached out with her finger and ran it over his written name. When she finished, she folded the letter back and held it close to her heart. She did not know if she was more touched by Georgiana's warmth or her words of her brother.

"I must write her back directly!" thought Elizabeth aloud.

She put her needlework down and drew out some stationary and pen. *Now, what to write!* She looked at the blank sheet of stationary, and words began pouring out from her and she quickly wrote them down.

Dearest Georgiana,

How pleased I was to receive your letter. I have thought often of you since returning to Longbourn and wondered how you were doing. It appears from your letter that you and your brother are doing well. I am grateful he is so well recovered.

Here at Longbourn we have been busy, of course, with wedding plans. Mr. Bingley was in London for most of the week, and Jane and I spent much time together making plans for their wedding. Now that he has returned, I see her rarely. I must admit that I miss her and know that once she is married, things will be different. I am saddened by the thought of how things will change for us, but I am still very pleased for her. She and Charles are very happy!

I am delighted that you are keeping a journal and find it beneficial. I can tell you from personal experience that when I have gone through a difficult time, a journal was what I often found useful to help me sort through my feelings. There was many a time when I would write down my thoughts as they poured from me, not truly making any sense. But then later when I read it, I could more accurately determine what I was feeling at the time, and even decide on a course of action to take to help me get through it.

I am also pleased that you are enjoying this extended time with your brother. I am very much aware of your high esteem of him, and I know that this must bring great joy to you; both his full recovery and his presence there with you.

I cannot help but to joyously anticipate your visit next month. And I shall, if you insist, play and sing for you. Please do not hold your expectations too high, I am not as proficient as you are. But as you played for me, so shall I play for you.

Georgiana, I concur with you, that the first letter you sent to me must have been providential. So much came to pass because of our coming to Pemberley, I cannot imagine what things would be like if we had not come. So again, I thank you from the bottom of my heart. Most of all, having the privilege of making your acquaintance was one of the highlights.

My family is anxious to meet you, as well, as I have often spoken of you to them with great admiration. We shall look forward, then, to you and your brother coming. Our family sends you both their warmest greeting.

With fond regard, Elizabeth

Elizabeth reread it, wondering if her comments about Darcy were too revealing, too personal. No, everything in it was fitting. She sealed the envelope and put the address directions on the front. She decided she would walk it into town herself to post it.

She found her father in his library and let him know what she was going to do. "Would you not prefer one of your sisters to go into town with you?" he asked. "Your two youngest sisters are always looking for an opportunity to go into Meryton."

"Yes, but they are not as anxious these days with the militia gone. I think I shall prefer to go on my own."

"Very well, dearest Lizzy. Do not be gone too long."

Elizabeth left the house with her letter in hand and stepped outdoors greeting the warmth of the summer day. It had been days since she had gone out on one of her walks; she was grateful for the solitary ambience. It gave her time to stroll leisurely and gather her thoughts. She reflected back to her walks at Rosings Park and her encounters with Darcy there. She secretly wished that there was a chance that now she would encounter him; walk past some tree or outcropping and find him standing there. But no, it would still be some weeks before he would come.

The thoughts and feelings that intruded caused her to both wish and fear his presence. She wanted another chance to treat him differently; to treat him as she ought to have done all along. She wanted another chance to show him that her feelings toward him had changed. But did she dare take that risk? Did she dare put her whole heart into this, as there was yet the chance that he would still carry much resentment toward her?

As she walked along, she heard the sound of horses coming from behind and walked over to the side of the road. She stretched out her hand and let it slide against the trunk of a tree as she strode past, pulling it along a long branch and gathering some of its leaves in her fingers along the way.

The carriage came alongside her and abruptly stopped. A voice called out, "Why Miss Bennet!"

Elizabeth turned and saw that it was Caroline Bingley. She nodded her head, "Miss Bingley." She looked at the direction of Miss Bingleys eyes to the gathering of leaves in her hand and quickly dropped them, wiping her hand against her dress to rid them of the bits and pieces that remained.

"I see you still enjoy long, solitary walks. How pleasant you must find them!"

Elizabeth looked down and bit her top lip. She finally looked up and smiled. "Yes, it gives me time to reflect and think."

"Yes, I am sure it must be required of you to get out of your household in order to have the peace and quiet that enables one to think clearly."

Elizabeth took a deep breath, knowing that she was snidely commenting on the excessive and often loud behaviour of her family. She politely refrained from making the response that came to her mind.

"I understand that you were quite the heroine for Mr. Darcy at Pemberley a few weeks back. I am sure he must feel very indebted to you."

"I did nothing out of the ordinary."

"Oh, but according to my brother, you did! How do you think Mr. Darcy will ever be able to repay you for your presence of mind and actions? Such a good nurse to him; have you ever considered going into that line of work, my dear?"

Elizabeth kept her composure, being fully aware that this woman would soon be Jane's sister-in-law and did not want to do anything to rile her. But oh, how she wanted to speak her mind!

Suddenly Miss Bingley caught sight of the envelope in Elizabeth's hand, and turned her head to read the name on it. "A letter to Georgiana! You are sending a letter to Georgiana?" The look on her face betrayed a sense of jealousy and annoyance.

With a forced interest she asked, "How did you find Georgiana? She is a sweet girl, is she not? I am rather disappointed that she and... well, never mind. I so enjoy her company and I am convinced that if I had been there... oh how upset I was at Charles for not informing me sooner about the accident... I am sure I would have been most supportive to her. She is like a younger sister to me."

Elizabeth only nodded and replied, "I am sure."

"But Miss Bennet, there is one thing I do not understand. How is it that you and your sister travelled to Pemberley? I find the situation very indelicate indeed that you both were there."

Elizabeth did not know what to say. She could not tell her all that led to their journey to Pemberley, especially that it was her mother's reckless decision that allowed them to go and Georgiana's misunderstanding that began the whole thing.

"I... uh... it is a rather long story."

"Oh, yes, well, I am sure someday you must tell me all about it. My brother has certainly not obliged me with the answers to my questions. I have my own ideas about it, but... well, I shall be on my way. You would not wish to ride, would you?"

Elizabeth could see through the insincerity in her offer and refused, preferring to walk anyway. "No, but I thank you."

The carriage departed, and Elizabeth shook her fists and kicked her foot through the dirt. *How dare she!* she thought. *To infer that Darcy should only feel indebted to me!* She tried to tell herself that it was only Caroline Bingley, and not to pay any attention to what she said. But would that indeed be all he felt? What if Bingley had said something to her to that effect? Unfortunately her words rang true about her family. Suddenly her heart was troubled again.

She found herself walking aimlessly, paying no heed to her surroundings. She passed trees and flowers and interesting outcroppings of rocks without noticing them. Her eyes grew moist as she contemplated the words that Caroline spoke. She looked down at the letter in her hand, finding it more difficult to read the words through her tears. If it had not been her greatest desire to send it off on the next post, she would have turned right around and gone home.

Oh Jane, how will you bear that woman's ill manners? I do not envy you one bit! Caroline's remarks stung. She reached into her pocket and pulled out a tattered handkerchief, to gently wipe her eyes. She looked at it, suddenly thinking of her lost one. Since Georgiana had not mentioned it, she assumed it had not been found, and probably would not be now. As she dabbed her eyes, she breathed in the scent of the gardenia toilet water that she always sprinkled on it. It had a comforting effect on her. She took her handkerchief and, along with the letter to Georgiana, stuffed them into her pocket.

As she came into town, she saw the carriage in which Caroline had been riding and Elizabeth went around another way to avoid it. The last thing she wanted was another encounter with her. She quickly posted the letter and then set out to return home.

As she walked back to Longbourn, she again pondered the words of Caroline. As her thoughts approached that tall, dark man who had time and again been thrown into her life, she dared not allow herself to think that he would continue to think favourably of her. When they were together last, it had been disastrous! The first time, she refused his offer of proposal with very scathing words. Then, he rightly accused her of manipulating Jane and Charles, as well as deceiving his sister and causing her great distress.

No, it did not look good, and she resolved to put him out of her mind. If she could.

~~*

As Fitzwilliam entered the study to join Darcy, he knew that the teasing must cease, and he must put on his business air. His cousin always trusted his business sense, preferring to have a differing point of view on some particular business question or transaction. Fitzwilliam always obliged him; however very rarely did Darcy take his counsel if it differed from his.

"So what is this that you want to talk with me about, Darcy?"

Darcy took a deep breath, holding it a few seconds before releasing it. "I know that right now you are in the mood to tease me, but what I am about to say, I am very serious about."

"Go on."

"I was in Cambridge these past few days, talking with an old friend of mine who now works in the offices at the university. I also spent some time in the library doing some research." He glanced up at Fitzwilliam. "I was doing some research… on communicating with the deaf."

Fitzwilliam's jaw dropped and his eyes widened. Then, out of incredulous humour, said, "My name is Richard Fitzwilliam, Sir. I do not believe I have made your acquaintance. You are…?" He held out his hand as if to shake it.

Darcy continued, ignoring his taunt. "I am in earnest, Fitz. This all began when I found out that the four-year-old daughter of my head stable hand is deaf. They cannot communicate with her. She cannot communicate with them. But I found out there is a school in France where they teach communication to the deaf by using signs with the hands."

He pulled out a packet of papers, and took one out, giving it to Fitzwilliam. On it were drawings of hands in different positions, and words, or letters of the alphabet that signified what they mean. "This friend of mine in Cambridge had inherited some land years ago on the south end of Derbyshire. He has never done anything with it. He has always been after me to buy it, as he has no interest in it." He pulled out a business transaction. "I would like to buy that land, and then donate it to start a similar school here. Upon checking, I have discovered that there are several deaf people in and around Derbyshire that would benefit from such a school. In the neighbouring counties I am sure there are even more."

"Are you serious, Darcy? I know that you have always been generous... you have always given to charity without blinking an eye, but this... You have taken, dare I say it, an active interest in them!" He recalled Georgiana's telling him of their visits to the poor and marvelled at this attempt both on his part and his sister's to transform him. "What is going on Darce? Georgiana told me of her taking you with her on her visits. Could you miraculously be getting involved personally in people's lives? Particularly those of inferior circumstance?"

"Do you find anything wrong in that, Fitzwilliam?" He seriously wanted his cousin's opinion on the matter.

"No, of course not. It is just a little out of character, out of *your* character. I am just wondering why. This, by any chance, does not have anything to do with Miss Elizabeth Bennet, does it?"

"Why does Miss Bennet always have to be the reason for something?" he answered defensively. "You know I am always trying to improve myself."

"So you are saying this has nothing to do with her?"

Darcy felt pushed to the limit. *Yes!* he wanted to scream. *It has everything to do with her! She opened my eyes to who I really am!* He stuffed his hands into his pocket, and grabbed the handkerchief that remained his constant companion. He fingered it inside his pocket as he said, "Fitzwilliam, my desire to improve myself at this moment is partly because it is Georgiana's wish. You may also attribute it to being so close to death. Things look differently to me now."

His answer was only partly true. Much had to do with Miss Bennet. He hoped his words sounded convincing.

"But if Miss Bennet *does* notice an improvement in your character, that is an added benefit, is it not?" He gave his cousin a shrewd smile, raising his eyebrows at him in question.

Darcy scrutinized Fitzwilliam to determine whether he was teasing or serious. Darcy decided to be honest and vulnerable in his answer, hoping it would diffuse the teasing. Softly, he said, "I cannot count on that, but yes. I would consider it to be a most desirable benefit. Although I am not holding my breath that she will change her opinion of me."

"Tell me, Darcy." Fitzwilliam was serious now. "I thought we were close, that we shared everything. Why did you not share with me what was going on between the two of you at Rosings? When we left, I noticed you were upset, yet you refused to confide in me what was disturbing you. I thought we were better friends than that."

"I was going to tell you."

"And when exactly was that going to be?"

"Probably not for about twenty years." Darcy looked at him and a smile came across his face. "Now, let us go look over this paperwork and tell me what you think."

~~*

The next morning Darcy walked into the dining room to find Fitzwilliam and Georgiana laughing. His first inclination was that they were laughing at his expense and he almost did not continue in, but after a thought, changed his mind and entered. "Good morning, Fitz. Good morning, Georgiana."

Georgiana looked at him with eyes filling with tears as her laughter continued. "Good morning, Brother."

"Good morning, Darce. Come right in. Your sister and I were just reflecting on what life will be like in twenty years here at Pemberley, with all your charitable causes in which you will be involved. Shall we have picnics on the grounds for all of Lambton, bringing in clowns and ponies for the children, and maybe merry-go-rounds and…" He laughed as he winked at Georgiana, "You could start a food kitchen, providing warm meals in the winter for the destitute."

"Enough, Fitz. I do not think Pemberley is going to become some sort of social goodwill club for the general populace. You find it so amusing that I am doing a few acts of charity?"

"I was just telling your sister about your proposal for the school. Even she is overtaken with astonishment by such prodigious actions."

Darcy looked at his sister who returned his gaze with much admiration in her eyes. "This is why you went to Cambridge?"

"Not wholly; I was not certain what I would discover. I went mainly to do some research. With what I did find out, though, I wondered if you and I could pay another visit to the Franks today and give them this preliminary information on communicating with the deaf; see what their thoughts on a school would be."

"Oh, yes! I would love to!"

"Fitzwilliam will you join us?"

"Sorry, no. I need to check in with my regiment. I shall try to return on Monday. But please give me advance warning what to expect from you when I come next; whether it is Monday or at a later time. It has always been so comforting to know what to anticipate when I see you. You have always been so constant, so steadfast, so boring! But the last few times I have been with you -- your behaviour at Rosings, going north with you, and then coming here and seeing you like this -- have me absolutely baffled! It is too much to bear!"

Georgiana giggled and looked to her brother who was shaking his head at his cousin. "You are too severe on me, but I believe you actually like the change you see in me."

"Like it, Ol' Darce. I love it!"

Later that day Georgiana and Darcy set out for the Franks. As they settled in the carriage, Georgiana looked at him and began, "William, there is something I would like to ask you."

"Certainly. What is it?"

"I felt I needed to wait until Richard was no longer with us. If he heard what I asked, I know that he would never cease teasing you."

"Well, I am now both curious *and* worried!"

"Do you remember when it was that you first noticed Elizabeth's scent? I mean the gardenia scent?"

Darcy narrowed his eyes at her, trying to calculate what thoughts were now occupying her mind. But yes, he remembered, vividly.

"It was the evening I met her. When we were first introduced, I was standing too far away to notice. It was not until she walked past me later in the evening that I first caught a whiff of it. It was just after Bingley and I..." he stopped in mid sentence. "Never mind."

"Never mind what? What were you and Bingley doing?"

"It is not important." Darcy shifted his weight and looked away. Georgiana recognized this Darcy trait of hiding something.

"What happened, Will?"

He looked back at her and looked down, shaking his head. "Just another one of my blunders."

"What did you do?"

He was silent for a moment and then calmly, penitently confessed, "Bingley was prodding me to dance. I wanted to do nothing of the sort. He had been dancing with Miss Jane Bennet and he suddenly saw Miss Elizabeth sitting out the dance just in front of us. He pointed her out saying she was quite agreeable."

He looked at Georgiana, and paused as he took in a deep breath. As he let it out, he said, "I replied that she was tolerable, but not handsome enough to tempt me."

Georgiana gasped, bringing her hand to her mouth. "No! William, I cannot believe it! Your behaviour! I simply cannot comprehend it!"

"Well, I am not proud of it, either. She obviously overheard my comment, and after Bingley departed, she strolled past me. That is when I first smelled the gardenia."

"With this knowledge, Brother, I think more lessons may be required to change Miss Bennet's opinion of you. Shall we have a lesson on giving a compliment? Repeat after me, 'You look very pretty tonight Miss Bennet'."

A look of resignation came across Darcy's face. "Now that we have digressed from your original question, why did you ask when I first noticed her scent?"

"Oh, yes. I found out a few days ago that gardenia was the scent our mother used to wear. Were you aware of that?"

He suddenly sat upright in his seat. "Who told you that?"

"Mrs. Reynolds, but it was only after one of the under gardeners told me he thought that the reason you planted the gardenia bushes was because of Mother's fondness for them."

"So it *was* gardenia!" He looked at Georgiana and continued, "Last week when I was in my study, I had a memory of our mother when I saw the cut gardenias in my study. I remembered she wore a particular scent. After she died I often went into her closet to smell her clothes just to feel close to her. But I could not remember whether or not it was gardenia."

"That is why I asked Mrs. Reynolds. I had to know for sure. I thought that it would be quite interesting if it was. You may have noticed Elizabeth for the first time because you were drawn to her scent."

"But my feelings toward her and my attraction to her certainly are not that for a mother!"

Georgiana laughed. "I would hope not! But think about it. What was it that first caught your attention about her?"

Darcy thought of her walking past him with that insolent smile after she had overheard his insult. As she strolled past him, something about her caught his attention. His eyes had followed her, and when he tried to look away, they unwillingly turned back to her. Yes, he distinctly remembered being drawn to her; her eyes, her impertinence, her smile, and yes, most assuredly, her scent!

Chapter 13

The news that the Darcys brought to the Franks was received with grateful astonishment. They were most appreciative of the information he gave them regarding the method of communicating using hand signs. He handed them the papers he had brought from Cambridge with pictures of the more common signs, and encouraged them to give it a try. He even got down on his knees with a book, and signed the word to their daughter, as he had practiced it on the way.

The Franks thought it quite extraordinary; the extra effort Darcy was taking on their behalf. They knew him to be generous, but could hardly believe that he would take such a personal interest in their deaf daughter that he would have gone to all this trouble. His idea for a school for the deaf also left them overwhelmed. Mrs. Frank broke down as she realized what this would mean for them. Georgiana quickly went to her side and put her arms around her, letting her tears of joy fall uninterrupted.

The ride home was one of great elation. Darcy was thrilled that they appeared to be so receptive and grateful.

Although he fully related to them that the idea for a school in Derbyshire was his idea, he made sure that they were not aware of his total involvement in it. They were not aware that he was purchasing the land or contributing the money to get it started. He did not want to be credited for it.

The land he purchased from his friend, with the intent to use it for the school, would not be listed under his name. As far as anyone was concerned, an unnamed person donated it. Any funds he contributed toward the school would not bear his name either.

Sunday began again with attendance at church, and again Georgiana arranged for them to visit two more families. This day's visitation "lesson" for Darcy proved less traumatic, in that he was not surprised by anything. He felt that he was more able to look past the differences in their society and see them for who they were. He made every attempt at conversation, usually with the man of the house, but being very cordial to everyone else. Georgiana was well pleased with his effort.

The next morning brought the return of Colonel Fitzwilliam. He was only able to stay on a few days as he was just passing through, but looked forward to their time together. After Georgiana's lessons with Miss Annesley, the three of them withdrew to the dining room to have an afternoon meal.

As they were dining, Mrs. Reynolds entered and presented a letter to Georgiana. "From Miss Bennett," she informed her.

From Fitzwilliam's perspective at the table, he readily noticed the similar reaction from both of his cousins. Georgiana and Darcy at once were both upright and alert. The only difference was the Georgiana smiled and Darcy kept an unreadable expression on his face.

Georgiana thanked Mrs. Reynolds and took the letter. She opened it, looked at her brother and Fitzwilliam, and said politely, "Excuse me, please, while I read my letter."

Fitzwilliam looked on at Darcy in amusement as he noticed him nervously rubbing his fingers together. That was the only movement from him. He could see that he was anxious, but was trying very hard not to show it.

Finally, after assuring himself that his composure was what it should be, Darcy asked in a very cool, deliberate voice, "What does Miss Bennet have to say?"

"Oh, just that plans for the wedding are coming along and she looks forward to seeing me again." Georgiana looked up and met Fitzwilliam's knowing grin and Darcy's look of impatience. She placed the letter down on the table next to her.

"Is that all?" He asked.

"Were you expecting anything else, Darce?" interjected Fitzwilliam? "Were you, perhaps, expecting a personal greeting to yourself?" He looked at him with an amused grin.

Darcy returned a sardonic look to his cousin, took in an anxious breath, and tried to change the subject. "Fitzwilliam, tell me, when is it again you are leaving?"

"I plan to leave tomorrow afternoon. You are not anxious for me to be gone, are you?"

"Of course not."

"But I am afraid it shall be a while before I am able to return." He turned to Georgiana and added, "And because of that, I should enjoy hearing you play for me, Georgiana. Would you do that for me right now?" he asked, looking at his young cousin. Darcy could not have been more relieved to see that the subject of the previous conversation had changed and already forgotten.

"Right at this moment?" she asked.

He nodded.

"If you wish." They both rose, and Fitzwilliam looked at Darcy to excuse them.

As they walked out the door, Fitzwilliam pulled Georgiana back as she began walking toward the stairs. He pointed to the edge of the door, where they could peer in and observe Darcy sitting at the table, his back to them. He put his finger to his lips as to silence her, and they watched.

Darcy sat there for a few moments, taking a final sip of his tea. After a few moments he gradually he leaned forward, reaching out his arm toward the letter. He paused, turned his head to the side as if listening, and lifted himself from the chair just to give him the added length he needed to reach the letter. He placed his hand on it for a few seconds and then slid it slowly towards himself. Fitzwilliam began shaking his head, as if he knew all along what Darcy would do. Georgiana covered her mouth her hand to keep from giggling.

Darcy drew back the letter and opened it. He slowly read the words of Elizabeth, looking at each word, rereading the portions where he was mentioned, and endeavouring to determine how she might feel. It was all very civil and polite; nothing into which he could read too much or too little.

Without giving much thought to it, he raised the letter to his nose and was pleasantly surprised to find that it had the faint scent with which he had become so familiar. He leaned back in his chair, stretching his legs out before him, breathing in the scent.

A sudden burst of laughter came from just outside the dining room door. "I am sorry, Darce, I just could not hold it in any longer!" Fitzwilliam came charging back into the room unable to control his laughter.

Georgiana looked sheepish, knowing she was part of her cousin's spying escapade. Now she felt guilty again, allowing her cousin to draw her in and giving him ample ammunition to tease.

"So, did Miss Bennet have anything to say to you, Darce?" Fitzwilliam took the letter from him and waved it beneath his nose. "Or do you think this scent was added for your benefit?"

Darcy grinned. "It was a very nice letter to my sister; no there was nothing personal in it for me, and I doubt that she put any fragrance on it to attract my attention."

"But were you possibly hoping for more? Maybe hoping to read something between the lines?"

"Actually Fitz, I picked up the letter and read it because I knew you and Georgiana were behind that door watching me, just waiting for me to do it. I merely obliged you." With that, Darcy chuckled.

Fitzwilliam looked at Georgiana and then back at Darcy. "Excellent try, but it will not work."

"Well, you cannot say I did not try." He took the letter out of Fitzwilliam's hand and handed it back to his sister.

"I would keep this with you. If you lose it, I do not want to be accused of stealing it." He stood up to take leave of the room. As his frame filled the doorway on his way out, he turned and addressed Georgiana. "I am off to send a post to Bingley letting him know we shall arrive the Wednesday prior to the wedding. When you write Miss Bennet back, you may inform her of that. And please send a greeting to her for me; inform her how grateful I am for all she did while she was here."

~~*

The next few weeks at Pemberley involved more *caring calls* and Darcy made further contacts in London regarding his idea for the school. He had Mr. Bostwick, his head gardener take a few of his young under gardeners with him to see what they could do initially to improve the natural landscaping of the land

Darcy had purchased. He hired some builders to come out and design a structure for the school and housing that would best fit on the land.

Later, when Mr. Bostwick returned, he approached Darcy to give an update of the work accomplished and also to request some time off as the day of his son's wedding was approaching. Darcy was very obliging and offered him any time off that was needed.

Georgiana happened past at this point and informed Mr. Bostwick, to Darcy's surprise, that they would both be in attendance at the wedding and at the wedding breakfast following.

Darcy flinched, but said nothing. Mr. Bostwick expressed his appreciation and left. "What is this? We are going to a wedding?"

"Yes. You have spent the past few weeks visiting people in their homes, practicing sociability on a limited basis. I feel that you need more of a similar experience as to what it will be like in Hertfordshire at Jane and Mr. Bingley's wedding. Being in a large group and knowing how to behave is a great deal different than talking with a small party. I speak for myself that I need the experience and practice just as much as you do."

"But Georgiana, could we not just send a gift? That is what I normally do!"

"I think not. I believe our presence would be more greatly appreciated than a gift. After all, he is the son of your head gardener."

"Well then we can just go to the wedding. I do not think it is necessary for us to attend the wedding breakfast. You know I do not have that talent of conversing with strangers. I would not be comfortable especially…" He paused and looked down at his sister. She had that look on her face that said she had heard enough excuses and the only way to learn anything was to just do it!

"All right, Georgiana. I will agree, but promise me one thing. Let us just stay an acceptable amount of time after the meal, no longer. Agree to that for me, please."

"If you insist, we shall just stay until after the meal."

"Thank you."

When she walked away, Darcy felt himself grow uneasy. He told himself it would all be fine, as he would certainly know a few people with whom he would be able to converse. He knew what he talked about with men of education, but had no idea about what most of these people talked. He hoped he would be able to find topics of conversation with them.

He knew his tendency would be to put that blasted wall around himself that he usually did at functions like this. He would have to keep from doing that for Georgiana, and as much as he did not want to admit it, it would not be easy. But it was also for Elizabeth. He hoped that she would notice the transformation in him, which would, he also hoped, transform her opinion of him.

The day before the Bostwick wedding, Darcy was out riding, and Georgiana was reading in the sitting room. She heard some excited voices coming from the front door. Mrs. Reynolds came in and announced to her that the young Mr. David Bostwick was at the door and needed to speak to her or her brother.

She quickly went out to the entry way to greet a very distressed Mr. Bostwick. "Good morning, Miss Darcy," he bowed before her. "I regret to have to tell you that there was a fire in town last night, and the Lambton Assembly Hall, where we were to have our wedding breakfast, was partially destroyed by it. The only other place to have it is the smaller Lambton Inn. We are not sure how it will work out, but that is the only option we have. We were trying to let everyone know."

"I am so sorry, Mr. Bostwick. Is there anything we can do?"

He looked at her as if to say something, but only shook his head. "No, it will not be as nice as had originally been planned, but we will just have to make do."

Georgiana thanked him for relaying the news, and he excused himself.

What are the chances… thought Georgiana, *that my brother would allow the wedding breakfast to be held here?* She grimaced as she considered what he would say. *This may be asking a little too much from him, but oh, how I wish we could offer them the use of Pemberley!*

Later, when her brother came in from riding, he entered the front door, removed his hat and gloves, and was met by Georgiana. "William, I have something to tell you, as well as something to ask."

He walked over to her and took her hand, squeezing it. "Yes, my dear. What is it?"

"I was just now informed that last night the Lambton Assembly Hall had a small fire. It was not too large, but it did enough damage to prevent the wedding breakfast from being held there." She squeezed his hand back and looked at him with big, wide eyes. Darcy drew back and he gave her a furtive glance. "The only other place that they can have it is at the Inn, but that is quite a bit smaller, and not as nice."

"I am sorry to hear that," Darcy said, releasing her hand.

"William, is there any possibility we can have it here?" she asked quickly, not letting herself look at him.

"No!" The word was out of his mouth barely before Georgiana had finished asking the question. "I am sorry, Georgiana, I cannot allow that. That is out of the question." She could easily see that he was agitated, that the thought was truly bothersome to him. "Did they ask to use Pemberley?"

"No, of course not, and I did not offer. I thought it would be a nice gesture."

"There are just some things you do not understand. I hate to have to be so adamant, but it cannot be!"

Darcy could tell his sister was disappointed, but he did not see how he could allow it. He knew there would be much work that would have to be done, although he knew his staff to be most capable. He also judged it very imprudent to host a houseful of people from who knows what connections. But he also wondered how he would ever be able to handle being congenial throughout the entire event. He would be obliged to be amongst them the whole time. No, this was simply out of the question. They would have to go ahead as they now had it planned and have it at the inn.

That morning gave way to afternoon and the afternoon slowly dragged on, with Georgiana becoming very quiet and not knowing what to say to her brother. Darcy reciprocated the silence. They each took refuge in their favourite room; Darcy in his study, Georgiana in the sitting room. They each tried to read but with little success. Darcy was not happy that Georgiana was distressed about his decision, but he could not change his mind.

Georgiana knew it had been a major request, but was inwardly hoping that he would have allowed it. How much it would have said to the people. How she prayed something would change his mind!

~~*

The next day Fitzwilliam and Georgiana Darcy stood in the entry to their house waiting as the first wedding guests arrived. He stood stiffly, shaking his head at the turn of events that brought this about.

His house had been in a flurry of activity late into the evening yesterday and early this morning. But thanks to his excellent staff and those who had originally planned to put on the dinner at the Assembly Hall, things were ready just as the first guests pulled up. Darcy was convinced that more people attended this wedding than usual, as word spread throughout the area that the Darcys had agreed to host the wedding breakfast at Pemberley.

He shifted from one foot to another, feeling that natural tendency he owned to draw away; be left to himself. But he could not, and would not, for his sister's sake. He thought back to the alternative that presented itself the day before and wondered which would have been the greater of the two evils.

Yesterday afternoon, Darcy and Georgiana had gone their separate ways, both with strained feelings toward the other. Darcy locked himself in his study and Georgiana found herself in the sitting room. Both had books in front of them, but perceived very few words.

Georgiana was stirred by the sound of a carriage pulling up front. She wondered if it could be someone again regarding the Bostwick wedding. She heard the door open and began to stand when she heard a very familiar, harsh voice say, "Where is my nephew?"

Georgiana began to shudder as she instantly knew it was her aunt, Lady Catherine. Her heart sank as she suddenly realized this could be disastrous to her plans to get her brother to even attend the wedding. She sat back down, frozen to the chair.

"Darcy, where are you? Where is my niece? Georgiana!"

Mrs. Reynolds quickly came into the sitting room, saw Georgiana, and looked at her helplessly. "You aunt is here Miss Darcy. Why do you not wait until your brother sees her first? There is no sense in you having to deal with her on your own. She is terribly upset!"

Georgiana gratefully nodded.

Darcy heard his aunt's voice and closed his book. With his elbows on the desk, he put his head into his hands. He was not in any disposition to deal with his aunt. *Why did she have to appear now?* Mrs. Reynolds came in and Darcy looked up.

"I heard."

She nodded and quickly backed out of the room. Darcy took his time, wringing his hands together as he walked toward the door. Before reaching out to grasp the door handle, his hand took a little detour to his pocket. He pulled out the handkerchief and fingered it gently between his thumb and finger. Then he slipped it back into his pocket. "It is now or never!" he said to himself in a frustrated tone.

He walked out and met his aunt in the drawing room. He saw immediately that she was upset. Her body was tense; she was sitting upright, her head cocked to the side. Her hand tightly gripped her cane, as if she was ready to pound it for emphasis. Darcy toughened his nerve as he walked in.

"Good afternoon, Aunt. This is a surprise. How are you?"

"Not well at all! I have had the most distressing news, and I do not know how I can bear it all!"

Georgiana walked in meekly, keeping herself at a distance, behind her brother. "Good afternoon, Aunt." She curtseyed.

"Georgiana." Her response was very short.

"May I ask what brings you here today?" asked Darcy.

"It is insupportable! How is it to be endured? A report of a most alarming nature reached me." She turned her head to glare at Georgiana. "Why was I not informed of my nephew's accident, considering how seriously injured he was? I have not been accustomed to being neglected like this! Georgiana, what have you to say for yourself, girl?"

"I... uh..." Georgiana stepped even further behind her brother, holding on to him as she felt herself growing weak.

"Aunt Catherine, I beg you to not address my sister in that manner."

"But such thoughtlessness! It makes me wonder, Nephew, of her upbringing. I cannot help but think she would have been better off if she had been put in my care when your father passed on. Having had no mother from an early age, and then to be raised by a brother! I do not believe you have exercised the most prudent wisdom in her upbringing!"

Darcy, furious by now at his aunt, but concerned for his sister, turned to Georgiana. Her eyes were swelling with tears at her aunt's words. "Georgiana, go to your room, right now," he said to her in a firm voice.

"But William..."

"I do not want to talk about it now. I want you there immediately!"

When she left the room, Darcy turned back to his aunt. "I have never heard such absurdities in my life. I will *not* allow you to talk about her like that. Georgiana is young, and she did what she thought was best when I was ill. It would not have done me any good to have you here; there was nothing you could have done!" Darcy pondered how disastrous it would have been if she had come. To have had her here without his presence of mind to ward off her tirades, Georgiana would have not have fared well at all.

"Nephew! You are missing the whole point! I am your closest family! I should have been informed!" She stood up and stormed across to the other side of the room. "But this is not the only thing of which I have become aware that she has done. It has been brought to my attention that she is mingling with the most inferior..."

Darcy turned away from her and tried to cut her off with, "That is enough, Aunt Catherine!"

"I will not be interrupted! The disrespect you show!" She looked at him through piercing eyes. "I understand that she has been associating with those of the most inferior station and connections, actually going into their homes. And now I come to hear that she has been taking you along with her. Darcy, you know that such associations must not pollute our family. And I will not allow you to continue to do such a thing, knowing that such behaviour would be polluting my own daughter when you marry her! This is…"

Darcy turned on her in anger. "Aunt Catherine! We have been through this again and again! I have no intention; have never had any intention of marrying your daughter!"

"But Nephew, you must! It was your mother's favourite wish as well as my own, intended from your infancy. You cannot go against your mother's wish!"

Darcy drew in a very raspy breath. He knew he had to calm down, but had little hope of doing so on his own. "I have only heard from you that it was her wish. I never heard of any such thing until after her death. I cannot believe my mother would have been a part of such a scheme. Even in her own marriage, she married for love. I could not marry for anything less!"

"This is not to be borne! I never thought I would hear such words from you! Who you marry is of utmost concern to me… to the family name!"

"Aunt Catherine, you have no say in whom I marry. If I choose to marry someone of the poorest connections, that is my business, not your concern at all, but I am not marrying your daughter!"

"Oh! You are just as insolent as your sister! But let me be rightly understood, in this other matter of your consorting with those inferior to our name. I do not know what has befallen you, but I must insist that it stop! If you were sensible of the sphere in which you were brought up, you would discontinue these disgraceful associations immediately!"

"We have no intention of stopping them, and now I am afraid that I must ask you to leave. Immediately! I will not have you remain in this household as long as you continue in this way."

"You are turning me out? I will not be trifled with! I have every intention to remain here at Pemberley as long as I wish!"

"You will not, Aunt. Pemberley is my home and I am asking you to leave."

"Darcy, you are not serious. You cannot put me out at this time of day!"

"Granted, Aunt. You are correct. I am not that inhospitable. I will have the kitchen staff prepare you a meal and then you must be off."

"This is a disgrace indeed, Nephew. I see the shades of Pemberley are already polluted. But," she suddenly decided to change her tactics, "let me appeal to your sense of family, of goodness, and allow me to remain on. Only for a few more days to see for myself just how Georgiana is coming along."

"No, Aunt. You are not to see Georgiana. I am sorry, you must leave today."

"I cannot believe that you are so stubborn. I will leave when I am ready!"

By now Darcy was frustrated, but knew he could not allow his aunt to remain here, if not for his sake, for Georgiana's.

He suddenly had an idea. "Aunt Catherine, if I were you, I would make plans to leave as soon as possible. I cannot guarantee that you will not be polluted yourself by what is taking place here tomorrow.

"And what would that be?"

"Tomorrow is a wedding that Georgiana and I will be attending. Then everyone from that wedding, people who would be considered by you to be most inferior to yourself and your station, will be coming to Pemberley for the wedding breakfast! In fact," Darcy pulled out his pocket watch, "they will be arriving at any time now to start preparing for it!"

~~*

Yes, Darcy knew he had done the right thing. He could not allow his aunt to remain in his house and lay scathing censure on him and Georgiana as she did. So now he was standing in a receiving line, welcoming people from neighbouring towns and villages into his elegant house. Darcy had to chuckle to himself that his proclamation that the wedding breakfast was being held at Pemberley had the desired effect. His aunt stormed out, not even accepting his generous offer to feed her first.

The first guests were now arriving, and Georgiana turned to her brother whispering, "You do not have to stand so stiff. You can be formal if you wish, but relax. And try to smile; it does wonders for your countenance. These people are not going to bite you!"

Darcy took in a deep breath to compensate for the long one he had been holding. He relaxed his shoulders as Georgiana slipped her arm through his. She looked at him and a warm, encouraging smile spread across her face. Darcy reciprocated, but Georgiana shook her head.

She fervently whispered, "Do not coerce it! It must be more natural! Think of that one thing, perhaps that one *person* that makes you happy."

Georgiana turned away to greet the first of the arriving guests. As she turned back to Darcy for the introduction, she was surprised to actually see him smile; a thoughtful, genuine smile. *He needs to do that more often!* she thought to herself. When the party left them to move into the house, she commented, "Now, that was not difficult, was it?" The smile on her face gave him even more reason to smile, and he felt so proud of his sister who was such an endearing hostess.

Darcy thought back to the previous day, after his aunt thundered out. He ran upstairs to Georgiana's room, finding her terribly distraught. She tried to apologize to him for this oversight of not informing their aunt of his accident, thinking he was upset by it. Darcy shook his head, reassuring her that he was actually grateful she had not notified her. That was not the reason he sent her out of the room. He wanted to spare her their aunt's callous remarks. She was thankful, for she had intentionally not informed their aunt of his condition.

He then told Georgiana of his decision to allow the wedding breakfast to be held at Pemberley, and at once, preparations began. The servants used their expertise to begin working even before those who were already involved in the plans arrived from Lambton. Darcy was amazed at how well they all worked together and brought it to pass.

He looked back down to Georgiana at his side. Having her there to give him words of encouragement and downright practical advice helped him immensely.

So far, it had really not been terribly difficult. At least *this* part. He knew that once the introductions were over, he would have to socialize, and more would be required of him. It would require more of an effort.

As the last of the wedding guests were welcomed, Georgiana and Darcy turned and walked together into the large dining hall at Pemberley. It had been set up and beautifully decorated for the meal. Most people stood around, visiting. Georgiana could not get over how beautiful things looked, how everything had been transformed in less than twenty-four hours.

Georgiana quietly observed her brother tense again, and she tightened her grip on his arm as he escorted her into the room. He looked down and felt strengthened by her smile. There were small pockets of people conversing. Darcy looked for a group that looked "safe" to him. He saw the parents of the groom, Mr. and Mrs. Bostwick, in a small tête-à-tête with two other couples whose names he could not remember. He walked over to join them, as Georgiana found her way to some young girls her age.

Darcy walked towards them and noticed their lively conversation with one another. As they saw him approach, they stopped and became more reserved in their manner. Darcy sensed that they were as uncomfortable as he himself was, and would have given anything to walk past them and bolster himself against the mantel or at a window. But he would not do that, and proceeded towards them.

He knew he had to break down his barrier so they would break down theirs. "That was a splendid wedding, Bostwick. You son appears to be very happy. She looks to be a very fine girl."

"Thank you, Sir. We are most pleased with his choice. And I cannot thank you enough for your generous hospitality in allowing us to come to Pemberley for the breakfast. We are most grateful." The conversation continued; they spoke of the estate and he spoke of their families.

He occasionally made eye contact with Georgiana, who appeared pleased with the way he handled himself. She smiled an exaggerated smile to remind him to do the same if she thought he was looking too severe, but that was needed less and less as the day progressed. He found it easier, by the end of the celebration, to move and talk more willingly and comfortably with those he previously would have considered himself too superior to intimately associate.

He learned a great deal that night. As Georgiana said on their very first *caring call*, these people had the same hopes, dreams, fears, and desires that he did. They lived simply; he was amazed at how it took very little to make them happy. They stood in awe of his great estate, but he knew that they would return to their homes and still be as happy in them as he might be here. In fact, he felt some of them could be happier than he, depending whether or not one certain lady would show any inclination of returning his regard when he saw her again in less than two weeks.

Chapter 14

Darcy helped Georgiana into their carriage as their luggage was loaded. Each had been secretly counting down the days before their departure, and felt such nervous anticipation, that the last few nights had granted them very little sleep.

This morning they both were quiet and reflective. The day had finally arrived. They settled themselves in the carriage; Darcy with a book in hand and Georgiana with her needlework. As he looked over at her laboriously working on each stitch, he thought of the handkerchief, which he had so painstakingly kept from everyone, save Georgiana, these two months. He patted his pocket absent-mindedly to reassure himself that it rested in its safe abode.

Occasionally Georgiana would speak out a thought of hers; about the wedding, wondering what Jane's dress looked like, or how everyone was doing. She smiled as she thought of the letter she had sent off to Elizabeth after receiving hers. Her brother told her to send his greeting. She sent his warmest greeting, along with some flattering information about him which might sway her feelings to his favour. Her smile was also indicative of her longing to speak with Elizabeth. She had so much she would like to talk with her about.

Georgiana looked over at her brother, who appeared calm save for the nervous rubbing together of his thumb and index finger. It was a habit she had come to recognize as meaning that although he appeared calm on the outside, on the inside he was quite anxious. Oh how she hoped and prayed he would be able to right things between himself and Elizabeth. He had been rather silent on that subject lately and she wondered whether she should broach it.

"William?"

He looked up from his book. "Mmm?"

"I am so looking forward to seeing the Bennet sisters again, especially Elizabeth. Do you believe we will be able to spend much time with them before the wedding?"

Darcy shifted his position and looked back down. Georgiana continued. "I know how much you want her to know that you have changed. I can testify myself that you are a different man than you were six months ago, even two months ago. I just hope she has the opportunity to take notice of it."

Yes, that was true. When he had been in Hertfordshire more than six months earlier, he thought he had his life together. He thought he knew exactly what he wanted and how to attain it. How wrong he was! His heart began pounding at the thought of seeing her again. The woman who had so thrown his life into turmoil! *This time it will be different,* he told himself. If only he could believe that!

"I am not certain what our schedule will be," he answered all too calmly. "I assume we will pay a call at Longbourn, but I must confess I am not totally confident that she will take the time to notice any change in me."

"Oh, I am sure she will."

"On that we shall see, but there is one thing I *am* concerned about that I had a very difficult time with before."

"What was that?"

"Tell me, Georgiana, how do I handle her mother?"

"Her mother?"

"Yes, she is truly quite annoying; practically uncivilized. She proved to be quite exasperating to me, actually."

"I doubt that she can be as bad as you say."

"Just you wait."

"Perhaps you could take a clue from how others respond to her. You may just have to politely… quietly and graciously endure her. Just do not put up that wall of yours. She is, after all, Elizabeth's mother."

He took in a quiet, deep breath. Georgiana noticed that his shoulders raised as he inhaled, and it seemed an eternity before he released it. He tilted his head at her and smiled. "You have grown up so much these past few months. I can scarce believe that you are not a little girl anymore; you have turned into quite the young lady."

Georgiana looked down, slightly embarrassed by her brother's words, but so very appreciative of them. Did he really know how much of what she had become these last few months was the direct result of Elizabeth? As she looked up and met his eyes, she felt sure he did. There was both admiration in them for her and a reflective faraway look that made her wonder if he was thinking of Elizabeth.

"William, the things Aunt Catherine said whilst she was here. About me not being raised properly…"

"She should have never said such things!" he responded harshly. He softened as he continued, "Yet, the truth is, I have often wondered that myself."

"No! You could not have done a better job, along with Cousin Richard, in providing guidance and direction for me… love and support. Please do not ever doubt that."

"Thank you, Georgiana. I have often wondered, though, the loss you must have felt in not having a mother. I had hoped that Miss Annesley would prove to be something akin to that for you."

"She is very good, very kind. But a mother, no. Maybe more like a great aunt, although very different from our own Aunt Catherine." She softly laughed. "I have often wished that I did have someone I could feel comfortable enough to confide in."

That reflective look crossed Darcy's face again. "I had hoped by now…" The silence that filled the carriage was very heavy. Georgiana knew he was thinking of Elizabeth and that he was just as aware that she was thinking of her, also.

"Yes," Georgiana replied softly.

They arrived at Netherfield just before the evening meal. As Darcy entered the large estate, he could not help but recall each room and the moments he had shared with Elizabeth, although they often resulted in a misunderstanding between the two of them. There was the dining room, the sitting room, the billiard room, the ballroom…

His reverie was short lived as Miss Bingley greeted them with her officious courtesy. "Why, Mr. Darcy, we almost gave up on your arrival! It has been absolutely dreadful here. And Georgiana, why how you have grown since last I saw you! Indeed, the very presence of you both shall bring much needed consequence here!"

"Miss Bingley," was his only reply.

Bingley entered the room as jubilantly as one would have expected, being just three days to his wedding. "Darcy! How good it is to see you again! I am so glad you are here at last! Come; let us go into the dining room for something to eat. I have so much to tell you!"

They were joined by the Hursts and departed to the dining room where a meal awaited them. Mr. Hurst displayed his usual self-indulgent manners, and the two Bingley sisters chatted incessantly of the pleasing prospect that their *superior* family and friends would soon be arriving for the wedding.

Darcy turned to Bingley and asked how plans for the wedding were coming. "Oh, just fine. I try to stay out of it as much as possible. Leave the decisions for the wedding to Jane and her mother; whatever she wants is fine with me."

"That is probably the most prudent course of action."

"Darcy, tomorrow I do need you to go into town with me for a few things."

"I see no problem with that."

"Good! And then tomorrow night we are all invited to the Bennets' home for dinner."

Bingley looked at Darcy for a reaction, but was interrupted from his scrutiny by Georgiana. "Oh, that sounds lovely. I look so forward to seeing them again."

Bingley's sisters looked at each other with raised eyebrows and a mocking sneer. With the engagement of their brother to the eldest Bennet daughter, their retorts concerning any of the Bennets could no longer be verbal in his presence. They had mastered their looks of disgust and condescension very well.

It did not escape Darcy's or Georgiana's notice. Bingley was too jovial and in high spirits to recognize that his sisters thought too well of themselves to sincerely approve of this match. Brother and sister looked at each other with concurring looks of displeasure at the ladies' response.

Bingley continued in his oblivious state, "Unfortunately, Miss Bennet was not able to join us this evening, as they expect the arrival of their aunt and uncle from London. How I wish she could have been here to join me in welcoming you." He turned to Georgiana and winked, "And I am privy to the knowledge that Miss Elizabeth is greatly looking forward to seeing you again, Georgiana."

Again there was a look exchanged between the sisters, and Darcy caught himself nervously tapping his fingers. Georgiana felt a very taut tension in the air at the mention of Elizabeth. She finally turned to Bingley and answered quietly, "I have long desired her company, as well."

Bingley looked at Darcy, searching his face for some sort of clue as to what the state of his feelings was toward his soon to be sister-in-law. He saw a particularly masked expression on his friend's face. Darcy either still had very strong feelings for her that he did not want anyone to see, or he had sorted through his feelings and they came up wanting. He wondered if his friend would confide what his feelings were for her now, after two months.

~~*

At the Bennet household, the Gardiners arrived in the middle of the evening meal, causing everyone to rise and leave the food on their plates, while the kitchen help quickly set more place settings for the couple and their children. Elizabeth was delighted to finally have her aunt and uncle here, whom she loved and admired deeply.

She felt that her aunt had always been her model of the mother and wife Elizabeth would want to be. The love and respect the Gardiners had for each other was very evident; very unlike the relationship between Mr. and Mrs. Bennet. For that reason, Elizabeth took every advantage of sitting, talking, watching, and learning from both of them. It would be good to have them in their home for these next few days. With Jane spending so much time recently with Charles, it left Elizabeth confined to the company of her mother and three younger sisters, which left her feeling much more alone.

They returned to the dining room, and were now joined at the table by the Gardiners. They talked of their travels that day and of such pleasantries as the weather, the wedding, and soon talked of the dinner that would be held there the following evening.

"Oh, how I hope our kitchen staff will get everything right!" lamented Mrs. Bennet. "You know how I would hate to have some major disaster with the food that is prepared."

"Do not you worry, Mrs. Bennet," said her husband quite unsympathetically. "Leave it to them. You have enough worries in these next few days; I should think you would have no room for more."

"And who all is invited tomorrow night?" asked Mrs. Gardiner to Jane.

"It shall be all of us, yourselves, Aunt and Uncle Phillips, the Bingleys and Hursts, the Lucases, and the Collinses."

"Oh, do not forget that Darcy fellow," chimed in Mrs. Bennet. "He and his sister, I suppose are coming too."

Elizabeth quickly looked down, hoping no one would notice her flushed face as she was struck by merely the mention of his name, but was also appalled that her mother still held such a contemptible view of him. It was probably due to the fact that Jane had returned from Pemberley engaged but she did not.

"He is the one from Pemberley, is he not?" asked Mrs. Gardiner.

Mrs. Bennet nodded. "Yes, he is that proud, disagreeable man whose accident took Jane and Elizabeth to Pemberley. I cannot say, though, that I am altogether displeased with their having to travel there. Look what it meant for our Jane.

Because of it she will soon be married!"

Elizabeth looked down and gently shook her head as she heard her mother's misinformation to the Gardiners regarding how they happened to go to Pemberley.

"I remember Pemberley as a child. Growing up in Lambton, just five miles away, we were very much aware of the prosperity that estate lent to our small town. I never knew the family, just of them. They were apparently very well esteemed."

She looked at Elizabeth and smiled, noting something peculiar in her niece's expression. "It is a shame that the new master is not as gracious as his father was."

"Oh, but he is." It was Jane this time, coming to Darcy's defence. "He is most good-natured and kind, as well as his sister. I think we have all been under the most incorrect presumption about him. Charles even shared with me that he and his sister make regular visits to those less fortunate than themselves. They both have a very generous spirit." Jane looked at Lizzy and noticed a startled look upon her face.

"And what is your opinion of the man, Lizzy?" asked Mrs. Gardiner, sensing something from Elizabeth that she could not quite make out.

Initially, Elizabeth knew not what she should say, as she had been arguing this very point in her mind for months now. "I know... that when he was here in Hertfordshire, he appeared to us all as being arrogant. But he does seem to have the respect of many people, including his sister and Mr. Bingley. Unfortunately, when he awakened from his coma while we were there, I did not stay long enough to form a complete, accurate opinion of him."

Conveniently for Elizabeth the conversation turned elsewhere and she was left with her own thoughts. She knew that he and Georgiana had most likely arrived at Netherfield by now. Her heart fluctuated between skipping a beat in anticipation of seeing Georgiana again and beating thunderously as she contemplated seeing her brother again. It was now less than a day away.

Mrs. Gardiner eyed her second eldest niece with a guarded look of suspicion, wondering what, indeed, her *heartfelt* opinion of him was.

~~*

Elizabeth did not sleep well at all that night. When she came to her room that evening, she pulled out the letter she had just received from Georgiana. It was short, but sweet. She looked over the words she had written.

Dearest Elizabeth,

How soon it shall be before we arrive! My brother tells me we should arrive the Wednesday before the wedding. I wish it could have been sooner, but there is some business he needs to tend to that prevents us from coming earlier. I look forward to visiting with you.

I would like to request some time with you alone, if you might spare it. I do not know what plans you have. I know that you will probably be quite busy before the wedding, but if you can make some time for me, I should like to pay you a call. I am quite unsure how long we will stay. My brother has said he will have to wait and see. I suppose it could be just through the weekend, or possibly longer. I am hoping it is longer.

Our cousin, Fitzwilliam, was here recently and he talked very animatedly about you. We had some good laughs at my brother's expense. I believe, after all these years, he is finally learning to laugh at himself, if only just a little, without losing too much dignity. It would have been wiser for him to have learned this years ago, as it would have lessened by cousin's enjoyment in teasing him so.

This letter shall be short, as we shall soon be in each other's company. My brother has most emphatically expressed the wish to extend his gratitude to you for all you did here a few months back. Again, you cannot know how much your presence here meant. He sends his warmest greeting.

With fond anticipation of our forthwith reunion,
&c, Georgiana

Elizabeth wondered at those words from her brother. *Could he be making certain she knew that now he merely felt gratitude toward her, as Caroline had suggested? But what was this - his warmest greeting?* Such conflicting pieces of information, how could she assess what it really meant?

Putting aside the letter, she climbed into her bed and tried to calm herself down. Her thoughts assaulted her and her nerves were taut. She tossed and turned, weighing every argument she could conceive both in his favour and against. By early morning she had resigned herself to simply wait and see, but she was certain he most likely would be the same man as he had been when he was here before.

She knew he felt disdain for her family and their behaviour. He had said so in his letter to her. She had witnessed him on more than one occasion walk away in disgust at something her mother or other member of her family said or did. She imagined that he would conveniently stay close to his sister, the Bingleys, and the Hursts, avoiding her family and friends as much as possible. And if that were the case, she could have no part of him. But why did that make her heart ache so much?

Chapter 15

When morning broke, Elizabeth was not yet ready to rise. She heard stirrings from other parts of the house; her mother's voice above all others. She could ascertain from her mother's tone that she was frantically giving orders; orders that, she was certain, did not need to be given, as the house staff usually did a very proficient job.

Elizabeth tugged off the blankets that covered her and she stretched her arms high above her, releasing an awakening yawn. She finally pulled herself out of bed and brought herself to her dressing table and looked in the mirror. "Oh!" she exclaimed as looked at herself. "Not good at all!" She eyed the dark circles under her eyes and hoped that time and some fresh air would help. She brushed out her hair, rinsed her face, and looked in the mirror again. Shaking her head half-heartedly, she proceeded to get dressed.

As she went downstairs, the clamour that her mother was creating by her rants and ravings was, in Elizabeth's opinion, causing more problems than solving them. She saw that her father's study was door closed, so she knocked on it softly.

"Come in," he answered softly.

Elizabeth opened the door and walked in, just as another one of Mrs. Bennet's overtures could be heard throughout the house. Both she and her father looked at each other with one mirroring eyebrow raised in consternation. "I sense that this is what things will be like for the next few days."

Elizabeth nodded, looking down. "Father…" Elizabeth paused, not knowing how to say what she wanted so much to say.

"What is it, my dear Lizzy?"

"Is there any way that you can talk to Mother, about… well tonight… at the dinner. Is there any way someone can talk to her about behaving a little more dignified than usual?" Her head went down, causing her to have to look up at her father with raised eyebrows as she awaited his response.

"I really do not know what good it would do, my sweet. But if you insist, I shall make every endeavour to please you. Perhaps she can get it all out of her today, before everyone arrives. What say you to that?"

"Anything is worth hoping for!" Elizabeth sighed. "I just feel that with all those who will be here tonight, if she could just be on her best… well, if she could just behave properly."

"I will see what I can do!"

"Thank you, Papa." She turned to exit the study, steeling herself for what she knew would be a terribly stressful day. As she stepped out, she was grateful to see her aunt walking past.

"Oh, Lizzy, you have finally risen. I have been waiting for you to come down. Shall we get something to eat, and then, how about a little walk?"

"That sounds wonderful, Aunt!" replied a delighted Elizabeth.

They went in to eat; most everyone else having eaten already. She looked at the clock and saw that it was ten o'clock. She rarely slept in this late. Her aunt noticed that she looked fatigued, as if she had not slept well. "Let me get you some tea," offered her aunt. "It will do wonders for you."

"I think this morning I need a little something special." Elizabeth walked over to the sideboard and pulled out some chamomile tea, adding a little honey, a touch of cream, and a small peppermint candy, which soon began to dissolve.

"Your special remedy, I see."

"Ah, yes. It is both soothing to calm the nerves, but the peppermint adds just the right refreshment to pick you up."

Elizabeth ate very little, but savoured her special cup of tea. Her stomach felt all tied up in knots, and she hoped this would help. When she finished the cup of tea, she stood up with her aunt and they linked arms as they took a turn outdoors.

They walked in silence at first, Elizabeth making only inconsequential conversation. As they reached the end of the drive, Mrs. Gardiner turned to her and took her hand in hers. "Tell me, Lizzy. Is there something you wish to talk with me about?" She paused, giving her niece time to think about it. "You appear a little less spirited than normal; I just wondered if anything was amiss."

"Oh, no, nothing is wrong." The flinch Elizabeth allowed to cross her face betrayed her true answer.

Mrs. Gardiner squeezed her hand. "Lizzy, if you do not want to talk about it, I will understand. But you know I have always been able to read you, and I am quite sure something is on your mind. I am available to hear you out, whatever you might be feeling."

"I do appreciate that, Aunt. You know that I have always been grateful to you for that. It is just that, well, I have been having a difficult time lately sorting out my feelings about a particular… subject. I have always thought I could so rightly determine the character of anyone -- of anything. I am just having more of a difficult time of it now, than usual."

Her aunt looked upon Elizabeth was much understanding. "Lizzy, perhaps when strong feelings get in the way, what we try to determine in our head does not make much sense. You either need to listen to your head or your heart, but whichever you listen to more, make sure it is the right one."

Elizabeth longed to tell her all, but not with the object of her confusion coming to their home that night. This would be all the details she could now give her, yet her few words spoke a considerable amount to her aunt.

~~*

121

As the time of the dinner neared, Elizabeth went to her room to ready herself. She perused her wardrobe, looking for just the right dress to wear. Everything suddenly looked dull to her. She thought of Mr. Darcy, as he would be so handsome in vest and jacket, and nothing that she owned would come close to the elegance that he would most likely be used to. She finally selected a blue dress which, when worn, often solicited comments about how it brought out the flecks of blue in her eyes.

She took down her hair and called for Sara, one of the younger maids, to help her put it up again. Sara came in with ribbons and gardenia petals, weaving them throughout her hair. When she had completed her task, Elizabeth went to the mirror and was relatively pleased with what she saw; at least she no longer looked weary. Looking down at her hands, however, she noticed they were shaking. *This will never do.* She had to calm down, or at least appear on the outside that she was calm. She would go downstairs and make herself another cup of her tea before anyone arrived.

Before leaving her room, she picked up her bottle of gardenia toilet water from her dressing table and lightly dabbed some on her wrists and neck. It was always so soothing for her to breathe in that flowery scent. The petals themselves were fragrant, but she could not smell them up in her hair. Sitting down, she closed her eyes and took in some slow, deep breaths. She brought her hand to her heart, bringing her fingers to her neck and holding it there ever so firmly, as if to compel her heart to stop its incessant pounding.

At length she knew she could delay the inevitable no longer. She must go downstairs and be available to greet the guests as they arrived. She shuddered unwittingly as a chill ran through her body. As she walked out of her door, she was joined by her sister, who was completely at ease and utterly calm. They took each other's hands, and as they walked down the stairs, Jane turned to Elizabeth.

"Lizzy, are you ready for this evening?"

"To be honest, I am quite nervous. I just wish the evening were over with." Jane gave Elizabeth a smile that was most genuine and heartfelt. Elizabeth returned one that was more forced.

Immediately after coming downstairs, Elizabeth poured herself a cup of tea and slowly sipped it in the dining room. She walked over to the tables and noticed that Darcy had been placed across from her. As she contemplated this, she tipped the cup and gulped down the rest of the tea. Why was her heart still pounding so?

Just as Elizabeth came back out to join the others, her Aunt and Uncle Phillips arrived. They were greeted by their mother with much enthusiasm. Mrs. Bennet was well pleased that they were the first guests to arrive.

They joined the Gardiners in conversation and Elizabeth saw the door open. Her heartbeat pounded in her chest until she saw that it was the Lucases. They entered, but Mr. and Mrs. Collins did not accompany them. They made the apology that Charlotte and her husband had just arrived from Hunsford. They were freshening up and would be joining them later. How Elizabeth wished Charlotte was there with her now.

Elizabeth was talking with her Aunt and Uncle Phillips when she noticed

Bingley walk in. Her heart momentarily stopped as she watched for the rest of his party. His sisters Caroline and Louisa and Mr. Hurst followed him, along with Georgiana. A few dreadfully long seconds later, Mr. Darcy finally appeared. As he entered the room he quickly scanned it; his eyes coming to rest on Elizabeth. It seemed as though the sight of her arrested his forward movement. He came to a brief stop as his tall frame passed through the door.

Mr. and Mrs. Bennet promptly greeted the whole party, along with an elated Jane. Bingley's smile did not depart his face as he greeted Jane and her family. The Bennets turned to introduce the party to the Gardiners. Darcy stepped forward to greet the Bennets and introduce his sister. She very graciously came forward to meet Elizabeth's parents, greet Jane, and then walked over to Elizabeth, holding out her hands to her.

"How are you, Georgiana?" As Elizabeth took her hands, she pulled her close and gave her a quick hug.

"It is so good to see you again, Elizabeth. My you smell simply delicious! Is that by any chance gardenia?"

"Yes, it is! My favourite scent."

"And a favourite around Pemberley also. You smell just like the fresh gardenias that line the front entry to our home."

Elizabeth looked at her quizzically as if trying to recall. "I do not remember any gardenias there. How odd! I am quite surprised I did not notice them."

Elizabeth suddenly felt herself grow flushed as she became aware of someone standing directly behind her. She heard the sound of a breath being taken in, and she slowly turned.

"Miss Elizabeth. Good evening." Darcy said as he slowly exhaled.

"Good evening, Mr. Darcy."

"It is good to see you again. I hope you are well."

"Yes, I am. Thank you. May I add that you are looking much improved from the last time I saw you."

"For that I am grateful. I regret that when you took leave of Pemberley, I neglected to thank you for all you did while you were there. You were a great help to my sister and also, apparently, to me."

"That is kind of you, Sir. I only did what needed to be done."

He stared at Elizabeth for a moment, took in a deep breath, and then turned to Georgiana, raising his eyebrows as if he was unsure what else to say.

Georgiana gave him a reassuring smile and addressed Elizabeth. "I understand that you will be standing up for your sister at her wedding. My brother is…"

As she spoke, Mr. Bennet came up to Darcy and pulled him off to the side. Darcy smiled apologetically and excused himself from the two ladies.

Georgiana looked back at Elizabeth and saw a brief look of disappointment crossing her face. "You have a lovely home here, Elizabeth. And you have a very loving family."

"Thank you."

They chatted for a little while longer and then Kitty and Lydia approached. Elizabeth introduced them to Georgiana. They each took an arm of the young girl and escorted her off to one side of the room. Elizabeth hoped they would behave in a most upright manner. She would have liked to talk more with Georgiana, but she would have time later.

Elizabeth looked at her father, who was now sequestered with Darcy and Mr. Gardiner in the corner. What they were talking about, she had no idea. But as she stole an occasional glimpse at Darcy, she noticed something very different about him. He appeared to enjoy the conversation. He was contributing, listening, and even smiling.

Jane and Bingley were sharing an animated conversation, completely oblivious to everyone else in the room. The Hursts and Miss Bingley had seated themselves in a secluded corner of the room where they scrutinized everyone that was present.

As Elizabeth walked around, her gaze kept returning to Darcy. She found herself surprised by his altered manner. She was drawn by his light, easygoing expression. Even his stance was less rigid, more relaxed. He seemed an altogether different man!

She watched him step over briefly and exchange conversation with Sir William and her uncle, Mr. Phillips. She realized none too soon that she had been neglecting the others, as she had been so transfixed by him. She had been watching him with the expectation that he would at any moment return to that proud demeanour they had come to expect when he was here previously.

She took a few strides over to her aunts who were enjoying a conversation with her mother. She noticed that her mother was also behaving far too self-controlled. Could her father have actually talked some sense into her? Elizabeth shook her head and thought, *No, it is just a matter of time.*

Darcy returned to Mr. Bennet and Mr. Gardiner, and was now joined by Bingley. The sound of hearty laughter from the men drew her notice to them. As her eyes came upon the group, Darcy was laughing. She looked again at him, never recalling seeing him thus. She had seen him smirk, smile slightly, but laugh? She could not recall. As she watched him, his eyes turned toward hers, holding them much like a magnet drawing metal to itself. To pull her eyes away took every ounce of resolve she could muster.

He was behaving most congenially. He did not have the sternness and reserve he had before. Elizabeth credited it to the civil behaviour of all those in her house. That her mother was behaving in a dignified way had her completely bewildered. Darcy was having far too easy of a time this evening. She knew her father could be very dignified, Bingley was his best friend, and her Uncle Gardiner was very distinguished, at least in her eyes.

Elizabeth stood to the side of the ladies, finding it difficult to participate in the conversation. Jane, who had been politely sitting with Bingley's sisters, came and joined the group. Elizabeth was grateful, as she needed the diversion, and apparently Jane had noticed.

"Lizzy, you are uncommonly quiet this evening. Are things well with you?"

"Oh, yes," she answered.

When she did not elaborate, Jane took advantage of the quiet. "He seems different, does he not?"

"Who?" asked Elizabeth, knowing full well about whom she was talking.

"Mr. Darcy, of course. Have you noticed how he appears to be a different man? I believe Charles must be correct about him."

"Jane, I am not convinced. The evening is still quite young."

"Are you not being a little too harsh on him?"

"No, I think not. He confirmed over and over again his arrogance and conceit when he was here last. I will not allow him to convince me otherwise in one evening spent with a small group of people, most of whom are actually being quite well-mannered." That last thought had her completely mystified.

"I think you may be a little too harsh on yourself, also."

"What do you mean?"

"I think you are afraid to trust your feelings. It is very apparent to me what your feelings are, and you are not giving them any credit."

Elizabeth blushed at her sister's words and did not answer. Jane turned to join in the conversation with her aunt and mother.

When Elizabeth turned back to take note of Darcy, the party of men had dispersed. She looked around and did not see him. She tried to join in the conversation going on about her, but found herself wondering where he might be.

After a while, she saw him re-enter the room. As he walked back in, he saw her eyes upon him. She quickly looked away, feeling colour rising to her cheeks. Her aunt peered at her through the corner of her eyes, looking then to the man who appeared to bring this all on.

Darcy walked over to Bingley, who had rejoined Jane and her mother. She watched him as he interacted with her mother, waiting for that moment when she would behave in a way that would drive him to the furthest part of the room. But her mother did not comply.

She suddenly had an idea that would truly test whether Darcy had changed.

Elizabeth excused herself, walking past the two Bingley sisters and Mr. Hurst. She walked into the dining room, going directly to Mr. Darcy's seat. She looked down at the place cards and thought to herself, *This will never do! Seated between Bingley and Mr. Gardiner; across from Georgiana and me. No! This would be far too easy for him!*

She quickly did some rearranging, placing him to the right of her mother at the far end of the table, and next to Mr. Collins. *Now we shall see the true character of Mr. Darcy and how he behaves when my mother's real behaviour is inevitably exhibited, along with our faithfully odious Mr. Collins!*

With this little bit of tomfoolery behind her, she walked back out into the room once more. As she came in, she saw Darcy was now standing off by himself. When he saw her walk in, he began walking slowly toward her. Their eyes met and locked as he closed the gap between them.

Just as he was about to take the final long stride and reach her, and her thunderous heartbeat was pounding loud in her ears, the Collinses were announced. Elizabeth looked quickly at Darcy, and excused herself to go greet her good friend. Introductions were made and Elizabeth was able to secure her friend's arm and take her off to one side.

"Charlotte! It is good to see you! How have you been?" Her hands shook slightly and her face flushed with colour.

"Oh, Lizzy. I am just so glad to be here. It had been most dreadful the past few weeks at Rosings."

"Oh, dear. What is wrong?" She looked to Mr. Collins, wondering what he may have done to upset Charlotte, or even worse, Lady Catherine.

"A few weeks ago Lady Catherine visited Mr. Darcy at Pemberley. She claims that he behaved in the most rude, offensive way towards her; even demanding that she leave his home. He refused to let her stay. Unsurprisingly, it has been very unpleasant to be around her. She was not the least bit pleased that we were coming here, knowing he would be here. My husband has been most perturbed about the whole thing, feeling it is his duty to set Mr. Darcy straight on the matter. I have tried to convince him to stay out of it. I think... I hope he will behave, as long as he does not come into too close contact with him.

At these words, Elizabeth thought of the dining room table and gasped. She truly believed that if Darcy had ordered his own aunt out of his house, it had to be for a good reason. She did not want to put him through *that* much torture, bearing Mr. Collins' unreasonable tirades from his aunt.

"Charlotte, excuse me. I must attend to something directly."

Mr. Bennet's words halted Elizabeth, "Let us adjourn to the dining room. Now that the last of our party has arrived, I believe we can eat." Everyone was quite eager to go in and find their seat.

Unfortunately, Elizabeth was toward the back and could not sneak in ahead of everyone, as she wished. When she entered the room, Darcy was ahead of her and she watched him walk around to the one end of the table where Bingley was seated. He took hold of the chair he had originally been placed at and looked down, suddenly taking note of the place card. Glancing at it again, he turned a puzzled gaze slowly down the length of the table. Elizabeth suddenly felt mortified as she realized he must have been in there earlier and seen where he was initially to be seated. He looked up and could easily see in Elizabeth's expression that she was the one who changed the seating arrangements.

As he walked down the length of the table, Elizabeth noticed him tense. He looked down at the place card for Mr. Collins and next to it was his. He looked to his left and saw that he was seated next to Mrs. Bennet. He took his seat, very gravely looking straight ahead.

Elizabeth quickly found her chair and slinked into it, not being able to look at him at all. Georgiana came and found her place next to Elizabeth. When Bingley and Jane walked in, he noticed Darcy at the far end and exclaimed, "That is odd," but said nothing more when the Hursts and Caroline sat down beside him.

Georgiana was pleased to be seated next to Elizabeth. She had not had the opportunity to really talk with her this evening. When Georgiana seated herself, Elizabeth discovered something terribly distressing. When she looked at Georgiana, Darcy was directly in her line of vision, and she could not look at her without noticing him.

As Georgiana expressed her joy again at meeting her family, Elizabeth tried to concentrate, but found her eyes focusing beyond the girl to her brother. He had a very solemn look about him. She took little pleasure in the truth that this would certainly be a test for him. She suddenly felt very remorseful for her impulsive, immature actions as she watched the scene take place before her eyes. Mr. Collins arrived to find that his place had been set directly next to Mr. Darcy.

Mr. Collins came to his place at the table and as Darcy turned to greet him, Collins very uncivilly uttered, "Mr. Darcy, I am afraid I do not come with greetings from your aunt, Lady Catherine de Bourgh. She is most distraught, and I am sure you must know the reason for her distress. I feel it is my duty to..."

Charlotte quickly came around and, gently nudging her husband away from Darcy, picked up her place card and switched it with his, placing herself next to Darcy. She then quickly pulled out the chair and sat in it, pointing to the chair next to her for her husband to take. Elizabeth breathed a sigh of relief, as at least now, he would be spared some discomfort.

Charlotte smiled apologetically at Darcy and turned to her husband to distract him from going any further with his intended rebuke.

Elizabeth noticed Darcy's hand upon the table, nervously rubbing his thumb and finger together. When he looked over at her and saw that her eyes were upon him, he quickly stopped and picked up his napkin, placing it in his lap. He took a deep breath and felt the urge to reach into his pocket to finger the handkerchief. But he would not. That would now have to cease. He would no longer find comfort in this ritual that had taken him through the last two months.

He looked over at his other table partners and felt as though he should make some attempt at conversation, but at this point he was really not in the mood. It was very obvious to him what had happened. He had walked through earlier and seen that he was placed to sit across from Elizabeth. He looked forward to the meal and being able to spend it in conversation with her. But he had seen her come out from the dining room earlier. She must have moved his place card down to the far end of the table, as far away from her as possible, so she would not have to endure his company during the course of the meal.

He felt a strange discomfort that took away most of his appetite. He looked at his sister who was so enjoying Elizabeth's company. As he watched her, he met Elizabeth's eyes, but could not tell whether she was looking at his sister, or beyond her at him. He still found himself drawn to those eyes, and with great pain, he realized this was going to be a very long evening.

Chapter 16

Charlotte turned to Mr. Darcy after noticing her husband had solicited the attention of the Gardiners, who were seated next to him. "I must apologize for my husband," she spoke softly. "He had no right to be so unkind toward you. It is just that we have endured several weeks of very taxing visits with Lady Catherine. Just to let you know, she has been telling some quite disturbing stories about you regarding her visit to Pemberley. I am quite sure that she has greatly exaggerated what happened there."

Looking straight ahead, Darcy nervously drew himself upright in his chair. "Quite the contrary, Mrs. Collins. I am in no doubt that everything she has told you is true." He turned to her, seeing her puzzled look.

"If she told you I was callously rude to her, removed my sister from her presence, and refused to allow her to see her, finally demanding that she leave my home, that is correct." His eyes narrowed as he recalled his anger that day.

"I am certain that there must have been a very good reason for it, Mr. Darcy." She did not want to pry, but if he wanted to share what happened, she would be willing to listen.

He was reassured by her look of compassion, and was aware again as he looked at Mrs. Collins, that he could easily watch Elizabeth without her taking notice. She may not want his company, but he was going to act as civil and polite to her family and friends, no matter what she thought of him at the moment. And what harm was there in looking upon her face? In spite of his distress over her actions, having her in his sight actually soothed his spirit.

He continued, "She insulted my sister, Mrs. Collins, bringing her to tears. She questioned my ability to raise her properly. I would not stand for it and I knew if she remained, her unjust, heartless accusations would not have ceased. I could not, *would* not, allow her to remain on at Pemberley." He spoke with intensity, but softly, so as not to draw Mr. Collins' attention.

Charlotte responded, "I was quite certain, Mr. Darcy, that whatever happened between the two of you was attributed to her behaviour."

She turned her head toward her husband, and unfortunately, she and Mr. Darcy overheard an occasional word whispered fervently by Mr. Collins to the Gardiners, "my patroness... such distress when one's own family members... her nephew... demanded she leave."

She looked from Mr. Collins back to Mr. Darcy. "Please allow me to apologize for my husband. If he had any good sense, he would be willing to listen to your account of what occurred."

As she turned to whisper something to her husband, Darcy kept his eyes in her direction, looking past her to Elizabeth. He observed that there was something in the way she and Georgiana seemed to enjoy each other's company that made it difficult to look away. The only time he had seen them together was when Elizabeth was leaving Pemberley, as he watched them say goodbye to each other from his study window.

He noticed the difference in his sister as she spoke with Elizabeth, and then as she turned to speak to Elizabeth's two youngest sisters. As she spoke to them, she appeared more shy and reserved, smiling politely, but struggling with conversation. Yet when she turned back to Elizabeth, she displayed more an air of assurance and he could detect a very eager spirit within her. She seemed to have no difficulty keeping up the conversation.

Darcy's thoughts were very much whirring around inside him now. Charlotte and her husband appeared to be discussing something while Darcy continued to contemplate the effect Miss Bennet had on his sister... the effect she still had on him!

Suddenly Mr. Collins arose, and in an apologetic voice uttered, "It is with deepest regret that we must take leave of you now. My devoted wife has just informed me that she has been taken suddenly ill, and desires to return directly to her parents' home to rest. Would you please excuse us for the evening?"

A general response of sympathetic words poured forth from the party, and they began to walk toward the door. Mr. Bennet rose from the table to escort them out. Elizabeth was up instantly as well.

As they drew into the entry, she pulled Charlotte off to the side, knowing she was not feeling ill at all. "Charlotte, you need not to do this. I do not want you to leave. I know you are not truly ill."

"It is best. It will be impossible for my husband to remain silent tonight on the subject of Mr. Darcy's behaviour toward his aunt, and he does not even know the truth of the matter." She looked at Elizabeth and whispered, "Mr. Darcy informed me that Lady Catherine was very critical of Georgiana, even bringing her to tears. He would not allow her to stay in the house because of the hurt she was inflicting on his sister."

"I am not surprised, knowing Lady Catherine as I do. Poor Georgiana!"

"Lizzy, I know that you have been very offended by Mr. Darcy's behaviour in the past. But let me assure you that tonight he seemed most amiable. I truly enjoyed his company."

Elizabeth smiled meekly. *Why did I ever change his seat?* she asked herself regretfully. *Everyone seems to have been able to enjoy his company but me.*

Elizabeth and her father bid the couple goodbye and walked back into the dining room. When she stepped in, she noticed that the Gardiners had moved over and were now seated next to Darcy, engaged in conversation with him.

Apparently they had not been able to get any kind of responsive conversation with the Hursts, who were seated on the far side of Mr. Gardiner. When

Elizabeth walked in, it did not escape Mrs. Gardiner's notice that Darcy's attention was immediately drawn to her. She noticed that the instant he looked over at Elizabeth, he closed his fist and nervously rubbed his thumb and index finger together. Oblivious to his actions and her notice of them, he quickly turned back to continue his conversation with her.

Darcy discovered that Mrs. Gardiner had grown up in Lambton and enjoyed sharing their favourite places of the area. They talked of people they knew, and whether the other might know them. When Mrs. Gardiner mentioned the Franks Darcy nodded fervently.

"Why he is my head stableman! He is such a fine man and has such a wonderful family, indeed!"

"His wife and I grew up together. I remember when she first met Mr. Frank. He was working at Pemberley back then as simply a hired hand to work the stables."

"Obviously my father saw great potential in him, eventually moving him up to be in charge of the stables and horses, which he still is today."

"Are you aware, Mr. Darcy, that their daughter is deaf?"

"Yes, I just recently was made aware of that. Since then I have been getting information on a school in France that teaches communication using hand signs. I informed them of this and they seemed most interested in finding out more."

"Yes, she wrote me about that. She said that someone was looking into starting such a school in Derbyshire itself." She looked at Darcy and saw a somewhat embarrassed reaction; he coloured slightly and looked down, making her wonder whether it may have been Mr. Darcy himself who was putting up the money to start the school.

"So I have heard." He neither confirmed nor denied that he was the one, but she felt strongly convinced that it most likely was he.

Darcy selfishly wished to tell Mrs. Gardiner all about his involvement, knowing she would most surely relay this information to her niece. But he knew that telling her would make him appear too proud and conceited. He did not even want the people of Derbyshire to know of his total responsibility for it. His eyes drifted over to Elizabeth, and he wondered what it would ever take to get her to notice him. But he had a strong impression it would not be because of things he did or what he had. It would only be because of who he was on the inside. He wondered whether he could ever be that person.

As they talked, Darcy began to feel a little less distressed, finding the company of this couple genuinely pleasant. He was amused to watch their interaction with Mrs. Bennet. Mrs. Gardiner truly had a gift as she dealt with her sister-in-law. Whenever Mrs. Bennet began to get a trifle too agitated about something, Mrs. Gardiner calmly responded with a gentle word and look, which helped keep Mrs. Bennet's boisterousness to a minimum.

Because of the calming effect of Mrs. Gardiner, Darcy was actually able to converse civilly with Mrs. Bennet, but he preferred the company of the couple on his right. He found the Gardiners more knowledgeable on many subjects, but it also allowed him to covertly observe Elizabeth across the table.

Mrs. Gardiner watched him intently, being ever so aware of the slight shift of his eyes as he talked to her. She knew that from her niece's behaviour the previous night, and *his* behaviour at the moment, there was more between them than either would admit.

Darcy was drawn into a conversation with the Bennets about Pemberley; Mr. Bennet inquiring how long it had been in his family. Darcy obliged them with the history of his family and Pemberley, going back some two hundred years. Mrs. Bennet obliged him with overstated details about how much her two daughters enjoyed their stay there and how they returned with unending praise about the place and its occupants, causing him a little discomfiture.

Darcy felt he had spoken enough on the subject of Pemberley and turned the subject matter to Longbourn. Mrs. Bennet answered obligingly, despite her wish to continue talking about him and his home.

"Mr. Darcy, our home, I am sure, is very modest compared to your great estate, and with it entailed away from the female line, I have long hoped and prayed that each of our lovely girls would be fortunate enough to enter into a most beneficial marriage." She smiled at him and looked as if she expected a response. She then turned her gaze down to the far end of the table where her second eldest daughter was sitting.

Elizabeth watched as her mother smiled at Darcy and then glanced down the table and smiled at her. She had been carefully scrutinizing this interaction between Darcy and her parents. Elizabeth did not like the look of that smile and felt her mother was beginning to get some ideas into her head about her and Darcy. She tried to give her a warning look, hoping she would stay away from any subject of marrying her daughters off, especially to *desirable rich men*!

Darcy felt himself colour and awkwardly sought something to say. He could easily have come up with a response to secure Mrs. Bennet's favour by stating his intentions toward their daughter. *I want nothing more than to ask for the hand of your second eldest daughter, Elizabeth!* or *Mrs. Bennet, is my ten thousand sufficient enough to win your favour?* Or possibly, *How can you help me secure the favour of you second eldest daughter when even my ten thousand is as nothing to her?* "How fortunate that you have five lovely daughters, Mrs. Bennet."

"Why thank you, Sir. You are too kind! But as Longbourn is entailed, I am most distressed." Darcy drew back a little from her as she became somewhat frantic. "Every time I see that Mr. Collins, who is so very anxious to kick us out and move right in, it just makes…" Suddenly she stopped, looked at her husband, and turned back to Darcy and smiled, picking up her cup of tea and taking a sip.

Elizabeth, from the other end of the table could not believe what she just witnessed. Her eyes widened as she contemplated what happened. Did her father actually do what she thought she saw him do? If she was not mistaken, he had given her mother a nudge with his knee underneath the table to silence her! And it must have worked! But did anyone else notice? Elizabeth looked immediately at Darcy, who brought his napkin up to his face and politely dabbed the corners of his mouth. Was that a smirk she saw peeking out from behind?

The meal was almost completed when Georgiana turned back to Elizabeth, after having had a lengthy conversation with her two younger sisters. "Elizabeth, would it be possible for me to call on you tomorrow morning. I would greatly enjoy the pleasure of your company for a while. There are some things I would like to talk with you about. We could go for a walk, if that would be acceptable."

"I would so enjoy that and am already looking forward to it. I think the morning would be just fine."

Georgiana smiled. "I do need to go to the church in the afternoon and practice playing the music for the wedding before the rehearsal, but my morning is free. How does ten o'clock sound?"

"Would you prefer that I come to Netherfield?" Elizabeth's heart pounded, hoping she would say no.

"I think I would prefer to walk the grounds around Longbourn. My carriage will bring me round."

"I shall be waiting."

As the meal ended, the men were escorted by Mr. Bennet to his study. Mrs. Gardiner quickly came up to Elizabeth as the women left the dining room. She put her arm through hers and gently nudged her off to the side.

"I am so glad to have been able to have some conversation with Mr. Darcy. I do not find him proud and disagreeable at all! I was disappointed when we first walked in and saw that we had been moved and were no longer seated next to him. I noticed earlier that we were." She paused, watching Elizabeth's reaction.

Elizabeth took a deep breath and looked away. Her aunt continued, "Do you know, Lizzy, how the seating arrangements came to be changed?"

Elizabeth did not answer, colouring slightly and she was unable to look at her aunt. The look on Elizabeth's face told her aunt she had been correct in her assumption. Finally her aunt tenderly whispered, "Why did you do it, Lizzy?"

"You knew it was me?"

"It was most obvious."

"Why... I... it was an impulsive, immature act to see whether Mr. Darcy's true character would emerge by seating him between Mr. Collins and my mother. He had been so easygoing and amiable all evening. Trust me, Aunt, he has been very different tonight than what he was when he was in the neighbourhood before."

"It appears to me that he passed your little test. Would you not say so?"

"He did, yes. Most admirably. Do you think he was aware of what I did?" Elizabeth asked, knowing that inwardly she felt he did know.

"I believe he was very much aware of it."

Elizabeth turned, feeling more remorse than satisfaction for her little trickery. "He must hate me for purposely placing him between them."

"No, Elizabeth, I do not think he hates you. I do not think he believes that is the reason you moved him."

"You do not? What other reason is there?"

"I believe he thinks you moved him as far away from you as possible because you wanted nothing to do with him."

With that, she turned away and Elizabeth was left with the stunning realization that, once again, she had caused another misunderstanding between the two of them. How many times had one or the other misconstrued the other's words or actions? And usually it was her! She wanted to argue her aunt's observation, but she could not. He had been so congenial the whole course of the evening, even after being seated where he was, and he believed the whole time that he had been moved because she did not want him near her!

She turned in great anger with herself to find Georgiana walking toward her. "Elizabeth, I see you have a piano in here. Would you do me the honour of playing and singing? You did promise me that you would when we parted last."

"Yes, I did, indeed." Her voice faltered as she spoke and she wondered how she would be able to play, let alone sing, when she felt so terribly distressed. Her heart pounded ferociously and she knew her fingers would not easily obey, let alone her voice. "Could you give me a few minutes? I should like a cup of tea, first."

Georgiana agreed and Elizabeth went back into the dining room to make herself a cup of her special brew of tea. She kept herself secluded in the dining room while she drank, savouring its calming effect. She looked back at the table and saw, in her mind, Mr. Darcy, as she had watched him furtively while she talked with Georgiana through the course of the meal. *So friendly, so amiable!* She took another sip of tea as she felt herself grow dizzy with confusion. She had to calm down!

When she finally returned, Georgiana was looking through the music and picked out a few songs that she liked, asking if Elizabeth could play any of them.

Elizabeth looked through them and found one that was a rather slow tune that was easy enough to sing. She hoped that the conversation in the room would continue, as she disliked the idea of performing before others. She would rather just provide some background music.

She placed the music upon the piano and began playing and singing. It was soothing to her and she closed her eyes as she continued, knowing most of the song by memory. Suddenly she felt her heart stir, as she felt the presence of someone behind her. She hoped it was not who she thought it might be, but was not going to look. The easy flow of her fingers across the keys became more of an effort; she struggled to keep her composure in singing, as well as playing.

She recalled Georgiana's account to her of how Darcy would often come up behind her whilst she was playing and he would quietly listen. Elizabeth had no idea why she thought he was there; she just did.

She had two more pages to play through before she was finished, and prayed she would make it through. She looked up at Georgiana, who returned an encouraging smile. She noticed her gaze move beyond her and another smile directed behind her; this time more serene. At the end of the song, the party of women politely responded with light applause. Elizabeth steeled herself, took a breath and turned around. There was no one there.

Her hands shook so greatly that she berated herself for imagining things. She rose and walked over to Georgiana, asking her if she would oblige her now and play. Elizabeth knew that Georgiana's ability greatly exceeded hers and knew she would be enjoyed by all in the room.

Georgiana reluctantly agreed to play only, not sing, and Elizabeth sat down to join the others. As Georgiana played, Caroline continually praised Miss Darcy's ability and how accomplished she was. Elizabeth was convinced that the woman was more enthralled with the sound of her voice than Georgiana's playing.

In the course of Georgiana's song, the men returned and seated themselves around the room. Darcy settled in a sofa off to the side of his sister, obviously enjoying her playing.

Caroline suddenly spoke up and said to Elizabeth, "Are not the militia removed from Meryton? They must be a great loss to your family."

At this, Lydia broke in. "Oh, it has been so unbearable since they left! And to think I had received a personal invitation from the Forsters to join them all in Brighton. But because of the wedding, I was not able to. How we miss all those fine, handsome officers! Mr. Wickham was by far the most handsome and charming!"

When Georgiana heard Lydia's remark, it caused her great distress and she suddenly lost her place in the song. She feebly tried to improvise, and Elizabeth rushed over to her immediately, putting her hand on her shoulder, and quickly pointing to the place on the page where she had last played. "I am sorry," Elizabeth said to her. "Let me help you by turning the pages."

Darcy's colour heightened at the mention of Wickham's name and he had immediately begun to rise from the sofa to come to Georgiana's rescue, but was halted in his actions by Elizabeth's quick response to his sister's distress. As Georgiana regained her composure, she looked up at Elizabeth, and then to her brother. At that moment she came to the startling realization that Elizabeth knew of the situation between herself and Wickham. She must have known all along! Everything inside her reeled of shame at Elizabeth knowing.

Elizabeth was aware of Georgiana's sudden comprehension of this, and the inner struggle she faced. She murmured to her that it was all right, she was doing fine. Elizabeth kept her one hand on the young lady's shoulder, patting it, and the other on the music, readying to turn its page. Her actions comforted Georgiana, at least outwardly, as she continued to play.

When Elizabeth was confident that Georgiana was composed, she dared herself to look up at Darcy. The look on his face made her feel as though he was wrapping his arms around her. She glanced back down at Georgiana, feeling that now *she* was the one who needed composing. Then she looked back up.

There may have been a hint of gratitude in his expression, but there was something else there that touched Elizabeth to her core. A hint of a smile played at the corners of his mouth, but seemed to be more recognizable in his eyes. With great feeling exuding to the surface from within, she returned a smile.

When Georgiana finished playing, everyone expressed their appreciation of her wonderful talent and applauded heartily. Elizabeth reached down and gave the girl an encouraging hug. "You played beautifully, Georgiana." Neither of them alluded to what happened beforehand at the mention of Wickham's name.

When the music was over, it seemed to signal an end of the evening, as everyone began to stand up and take leave. Elizabeth wished with all her heart to walk over to Mr. Darcy and apologize for her very immature actions earlier this evening, but he was suddenly surrounded by Caroline and Louisa. She decided it would have to wait. All she could do tonight was send him off with a polite farewell.

As everyone walked outside to their waiting carriages, Elizabeth came up to Georgiana, who was now standing aside her brother, and she gave her a hug. "I shall look forward to seeing you tomorrow morning, Georgiana." She looked up at Darcy and with her arm still resting on the girl's shoulder teasingly added, "…if *you* will permit me some time by myself with her, Sir. I promise I will take good care of her."

He looked upon his sister with a feeling of envy sweeping over him. If only he could be on the receiving end of a hug from Elizabeth. In a soft, husky voice he returned, "I do not doubt that you would."

Silence hung heavy in the air, as the two seemed locked in the other's gaze. Darcy, reeling from her scent due to her close proximity and the captivating look of her eyes, braced himself against the onslaught of feelings that urged him to take that one small step closer to bridge the distance between them. He was grateful for the throng of people around, particularly his sister, for that helped keep himself in check. How he wished they were alone, yet in reality he knew that if it were just the two of them right here this evening together, such actions would most likely be rebuffed by her.

Elizabeth struggled with what to say to him; wanting to throw caution to the wind and to let him know how sorry she was for causing any misunderstanding this evening. Yet it was difficult for her to come up with words that came from her heart. She could easily banter with him, tease him, and make light conversation with him. But for some reason, to speak from her heart caused her much uneasiness.

"Good night, then." Again she returned a nervous smile to him, hoping that the stirrings she felt deep within were not apparent on her face. He rewarded her with one back, however slight, and it reflected much of the inner turmoil he was striving so hard to conceal.

Darcy and Georgiana, joined by Bingley, turned to climb up into the carriage. Caroline and her sister and Mr. Hurst rode in a second one. As their carriage began to pull away, Darcy leaned forward to the window and looked out, hoping to catch one last glimpse of Elizabeth. She stood back with Jane, the two of them watching until that one particular carriage was out of sight.

As soon as they were off, Bingley cried, "I do not understand what happened in there Darcy! You were supposed to sit beside me at dinner and across from Miss Elizabeth."

Darcy looked up at him and in a very matter-of-fact voice stated, "She switched the place cards."

"What?" asked Bingley and Georgiana together.

"You heard what I said. Miss Elizabeth switched the place cards and moved me to the far end of the table."

"I do not believe it! Why would she do something like that?" Bingley asked incredulously.

"Brother, are you quite certain?"

"Yes. It was very apparent that she did not wish to sit through the whole course of the meal with me seated across from her. She put me as far away as possible from her."

Georgiana looked down, feeling very distressed by this. Bingley was still unbelieving. "Darcy, with all the positive accounts I have been passing on to Jane concerning you, and how good-natured you were tonight, I find it hard to believe she still feels the same way! Might you not be mistaken?"

"I walked through the dining room myself and saw my place card next to you and across from hers. A short while later I saw her coming out of the dining room, and within just a few minutes we went in to eat. The place cards had already been changed. When she saw me set out directly for the chair I was originally to sit in, I could see in her face her alarm when she realized I knew my place had been moved."

At that moment he reached into his pocket. He pulled out Elizabeth's handkerchief and gave it to Georgiana. "Georgiana, if you would be so kind as to return this to Miss Elizabeth in the morning. I do not think I shall be requiring it any longer."

Georgiana slowly took it from her brother's hand. "William, this does not mean that you are giving up, does it?" she asked as her heart began to sink.

"What is that?" broke in Bingley. He could not see very well because of the darkness of the carriage. But as the carriage turned, suddenly the light from the moon on the horizon lit up the cab. He then was able to see the handkerchief with the initials *EB* and flowers embroidered in the corner. "It looks like a handkerchief with Miss Elizabeth's initials on it!

"You are very observant, friend. That is exactly what it is."

"And why do *you* have it?"

"It is a rather long, complicated story." He looked to his sister. "Now as for your question, Georgiana. I shall not need to carry this handkerchief any longer, because if she never returns my favour, having it in my possession shall serve only to torment me."

He turned to look out the window and saw that it was an almost full moon on the eastern horizon. He was immediately struck by its size and beauty and involuntarily wondered whether Elizabeth had noticed it. He turned back to the two and continued, "But if she does return my favour, I will no longer need the handkerchief, as having her will be much more preferable."

He reached out again and touched the handkerchief in his sister's hand. "Georgiana, you ask am I giving up? No, I am not. I intend to remain here as long as need be. I am going to try my hardest, do everything in my power, to win Miss Elizabeth Bennet's affections!"

Chapter 17

Elizabeth awoke early. The sun was slowly emerging as a golden orb up from the distant horizon. She could tell from the feel of the air that it had not cooled down much the night before, and today would probably be exceptionally warm. She threw off the light coverlet that had been atop her and stretched. Walking over to the window, she looked out to a virtual rainbow of reds, oranges and yellow, colliding with the new morning blue of the sky.

Elizabeth stood poised for a few moments and watched, enjoying the changing display as the sun progressed upward; clouds lazily taking on different shapes, and colours reaching their peak before slowly fading away. She wondered whether anyone else was up and debated whether to venture down and make herself some tea. She did not wish to waken anyone, but she knew that she would not be able to go back to sleep.

She painstakingly opened the door so no one would hear, and tiptoed down the hall and to the stairs. From the top she could see her father's study, and though the door was closed, she could see a faint light coming from beneath. She knew him to always rise early, and smiled that he had probably awakened while it was still dark.

She came down and found that some water was already heated and poured herself some tea. Wrapping her hands around the cup, she breathed in the brewing aroma. She carefully carried it with her as she walked to the study and knocked.

"Come in," came the gentle reply.

When Elizabeth walked in, her father was reading. He looked up from his book. "Good morning, Lizzy. I strongly suspected it was you. No one else would be awake this early. Come, sit down." He closed the book, giving her the assurance that he was willing to give her his undivided attention.

Elizabeth sat down with her tea in one of his deep leather chairs. How she used to love to come in here as a child and watch her father read or work. The smells that she remembered from this room still lingered. There was something comforting about being with her father in this room. They did not need to talk; they just enjoyed each other's presence.

It was her father that broke through her reverie. "Your mother and I were quite pleasantly surprised last night by Mr. Darcy. I wonder if the accident that left him so near death two months ago could have wrought this change in him. He certainly seemed a different man last night. I cannot believe I am saying this, but I thoroughly enjoyed his company."

So, it seems, did everyone else! "I am afraid that I did not have the opportunity to visit with him to any great extent last night, so I really could not say."

"What about during your stay at Pemberley?"

"My association with him there was very minimal. Once he awakened, Jane and I did not remain much longer. He and I only had two short conversations there." *And only one of them was civil!*

"That is a shame. You really ought to get to know him, Lizzy."

Elizabeth looked down, staring into her cup of tea. *If only he knew how much I tried!*

~~*

Georgiana arrived promptly at ten o'clock. She was let in and greeted Mr. and Mrs. Bennet and Elizabeth's younger sisters. Then she and Elizabeth set out for a walk around Longbourn.

Almost as soon as they were outside, Georgiana looked around to ensure no one else was around. She took Elizabeth's arm and held it tightly, as if needing her support and strength.

She looked up at Elizabeth and then looked away. Elizabeth waited, knowing that the young girl was struggling with what she was about to say to her. Elizabeth waited patiently for her to either formulate the right words, or to summon enough nerve to begin.

"Elizabeth…" Georgiana began, but paused, taking in a deep breath, and looked away. "You knew, did you not?"

"Knew?"

"About Wickham and me."

Elizabeth had an idea this was what Georgiana was struggling with, but still she was pierced with pain as she heard the grief in the young lady's voice. As gently and compassionately as she could, Elizabeth tenderly answered, "Yes, I did."

Georgiana grimaced and colour spread across her face. "My brother told you?"

Elizabeth murmured an affirmative.

"How long have you known? When did he tell you?"

Now it was Elizabeth's turn to take a deep breath. "It was only after I refused his proposal at Rosings. In truth, he did not tell me, but wrote me of it in a letter." Elizabeth halted her steps and turned to her. "Georgiana, as you know, Wickham was here with the militia. He seemed to be so charming, fooling everyone, including myself. He led me to believe that your brother had done him great wrong. He told us that your brother refused to provide for him as your father had promised him."

Georgiana was now looking up at Elizabeth. "He told you that?"

"He charmed us all with his attempt to make himself look good and your brother look the villain." Elizabeth took her hand and smiled. "I fell for his deceitful charm just as you did, Georgiana. When I told you that one of the reasons I did not accept your brother's offer of marriage was due to a misunderstanding, it was based on what Wickham had told me. I believed your brother was a most unfeeling, arrogant, cruel man. He later wrote me a letter to set the record straight regarding Wickham and himself. I believe he only told me to reinforce the fact that Wickham was truly a scoundrel down to the core."

"Did you really believe the lies he told you?"

"Unfortunately I did. So do not be so dreadfully hard on yourself, Georgiana. I made a very similar mistake as you."

"Yes, but I almost threw away my reputation!"

"No, *he* almost took it away!" Elizabeth said angrily. "But we can be grateful that your brother found out in time to prevent that."

"I have often thought that the good Lord must have been watching over me, for him to have shown up so unexpectedly and yet at such a crucial time. But still, ever since then, I have felt so ashamed, and I believe my brother still considers me very immature and is overly protective of me."

"Why do you say that?"

Georgiana stopped and turned toward her. "I think he struggles with trusting me… trusting my judgment. I am sixteen years old and he seems to avoid discussing with me my presentation at court for my first season of coming out."

"Hmm. So you believe he still considers you too young?"

Georgiana nodded. "Yet he claims otherwise. Even the other day on the way to Hertfordshire he commented on how grown up I am. But he does not seem to recognize that I am a woman, no longer a girl when it comes to…"

Elizabeth waited for her to finish, but when she could not, she helped her along. "When it comes to men?"

"Yes," she whispered.

Elizabeth could read in Georgiana's face that she had so much she wanted to impart to her, but knew not how to begin. "Is there something, or possibly *someone* in particular, that has prompted these feelings?"

"Oh, I do not know." Georgiana took in a frustrated breath. "I think it is more that I have so little contact with gentlemen my age or a little older, that when I am around one, I do not know what to say or how to behave. I feel so confused."

"Is there a certain one you are speaking of?"

"No, because it could never be."

"Who is he?" asked Elizabeth discerningly.

"He is an under gardener that I have known since my childhood. His father is the head gardener and when we were children he would often come to Pemberley while his father worked and we played together."

She looked at Elizabeth waiting for a response. "I had not seen him for quite some time. I saw him again just after you left Pemberley. Elizabeth, I did not know what to say to him; he was so tall and handsome! But I became so nervous I could not even look him in the eye."

"So what did you do?"

"We walked around the house. He described some of the work he had been doing on the grounds and then he told me what he remembered of my mother. I was too much afraid to say much of anything, so I just listened."

Elizabeth knew that the next words she said to this girl would be very crucial. It was one thing for Darcy to have asked a woman of no fortune to be his wife, but it would be altogether a different story for Miss Darcy to entertain any thoughts about someone who merely worked at Pemberley as an under gardener.

"Georgiana, there are different things that can cause a man and woman to be attracted to each other. The most obvious -- usually the first -- is finding the other person attractive. But there is also character, personality, and then sometimes some little connection that draws two people together. For example, sharing a memory, like the memory of your mother. But in the midst of that, it is very essential that you remember who you are."

"And who the other person is."

"Yes."

"Elizabeth, I know I have not fallen in love; it is simply that when he talked to me and looked at me, I felt things I had never felt before. Even with Mr. Wickham."

Elizabeth looked at her, somewhat surprised.

She continued, "I think I was too young to really understand what was going on with Mr. Wickham. I had known him all my life, grown up with him as a child. All of a sudden he was treating me like a lady; like I was all grown up, and no one had ever done that before. I liked that. He was offering himself to me in marriage, and I knew that since I would be getting married one day anyway, I reasoned it might be so much easier to marry someone I already knew."

"And you had no idea that he had ulterior motives in wanting you to elope with him."

"If you mean that he intended to get revenge on my brother through me and my fortune, no. I was very humiliated when William found out about us, and then Mr. Wickham confessed that he did not truly love me. I cannot know for certain that he ever intended to marry me, either."

"So now you feel as though your brother is delaying bringing you out into society, fearing you are still too young and immature."

"I am not certain. I do not feel as though I can talk to him about it. And I cannot talk with Miss Annesley about all of these things. I am not sure she would understand how I feel."

"What *are* your feelings, Georgiana?"

"I feel very flattered that a young man seems to enjoy my company. I find myself wanting to take walks around the grounds in hope that I will encounter him, but at the same time, very fearful of it. When I do see him I find it difficult to even begin a civil conversation with him."

"Georgiana, this young man will be only the first of many admirers you will likely have. There will be several more. But you can learn from it. You will learn what you like and what you do not like in a young gentleman. Just be careful. You recognize this relationship cannot go anywhere. That shows much wisdom. Be willing to learn from it, appreciate it, but do not try to pursue it."

"It would be easier if I were able to go out into the company of young men my age and of equal connections if I had more opportunity. Elizabeth, could I ask you to do something?"

"What would you have me do?"

"Talk to my brother."

Elizabeth suddenly felt her chest compress, as she thought of how she would even begin to talk to Darcy about this. "Georgiana, I do not think that I am the one…"

"Oh, yes I am sure you could make him understand."

Elizabeth's heart pounded inside her, just contemplating the idea. How would she ever handle talking to him on this subject?

"Would you, please? I believe that he would trust your opinion and listen to you."

"Oh, no Georgiana. You are not aware of the history between your brother and me. We continually misunderstand one another." She laughed as she continued, "We do a much better job of confusing the issues than making them clear."

"But please tell me you will try. You are the only one who knows and understands the whole situation."

"Georgiana, I cannot promise anything, but I shall see what I can do."

"Good. Good," she responded with much pleasure.

The two walked along in silence for awhile, Elizabeth feeling much anxiety over the previous conversation and Georgiana feeling very elated.

They had almost reached Oakham Mount, when the sight of Darcy approaching on horseback interrupted Elizabeth's steps. As Georgiana was holding Elizabeth's arm, she was very much aware of a slight tension in it as he appeared. Darcy saw the two ladies, and in a liquid motion alit from his horse.

He took the reins in one hand, and waited for them to reach him. He removed his hat and bowed. "Good morning. Have you two been enjoying your walk?"

"Yes we have, William."

Georgiana rushed up to him, and as he turned to walk in their direction, she slipped her hand in his arm. Elizabeth caught up more slowly, giving herself time to gather her composure and quiet her nerves. Georgiana looked behind her and called out, "Elizabeth, are you coming?"

"Ah, yes." There was nothing for her to do now but quicken her steps and catch up with them.

"What were you two ladies talking about?" he asked with a sly smile at his sister.

"Oh," Georgiana giggled. "Just things ladies talk about together. You would not be interested."

"Oh, you think not?" He looked over at Elizabeth, trying to read her expression. He trusted that Georgiana would not have said anything to Elizabeth that would betray his confidence regarding his feelings. As he saw Elizabeth smile at Georgiana's remark, he felt sure his sister had not.

As they walked, Georgiana suddenly chided herself for taking her brother's arm so quickly. He was leading the horse with one hand, and she had monopolized his other. How could she arrange for Elizabeth to take it?

As they reached the summit of Oakham Mount, Darcy and Georgiana expressed great admiration of the view it afforded them of the surrounding countryside. It was actually a flat mount that when walked completely around, provided a beautiful view of Hertfordshire below. The houses looked like little miniatures, and an occasional person could be seen as a small moving speck.

Georgiana found a rock to sit upon that gave her a splendid view and allowed her to rest. Darcy and Elizabeth had drifted apart and were taking in the view separately. Darcy finally returned and asked Georgiana how she was doing.

"I am quite tired, William. Do you suppose I could sit upon the horse on the return? I fear my legs are a bit unsteady from the walk up here."

"If you are careful, I am sure ol' Danbury here will be gentle enough."

When Elizabeth returned, Darcy commented, "It is a wonderful prospect from up here, Miss Bennet. Do you walk up here often?"

"I do. Coming up here allows me to think. If something is on my mind, the walk and solitude clear my thoughts and help me discern things more clearly. I had not intended for us to walk all the way up here; I think I just lost all track of time while we were talking and the next thing I knew, here we were!"

She looked over at the young girl. "Georgiana, you are not too tired, are you?"

"I am a bit weary. I have talked with William about riding on the way down."

"I am so sorry, Georgiana. It was very foolish of me to bring you all the way up here."

"No, I am glad to have seen the view. I shall be fine on the horse."

"Better you than me," laughed Elizabeth.

Darcy looked at her amused. "You do not like horses, Miss Bennet?"

"Oh, I think they are fine for ploughing fields and pulling carriages and heavy loads. Maybe for an occasional ride, but not for me."

"Perhaps it is because you are afraid of them. They are large animals, but if they are trained well, they can be most gentle. Come see. Danbury will not hurt you." He urged her toward the huge beast by gently nudging her with his hand pressing against the small of her back. The light touch of his fingers prompted Elizabeth to falter, as feelings suddenly surged through her.

"Here, stroke his nose, like this." Darcy lifted her hand and brought it down along the long length of the horse's head. "You see? He is quite friendly."

"Thank you, Mr. Darcy for completely ridding me of my fear of horses," laughed Elizabeth. "But, alas, I have no fear of them. I actually have a healthy respect for them. I merely prefer to walk, if I have the chance."

Darcy felt a little foolish for assuming she had a fear of horses, but he had to admit to himself that he enjoyed the small contact with her that his incorrect assumption had allowed him.

As they prepared to walk down from the mount, Darcy lifted his sister up onto Danbury. She settled comfortably on the horse, sitting side-saddle and allowing her brother to lead the horse with the rein.

As they began walking, Elizabeth took a few quick steps to put herself in front of the others. Georgiana nudged her brother and indicated with gestures for him to offer her his arm. He furrowed his brow at her, and she defiantly looked at him, urging him forward. Darcy looked at Elizabeth, who was now quite a few steps ahead of them. "Miss Bennet, may I offer you my arm as we descend?"

Elizabeth felt her heart flutter and wondered why something as commonplace as a polite gesture suddenly evoked such overwhelming feelings? His offer did little to help her put to rest those thoughts and questions that assaulted her. She paused, waiting for them to reach her, and very warily slipped her hand inside his arm, barely letting her fingers touch him.

Darcy was aware that she barely touched his arm. He knew she probably did not need his assistance, having walked this way alone an endless number of times, and was, in effect, letting him know she could have walked down unattended. How he wished he could have reached over with his other hand and joined his fingers with hers. He glanced down at her, admiring her dark hair. The sunlight highlighted each wayward curl as it bounced around with each step that she took.

They walked in silence, unaware that the young girl sitting atop the horse was carefully scrutinizing their behaviour.

Georgiana, being in an even better position to watch what was going on, found their conduct very strange indeed. She had very little experience in these matters, but felt that her brother was certainly not going about the right way of making any progress with Elizabeth.

The walk back was spent with talk of inconsequential subjects that had little bearing on any of them, but merely helped to pass the time.

When they arrived back at Longbourn, Darcy carefully helped Georgiana down off the horse. She reached up and gave him a hug, and then completely caught Elizabeth off guard with a request. "William, Elizabeth has something she wishes to speak with you about. I must leave to go to the church so I can practice my music for the wedding. But do you have some time to talk to her now?"

Elizabeth's eyes widened and her heart stopped as she realized what Georgiana was asking her to do. "Georgiana," she said nervously, "I am certain your brother must be busy. I do not want to take up any more of his time."

"On the contrary, I have no plans at the moment." He turned to Georgiana, "I shall see you back at Netherfield later." He leaned over and kissed her on the forehead. As he pulled away, he looked at her with brotherly suspicion.

"Goodbye, Elizabeth." Georgiana raised her eyebrows at her, so as to encourage her to talk with her brother about what they had discussed earlier.

"Goodbye, Georgiana."

The two stood for the longest time watching as the carriage rolled away, unable, unwilling to move. From the inside of the carriage, Georgiana looked back and thought to herself, *What will it take to bring these two together?* She reached into the pocket of her dress and pulled out the handkerchief. No, she decided not to return it to Elizabeth; not yet. She was of the firm belief that this handkerchief was the key to their getting together and she would wait for just the right time. As the carriage turned, Georgiana caught her last glimpse of the couple still steadfast in their places. She shook her head in bewilderment.

Finally, when the carriage had disappeared out of sight, Darcy turned to

Elizabeth and asked, "So what is this about which you want to speak with me?" He had a look of apprehension on his face. Was this something that Elizabeth desired to talk with him about or something his sister put her up to? As he waited for her to begin, he brought his hands together and nervously rubbed his thumbs and fingers together. When he realized he could not keep them still, he brought them behind his back so she would not see.

Elizabeth took in a breath, wondering where to start... how to start. They began walking, Darcy leading the two away from the house and over to a wildish area off to the side of the house.

"Your sister, Georgiana, feels that you... that you have a hard time accepting the fact that she is all grown up... that she is no longer a girl, but a young lady."

Darcy looked at her surprised. "I cannot understand why she would feel that way. I just told her the other day how grown up she is."

"But have you considered that she is grown up and mature enough to come out in society, to be presented at court and begin learning how to relate to young men her age?"

"Young men?"

"Yes. Do you have some objections to this? She is, after all, sixteen years old."

"I think she has plenty of time for that, yet."

"She is developing an awareness and feelings that need to be directed in the proper channel. And I think if you do not do it soon, and get her into society to meet eligible young men of similar connections and consequence, she may find the company of just any young man desirable." Elizabeth wondered if what she was saying made any sense.

"Are you inferring that she may run off with someone again of the likes of Wickham?"

"No, no. I do not believe that at all. But, she has confided in me that she has found the company of one young man, in particular, one of the hired hands at Pemberley, very pleasant."

"Who is it?" Darcy's eyes darkened.

"I do not think that is important. What is important right now is that he is the only young man who is paying her attention. Once she comes out in society and begins meeting other young men of similar standing, it will lessen that chance that her affections will be directed in the wrong way."

He turned and looked at her. "She has told you all this?"

"Yes, that is why she wanted to talk with me today."

"She seems to confide in you. She talks easily with you."

"So it seems."

"I have often thought Georgiana needed someone she could confide in. I had hoped she would have had that in the person of Miss Annesley. She is an excellent teacher but I fear she has not turned out to be the confidant I had hoped for her."

"Yes, and without having a mother or a sister, she does not really have anyone with whom she can openly share."

"I believe she may be right about my wanting to put off bringing her into society. It is not because I feel she is still too young and immature. It is because I am afraid of what that will mean for her. There will be things she will begin to experience, feelings that I will not be able to talk with her about, questions that I will be unable to answer."

He stopped and turned to Elizabeth. "One thing I have greatly wished for Georgiana is to have someone a little older and wiser that she felt comfortable enough to confide in. She finds it difficult to confide in most people. She needs someone with whom she feels at ease openly sharing. I would even be willing to hire someone to come in and do that if I found the right person."

He stopped walking and turned toward her. Elizabeth suddenly felt great fear rising up inside her. *No! Please do not!*

"Miss Bennet…"

"Mr. Darcy!" Elizabeth interjected frantically even before her name was completely out. She could not allow Darcy to formulate the question that was upon his lips. She knew that she had no reason to expect him ever to renew his address to her, but she could not allow him think of her now simply as a hired hand, a hired confidant for his sister. For her to have gone from being asked to be his wife, the mistress of Pemberley to now being a hired hand would be most distressing to her. Not that she would be unwilling to do it, but she did not want Mr. Darcy to view her from now on only in this way.

When she had cried out his name, he paused and waited for her to continue. When she did not, "Yes, Miss Bennet?"

What could she say now to him? How could she make it known to him that she harboured no ill feelings toward him any longer? Would it do any good?

"Mr. Darcy, I have a confession I must make to you."

"A confession?" This response caught him off guard.

"Yes." She turned from him and closed her eyes. Taking in a deep breath to calm herself, she proceeded. "Last night… at the dinner… I switched your place card."

"So it *was* you!" Now that he knew for certain that it had been her, he braced himself for her explanation.

Her eyes and lips tightened, feeling ashamed for what she had done, but she knew she must go on. She knew she must own up to the truth.

Darcy stood behind her, drawing ever so closely, wanting desperately to reach out and pull her back towards himself.

She turned toward him and laughed nervously when she found him so near. She hoped to make light of her impetuous action from the night before, but it did not help her excessive uneasiness. "It was very stupid of me, Sir. But I did it… I did it because I wanted to see your true character emerge."

"Pardon me, my true character?" He chuckled slightly from puzzlement.

"I know how you feel about my family, Mr. Darcy. I know how you behaved when you were here last. But last night you seemed to be too amiable with everyone and I felt that you would not be able to keep up that charade -- if indeed it was a charade -- if you were seated between my mother and Mr. Collins. At the time, I was unaware of what happened between you and your aunt, and so I had no idea that putting you next to Mr. Collins was the worst thing I could have done."

"So you were putting me to a test. Would that be a correct assessment?"

"Yes, and I am very sorry, indeed. It was wrong of me, Sir, and I apologize."

He lifted his eyes upward, and seemed to let out a breath that had been held for quite some time. With that breath being released, a smile came to his face and his eyes lit up.

Looking back down at her, he asked, "So did I pass your test, Miss Bennet?"

"Yes, you certainly did." She looked up at him with gratefulness in her eyes. "You were very gracious to my father *and* my mother. You were even cordial to Mr. Collins, however little he deserved it!" She laughed as she saw that he was accepting this very benevolently.

"Miss Bennet, let me tell you something. I do not claim to have patience with everyone. You mother may indeed push me to my limits. She has some eccentric ideas and becomes very passionate about some things according to the whim of the moment, but at least she does not have any evil intent in her motives or actions." As he said this, his eyes darkened. "My own aunt, on the other hand, can be very mean spirited. You may have heard Collins' remarks to the effect that I behaved rudely to her. I confess I did. But I do not regret my actions. I will not apologize for them. Not when she hurt my sister so deeply."

He went on to tell her the circumstances of his aunt's visit. "I still have a difficult time in certain people's company, not just from your family, but my own, as well. And Collins, well, he is just plain stupid." He paused, allowing himself to calm down. "I have to admit, however, that I had a little help last night on how to deal with your mother."

"You did?"

"Yes; the first was my sister. Georgiana advised me to watch others to see how they respond to your mother. So I did. Instead of turning away in frustration, I observed how others responded."

"Oh, you mean how they discreetly roll their eyes, put on a fake smile, and hope that she does not carry on much longer?"

Darcy laughed at her ability to make light of the situation. "Actually, it was observing Mrs. Gardiner that helped me. She had a way of responding to your mother calmly and very deliberately that really helped keep your mother more composed. Your aunt is quite a lady."

"Yes. I have often considered her as much my mother as my own mother is."

"There was one other response to your mother I observed, however, that I felt would be most prudent if I did *not* imitate myself."

"What was that?"

"It seems as though your father nudged her under the table with his knee when she became a little upset! It seemed to do the trick." He looked at her and smiled at her embarrassment. "But I did not feel as though I should behave in likewise manner."

"That is very wise of you, Sir." Elizabeth smiled at him and they both jointly broke into a hearty laugh. As they turned to walk back toward the house, they both independently realized what a turning point this moment had been between them. They just spent a good amount of time together and had carried on a civil, enjoyable conversation. Neither had gotten upset or misconstrued what the other said.

Darcy felt that much progress had been made. He was just not certain when the right time would be to approach her again with his feelings. Just the thought of it caused him great anxiety. He had a lot of stupid mistakes for which he had to make up. He knew she would most likely need time.

He was aware that he would see her later today as they went to the church to get things ready for the wedding. Later, there was also a small dinner party at Netherfield, although he most likely would not have the opportunity to see her alone and speak his heart. Tomorrow would be Jane and Bingley's wedding, so he would not do anything then, as that was to be their special day. That left Sunday; but would he be able to wait that long?

Chapter 18

Elizabeth watched as Darcy walked over and mounted his horse. When he was settled atop, he looked back at her, smiled, and brought his horse to a gallop, riding off. Her heart had not stopped pounding since she had first seen him atop the mount, and now she could only hope that for the next few hours she could regain what little composure she had left before she saw him once again.

As she entered the house, she hoped she could sneak in without anyone noticing. She was not in any mood to answer questions or to counter any suspicions that might have been aroused. She did not see anyone when she came in until she walked past the drawing room and found her aunt sitting there.

"Good morning, Lizzy. Or should I say afternoon? I imagine it is almost noon."

"Good morning Aunt. Where is everyone?"

"Jane left for Netherfield and will most likely go to the church from there. Your mother took both Kitty and Lydia into town to make some last minute purchases. I believe Mary is upstairs reading. And how has your morning been? You look as though you may have gotten a little too much sun."

Elizabeth did not know whether the colouring her aunt noticed was due to the sun or her heightened feelings resulting from her encounter with Mr. Darcy. "Georgiana and I had a very nice walk up to Oakham Mount, and a very good talk, as well."

"I am glad. She certainly seems to enjoy your company." Mrs. Gardiner continued to watch her niece, as if waiting for her to continue.

Lizzy had come to recognize that all-knowing look that her aunt gave her when she knew there was something left unsaid. "I imagine you saw me with Mr. Darcy."

"I did see you when the three of you returned from the walk, and then just now as he left."

"Georgiana asked me to speak with him about her wish that he begin to look upon her as a young lady, no longer as a girl."

"She asked *you* to speak with him about that?"

"Yes, partly because I am aware of some things of which most people are not aware." Elizabeth gave her aunt a smile. "And you will be happy to hear that I did apologize to him for switching his place card and I cleared up the reason for doing it."

"And how did he respond?"

"He seemed to accept it most graciously."

Her aunt nodded, again wearing that all knowing look on her face. "Well, Elizabeth, is there anything else we need to do before the wedding tomorrow?" she asked, abruptly changing the subject.

"I believe it is all taken care of. Everything is in good hands for the wedding breakfast here, so there is little for us to do now."

Elizabeth decided she would go upstairs and freshen up, after her long walk. "If you will excuse me, I shall be up in my room."

She found great solace in her room, sitting at her dressing table, and looking at her reflection in the mirror. She could see that her face was flushed. She felt it was a combination of being out in the sun and her emotions. *What had happened out there?* Could she, in her wildest imagination believe that he still cared? Or was his attention to her based strictly on his love for his sister and desire for her to have companionship?

She looked at herself in the mirror, taking a finger and winding it around a curl. Why did it seem she always had more questions than answers when she came away from him? She sighed as she contemplated what this could possibly mean. Did she dare hope…?

Her mother and sisters returned a bit later, and by mid afternoon the house was in a frenzy as everyone tried to get ready to go to the church and then to Netherfield. Elizabeth could only imagine what tomorrow would be like. But she had too much excitement for her sister to let it plague her.

The Bennets and the Gardiners, who had also been kindly invited to the dinner, boarded their waiting carriages, and they set out for the church. Elizabeth was anxious to see Jane, as she had not seen her all day. She tried to keep her mind focused on Jane's prospective joy and excitement, and keep her own thoughts and feelings pushed down.

When they arrived at the church, Jane and Bingley were already there. Georgiana was at the piano, going over her music one last time. The minister and his wife were talking with Jane about some of the things that would be happening throughout the course of the ceremony. When he had finished, Jane turned and saw her family, and she ran up to Lizzy and hugged her. "Oh, Lizzy, I am sorry I missed you this morning. I understand that you had a nice walk with Miss Darcy."

"Yes, we had a very nice visit."

"Is everyone here that needs to be?" asked Mrs. Burrton, the minister's wife.

"Mr. Darcy is not here yet," spoke up Bingley. "But he shall be soon."

"Well, let us first discuss the seating arrangements."

Mrs. Burrton went up to Mrs. Bennet and Jane and talked with them about where family should be seated. Elizabeth stood nearby waiting, but found it to be quite stifling. It had turned out to be another very warm day, and there was very little air reaching the front of the church, even with the back doors open. While her mother and sister were busy with details, she thought she would quickly walk toward the back to get some fresh air. As she came to the wide open doors, she practically collided with Darcy who was rushing in.

She put her hands up to stop her forward motion and they came to rest upon his solid chest. She let out an "Oh!" and felt his hand reach around her arm to steady her.

"I am sorry, Miss Bennet. I was in such a hurry; I did not see you coming. Am I very late?" His hand stayed around her arm as he waited for her to answer. His lingering touch made it difficult for her to formulate an answer.

"No, the reverend is talking with Jane and my mother. I was going to get some fresh air back here. It is quite warm up front." Suddenly he realized he was still holding on to her and quickly let go, stepping back. He looked up towards the front of the church.

"I do hope it will not be as warm tomorrow. With all our formal attire, it could become quite unbearable."

Their time spent at the church preparing for the wedding went as well as could be expected, with Mrs. Bennet getting highly excited several times. She had many questions for the reverend Burrton or his wife, and Darcy watched again in admiration as Mrs. Gardiner gently calmed her nerves and helped her understand.

He did not have to worry about his response to her today, as he was standing up front beside his friend. And Miss Bennet was right. It was excessively warm there!

By the time they finished going over the different aspects of the ceremony, Elizabeth was eager to rush to the back. She had been standing up there for some time, and was feeling flushed and light-headed. As she quickly moved to the open doors of the church, Darcy was right behind her, wiping his forehead that had beaded with perspiration.

As she finally felt the slightest breeze move past her, she said, "I certainly hope that if it is this hot tomorrow we will be fortunate enough to have a little more breeze to help us out up front."

Georgiana quickly joined them and they all concurred that should tomorrow be as warm as it was today, the back doors should definitely be left open for the whole of the ceremony. The wedding would take place in late morning, but in the past few days, it had been warmer than usual even that early in the day.

Jane and Mr. Bingley joined them outside the church, and they went over the details on getting to Longbourn after the ceremony for the wedding breakfast.

It was decided that Jane and Bingley would greet the guests outside the church, ensuring that they all knew they were invited to Longbourn after the ceremony and to a ball at Netherfield later in the evening. In that way, if anyone could not attend, they would at least have been able to greet them. Darcy, Elizabeth and Georgiana would leave immediately in order to greet the guests who should arrive at Longbourn first. The remaining family would follow quickly behind.

When all these details were taken care of, Bingley announced to everyone that they should immediately proceed to Netherfield, as a meal had been prepared for them.

When they arrived, Bingley's sisters greeted them. Several of his relatives had arrived, and introductions were soon being made all around. Elizabeth walked in and saw how they had already begun to decorate for the ball. Ribbons and lace accented the rooms, and fresh flowers had been put out. Everything looked beautiful.

Elizabeth made the acquaintance of two young ladies who turned out to be Bingley's cousins from the north. One was probably a little older and the other a little younger than herself. She was pleased to find them both very amiable and jovial, very much like Bingley himself, as opposed to his sisters.

From there she aimlessly wandered into the dining room which was set up for this evening's meal. She walked over to the tables and saw that they had set place cards out for everyone. Out of curiosity, she walked around to see where she was to be seated.

"You are not planning on changing the place cards again, are you Miss Bennet?"

Elizabeth felt warmth rise up her face as she recognized Mr. Darcy's voice from behind her. She slowly turned and smiled, "No, Sir. I was merely seeking out my own place."

He walked over to the end of the table and pointed to her place. "You are to be seated here, Miss Bennet. But I must warn you, I am seated across from you, unless of course, you choose to move me. But this time I shall know immediately it was you and I might protest."

"You need not fear, Sir. I have no intention of moving you or anyone else."

"I am glad to hear that. Shall we go back, then, and join the others?" He brought his hand up to her arm and gently propelled her toward the door.

Bingley's two cousins noticed her come out with Darcy and immediately came up to her, requesting an introduction. Elizabeth was amused by their very obvious interest in this tall, dark, and handsome man. She also noticed that he responded to them in a very guarded way. He actually looked uncomfortable. A rather amusing thought came to her. *Could he be shy?*

She stood back slightly, observing his look of... what was it? Feeling trapped with no way out? Wishing he were anywhere else but here?

The girls continued speaking politely to him, smiling warmly, and batting their eyes at him. At one point he looked at Elizabeth as if seeking her help in the situation, but she was having too much fun watching it to be of any assistance.

When Bingley announced the meal was about to be served and everyone should proceed to the dining room, Darcy was grateful for this excuse to leave his two admirers. He moved quickly to Elizabeth's side and in a mockingly severe voice said, "Thank you, Madam, for your help out there."

"What would you have me to do? You seemed to be doing just fine. At least they thought so." She looked up at him and laughed.

As they made their way to the table, Georgiana, who was to be seated by her brother, joined them. She seemed to be of very good spirits, and Elizabeth wondered whether she had talked with him about their conversation. To the left of her were her sisters and the Gardiners were across from her on the other side of Darcy.

Nothing monumental happened that evening, but by the end of it, both reflected back on yet another very pleasant time, enjoying each other's company and the company of those around them. Also, by the end of the evening, Bingley's two cousins noticed the way Elizabeth and Darcy looked and spoke to each other, and so gave up on their attempts to attract his attention.

At the end of the evening, as the Bennet family was departing, a very pensive Bingley said good night to his bride-to-be. Georgiana and Darcy stood off to one side, taking in this tender moment along with the Bennets.

Without much reserve and in front of all those looking on, he leaned over and kissed her gently. "Sleep well, my love."

Because of the darkness of the night, it was not apparent how much Jane blushed. But as Elizabeth watched, she thought about how this wedding almost did not happen. She looked over at Darcy, and wondered if he was thinking the same thing. She was sure there could not be a happier couple.

~~*

The day of the wedding finally arrived! Morning broke again with the declaration that it would be very warm day. But it would not be merely another ordinary day; it was a day of celebration. Even the birds seemed to take notice as they began to announce very early that something special was in the air as they flitted from tree to tree, chirping noisily.

Elizabeth awakened early, having actually slept very soundly, but she awoke with a fiercely beating heart. She thought of the joy her sister was experiencing and was so happy for her. She thought of the joy that seemed to be just barely lingering at her grasp. Was it real or just a figment of her imagination?

Today she would not try to ascertain his feelings. She would put everything into making this the day of her sister's dreams, and not be diverted by useless wondering.

As soon as the household began to stir, things became more and more hectic. As Mrs. Bennet went from ecstatic euphoria to vehement vexations, Elizabeth was most grateful that Mr. Darcy was not there to witness this. Even the calm, reassuring words of her aunt did little to quieten her mother's nerves. She could only hope that by the time they reached the church, she would be more composed.

Her father tried as much as he could to stay out of the way. He found solace in the study for a short time, but was called upon to help wherever he could. Elizabeth did her best, along with her aunt, to shield Jane from her mother's outbursts. Even when they were outbursts of joy and anticipation, it was enough to cause each person stress.

The warmth of the day also did not help matters. As the morning broke and the sun began to rise higher in the cloudless sky, the heat seemed to imprint itself on everyone in different ways.

It was difficult to get Elizabeth's two youngest sisters moving. Elizabeth was restless. Mrs. Bennet seemed more highly agitated than normal and Jane seemed oblivious to the heat, but very much aware of the effect it was having on everyone else.

Baths were drawn, clothes were set out, and hair was done up. Elizabeth's hair was pulled up with woven ribbons and flowers throughout. Some of her curls were left to hang loose. Her dress was a mint colour that brought out her rosy complexion and brightened her eyes.

When she had finished dressing, she stood back and looked at herself. She was pleased with how she appeared, and tried to think it was only because she wished to look nice for Jane's wedding day. She guardedly wondered, however, if *he* would be pleased with her appearance as well.

As everyone gathered downstairs to leave for the wedding, Elizabeth sought out Jane and took her hand. "Jane, you look simply beautiful! Without a doubt, Charles will think that you are the most beautiful bride that could ever be!"

"Oh, Lizzy, you are just saying that." With an added thought, she said, "I am so nervous!"

"As any bride usually is. Do not worry; everything shall go very smoothly. In just a short while, you shall be Jane Bingley. Mrs. Charles Bingley! You must start getting used to that!"

"It still seems so much a dream, Lizzy."

"I know. But it is *real*!"

When everyone was ready to leave and gathered downstairs, Mr. Bennet announced the carriages were ready. Elizabeth rode with Jane and she noticed Jane turn back and take one last look at what would now be her former home.

When they arrived at the church, they were ushered to a small room that had been set up for the bride and those in her party for last minute preparations. Jane remained in the room; not wanting to take the chance that Charles would see her before the wedding. Windows were opened and water was brought in to help alleviate the heat. Elizabeth was grateful that hers and Jane's dresses had short, puffed sleeves. She felt sorry for the men who would be wearing long sleeve shirts, vests and jackets. Though it was still morning, it would be most warm for them.

The sound of people entering the church raised the level of anxiety in the room. They heard the gentle playing of music by Georgiana at the piano. The reverend's wife came and announced to the family that they were now to be seated; all but Mr. Bennet, who would escort Jane in, and Elizabeth, who would stand up with her sister.

Elizabeth walked over and took Jane's hands in hers. "Today is the day of which you have often dreamed, Jane. Charles is the man of those dreams and I could not be happier for you."

As she reached out and hugged her, Jane said, "Lizzy, I only hope and pray that the man of your dreams will soon find his way into your heart." As they pulled away, Elizabeth did not know if she was speaking in general terms, or of someone specific.

"Come, ladies. It is about time for us to walk out."

Both Jane and Elizabeth felt their hearts tumble, as they realized the time had come. They were escorted to the back door, and stood off to the side as Georgiana began to play the special music they would walk in to. As the first chords began, Elizabeth took a deep breath and stepped out into the centre aisle. The walk toward the front seemed an eternity to her and she first saw Bingley, a smile lighting up his face. She glanced over to his side and saw Darcy, dressed so elegantly, and standing somewhat askew as if to afford him a better view. She saw him shift his weight from one foot to another and she smiled as she thought to herself, *He certainly seems to dislike standing up in front of everyone!*

Darcy watched Elizabeth glide down the aisle and he could not fathom how he could ever live without this woman who had so commandeered his senses. She beamed as she came toward them. Darcy, in his preoccupied state, almost took a step toward her, as if she was coming down the aisle to him as his bride. He stopped himself just in time, and shook his head in an attempt to rein his thoughts under control. As she stepped off to the left and turned to look back at Jane, she gave a quick glance over at him. He was not watching for the bride. He was looking at the woman he passionately desired for *his* bride.

Georgiana suddenly changed the volume of her music as Jane began her processional up the aisle. Everyone stood as she progressed forward, Bingley's smile growing larger and larger as she came closer and closer. Elizabeth felt her heart swell as the joy of this day reached its culmination.

When Jane arrived at the front with her father, he leaned over and kissed her, and then sat down. The minister opened in prayer, thanking God for this fine couple that He was about to join together, and asked His blessing upon this ceremony and their future married life together.

He read in the Scriptures from 1 Corinthians 13, which talks of love. "Love is patient, love is kind…" He extolled the virtues of paying heed to this passage on what love is and is not. As the ceremony went on, the heat pressed upon those in the front of the church and the air grew stifling.

When it came time for the vows, Bingley spoke his loudly and confidently; Jane spoke hers quietly and meekly. As they finished, they looked at each other and smiled. Charles placed a ring on Jane's finger as a symbol of his commitment to her.

Finally the minister called for everyone to bow their heads to pray. His words came forth, "Heavenly Father, our God in heaven, we thank Thee this day for this couple that has been joined together in holy matrimony…"

Elizabeth bowed her head and closed her eyes, but at the sound of movement across from her, she brought her glance up to Darcy.

Darcy, knowing that everyone would have their heads bowed, felt it would be a good opportunity to pull out his handkerchief from his pocket and wipe his forehead. In the course of an instant, he pulled it across his forehead, suddenly becoming very much aware of an overwhelming scent of gardenia. As he opened his eyes to ascertain why the scent was so overpowering, he discovered to his astonishment that he had just wiped his forehead with a handkerchief that bore the initials *EB*!

Elizabeth gasped as she recognized immediately that it was *her* handkerchief he was using. The corner of it hung down from his hand and she was able to see her initials very clearly. Upon hearing her gasp, Jane and Charles opened their eyes, looking first to Elizabeth. Noticing her wide eyed astonishment looking beyond them, they both turned to see a very mortified Darcy, handkerchief in hand, not knowing what to do!

The minister continued his prayer, unaware of what was taking place in front of him. Bingley began to lightly snicker, Jane's shoulders began to shake, and Elizabeth could only look on in wonderment at the man standing across from her. Darcy, on the other hand, harbouring such a strong tendency his whole life to avoid those weaknesses that give way to ridicule, wanted merely to disappear.

He quickly pocketed the handkerchief, all the while three pairs of eyes were on him. No, there were actually four pairs! He looked over at the piano and saw Georgiana's eyes peering over the top of it. He could only imagine that she was enjoying this all too immensely and most likely was the perpetrator of it. She was the last one who had the handkerchief in her possession and was supposed to have returned it to Miss Bennet! Obviously she gave it to Durnham to slip into his pocket after dousing it with gardenia scented toilet water!

Darcy relaxed a bit, and just as the prayer was about to end, looked down, feeling a bit foolish, but suddenly could not help himself. He began to chuckle, and then all of them up front found it very difficult to keep from joining him. As the reverend concluded with his, "Amen," he looked out to four beaming faces standing in front of him.

He pronounced Charles and Jane husband and wife, giving the groom license to kiss his bride. Charles leaned over and kissed her tenderly. If it were not for the fact that he was looking forward to this part of the ceremony the most, he feared he would not have been able to control the laughter that was about to burst forth from him.

Mr. and Mrs. Charles Bingley turned to everyone. As Georgiana began playing again, they marched, laughingly, back down the aisle. Darcy and Elizabeth stepped toward the centre, watching them. He would begin escorting her down the aisle after Charles and Jane had reached the door. He put his arm out for her, and she slipped her gloved hand through, again taking his arm so very slightly.

"You have my handkerchief, Mr. Darcy," she said under her breath to him, looking out to everyone else with a smile to hide her words.

"Caught red-handed, Miss Bennet!" he replied, nervously smiling back.

"You mean red-faced! Where did you find it? I lost it at Pemberley."

"Now we are to walk, Miss Bennet." They began walking down the aisle, and he brought his other hand over and reached for her fingers, pulling them forward and out over his arm. He wrapped his large fingers around her slender ones.

"Where did you find it?" she asked, while very conscious of the strength of his arm that her fingers were moulded against.

"By my pillow the morning I awoke." His hand around hers tightened.

She darted a glance at him, and he looked back. "Keep smiling, Miss Bennet; everyone is now looking upon you." They walked past the smiling faces of the guests in the church, but Elizabeth did not see them. They approached the open doors of the back of the church and a breeze soon washed over them, but Elizabeth did not feel it. The very happy newly married couple was at the back doors beaming widely, but she was not aware of them. All she was aware of was Darcy's gently caressing hand.

When they reached the back doors, Darcy released her hand and gave Bingley a fervent hand shake and a sincere, "Congratulations!" He then turned to

Jane and kissed her on the cheek. Elizabeth quickly composed herself and congratulated the couple also. They needed to quickly get to Longbourn, so Darcy hurriedly led Elizabeth to the waiting carriage and they climbed in. How she wanted him to take her hand again!

Darcy looked over the crowd of people exiting the church and searched for Georgiana, but he could not see her. When after a few moments she still did not appear, he made the decision that they should be on their way, as people were starting to head out for Longbourn.

"I wonder where she can be?" asked Elizabeth. "She knew she was to ride over with us!"

As Darcy looked back toward the church, he astutely shook his head at his conniving sister. He had a pretty good idea she never had any intention to join them, giving them another chance to be alone. And now with this handkerchief episode, he knew he would have some explaining to do to Elizabeth.

"Winston, I think we must be off. We are to greet the guests at Longbourn as they arrive, and some are already departing. Georgiana will have to find her way with someone else." He turned back to Elizabeth and shrugged his shoulders as if to indicate he did not know where his sister was and why she had not come out.

As they set off, Elizabeth turned to him and asked, "May I please have my handkerchief back now?"

Darcy looked at her and smiled a sheepish grin. "I think not. Let me have it cleaned first." He felt a little anxious now. He knew he would be able to make up some excuse for having her handkerchief on him, but it was the scent that would be more difficult to explain.

"I can do that just as easily, Sir. If you please." She held out her open hand.

Darcy took in a deep breath. He had already made a fool of himself in front of her, and now it was about to become worse. A small voice deep within his heart called out to him, *If I cannot be a fool in front of Elizabeth, who can I be a fool in front of?*

He slowly pulled out the handkerchief and handed it to her. She looked up at him and smiled, "Thank you. Now was that so hard?" When she took it, however, she at once noticed something, and brought the handkerchief up to her face and inhaled. "Oh my!" The scent was very overpowering, and very obviously the scent of gardenia.

Her look told him of her bewilderment, but she lightly teased him. "Tell me, Mr. Darcy. Is this some new London fashion for a man to carry a lady's embroidered handkerchief, scented at that, as part of his formal attire?" She brought it up to her face again and sniffed. "How could my handkerchief still have my fragrance on it? It has been two months! And it is so strong!"

Darcy began again nervously rubbing his thumbs and fingers together. *Do I tell her everything or try to come up with something that sounds relatively reasonable?* She looked at him with big beguiling eyes and he felt himself slowly being pulled in to her charm.

"No, it is not a new London fashion."

She began to formulate a teasing retort to him, but held herself back. His countenance suddenly changed, turning rather serious and reflective. Rather than speak what was on her mind, she decided to let him continue.

He reached over and took her hand. It was a few moments before he could summon the nerve to continue. "It has been my way of holding on to you these past two months."

Elizabeth's eyes opened wider and her heart raced wildly. She carefully listened to each word he said; afraid she did not fully comprehend his meaning.

"I found it the morning I awoke, underneath my pillow. I placed it in my pocket and it has been with me ever since."

Elizabeth studied his face as he spoke. Was he possibly feeling only gratitude? Was he still thinking only of Elizabeth as a close friend for his sister? No, she believed he was speaking out of a sustaining love and admiration for her.

She could not bring any sort of sensible response to her lips. She was finally able to barely mutter, "But the scent…"

"Yes, the scent." He squeezed her hand, and he again began kneading it with his thumb. "It is indeed your gardenia scent. In those first few days after you left, I found myself drawing out your handkerchief and inhaling this fragrance that was so very much a part of you. As it began to fade, I…"

As he looked at Elizabeth return his gaze, he found himself struggling with the desire to lean over and kiss her. His gaze dropped to her lips, which were slightly parted in awe at his words.

Taking in a deep breath, he continued. "I purchased some gardenia scented toilet water to keep the scent refreshed. He brought his arm up and put it behind her, taking one of her loose curls between his fingers and began twisting it. Elizabeth responded by arching her head against his fingers, feeling warmth permeate throughout her body as his hand occasionally brushed against her neck.

Her response to him unnerved him and prompted him to slowly pull her closer. With eyes locked on each other, he began to lower his face toward Elizabeth. She shook her head suddenly and brought up her hands to stop him.

"Mr. Darcy, today is Charles and Jane's wedding day. This is *their* day and I do not want to do anything that will take attention away from them."

He straightened up and turned forward, acknowledging her words and her request. Keeping the day set apart for Charles and Jane was something he had considered himself the other night. Elizabeth's request ensured he would abide by it. He decided to take another bold step of faith. The trembling of his voice betrayed the resolve he was about to make to her. "Would you allow me, Miss Bennet… would it be asking too much for me to call on you tomorrow, then, at Longbourn after morning services?"

With heart and head whirling, she answered, "I should like that very much."

As their eyes locked together, Darcy was just about to throw away his resolve. Every fibre of his body was screaming out to him to pull her into an embrace and kiss her. He was grateful, therefore, to see that the carriage had just pulled up in front of Longbourn. The elation he felt, knowing that she had accepted his request to call tomorrow, was enough to give him such great joy that would linger with him through the day and evening.

Chapter 19

Darcy helped Elizabeth out of the carriage, and the two walked up the front steps at Longbourn. They walked closely, occasionally brushing up against the other. Whereas before they would have kept a cautious distance between them, they seemed now to relish any close contact they could procure.

They situated themselves just inside the front door, waiting to greet those who arrived. Elizabeth made introductions when needed.

When Georgiana walked in with Bingley's sisters, Darcy noticed his sister smirking. He gave her a reprimanding smile, while Elizabeth asked her, "What happened to you Georgiana? We did not feel as though we could wait for you any longer as guests were already beginning to leave."

"I am so sorry, Elizabeth." She cast a sly glance at Darcy. "I was unavoidably detained. I hope it did not cause you any concern."

"Oh no, not at all," answered Elizabeth.

As she walked by, Georgiana whispered to her brother that she would see him later at the breakfast and then allowed a playful giggle to escape.

Once all the guests had arrived and were gathered for the wedding breakfast, Georgiana sought out her brother. Elizabeth had stepped away to visit with some friends. "Well?" she asked pointedly.

"Well what?" he responded.

"How was your carriage ride?"

Darcy looked at her through narrowing eyes and shook his head. "You are a mischievous little one." His voice was in a whisper so no one would hear.

"I believe it did get her attention! What happened on the way over here? Did the two of you have a nice ride? It was just the two of you, was it not?"

"As if you did not know!" He tried to appear serious, but the crinkle at the corner of his eyes gave him away.

"Did you talk? Did you tell her how you feel?"

Before he could answer, Elizabeth turned her attention back to Darcy and Georgiana. He looked at his sister and raised one eyebrow, giving her a smiling wink. Georgiana was not sure what this was supposed to mean, but she was sure it was good. In addition to his wink, she watched the two continually and found them to be very agreeably interacting together. She was also admittedly pleased with herself that her brother appeared to be behaving quite well in this crowd of country folk!

As the breakfast proceeded, Elizabeth watched Jane and Charles as they visited with those who had come. As much as Elizabeth wished to spend the whole time with Mr. Darcy, she knew she had obligations to the guests.

She noticed that Charlotte had come in with her husband, but they had not walked past her and Mr. Darcy as they greeted the guests. Charlotte was off by herself, so Elizabeth thought it would be a good time to go up to her.

"Charlotte! I am so glad to see you! I hope you are feeling better!" She gave her a conspiratorial look.

"Yes, well, I am sorry about leaving the other night."

"Is Mr. Collins any more appeased by the situation?"

"Considering he insisted we circumvent around you so we would not be greeted by Mr. Darcy, I think not. He will most likely harbour these feelings as long as Lady Catherine does. That is all there is to it."

"I am sorry to hear that."

"And how are things with you, Lizzy?"

Unexpectedly, Elizabeth blushed. Knowing that she did so caused her to look away.

"Lizzy, is there something you would like to talk about with me?"

"All I will say now is you had better get your husband's feelings about Mr. Darcy changed, or he may soon not let you ever visit me again."

"Tell me what has happened?"

"He asked to pay me a call tomorrow."

Charlotte grabbed her friend's hands tightly and smiled. "I just knew it. I knew it ever since the ball at Netherfield. You two were meant to be together!"

"Charlotte, nothing has happened. He merely asked…"

"Lizzy," Charlotte stopped her from proceeding any further. Elizabeth turned and was suddenly face to face with Mr. Collins.

"Mr. Collins," Elizabeth muttered politely.

"Cousin Elizabeth." He briefly bowed. "I cannot tell you how beautiful you and your sister look! It gives me such great honour to be a cousin to such charming ladies." With that he bowed again and took Charlotte's hand.

They spoke briefly, and then Elizabeth excused herself to go find Jane. Apart from their greeting at the back of the church and small greeting as they came in, she really had not had any time to visit with her. She looked around the room, and finally found her and Bingley in conversation with a small group of friends.

Elizabeth came and stood outside the group, waiting for Jane to finish and notice her. As the party of well wishers finally dispersed, Jane came up to Elizabeth and hugged her. "Oh, Lizzy, there are just so many people. I am so weary of smiling that my mouth hurts, and yet every time I look at my husband, it causes me to smile even more!"

"And that is the way it should be, Jane."

The two sisters hugged, very much aware that a significant change had occurred in their lives.

Mrs. Bennet need not have worried about any of the preparations for the wedding breakfast, as everyone enjoyed the food and lively celebrations. By early afternoon, everyone had departed to ready themselves for the wedding ball that would take place at Netherfield later that evening.

Darcy had behaved admirably at the breakfast, keeping his promise to Elizabeth that he would do nothing that would take away from Jane and Charles' special day. But as he prepared to leave, he came up alongside Elizabeth, looking down intently at her. "Would you save me a dance tonight at the ball, Miss Bennet?"

Elizabeth felt her heart flutter as she answered, "I would be most pleased to."

With that promise, Darcy was able to depart Longbourn with a joyful anticipation.

Jane and Charles lingered at Longbourn until all the guests had departed. They returned to Netherfield where they visited with friends and family for the remainder of the afternoon. Elizabeth knew it was going to be a long day for her sister, but she knew that her contentment at being married to Charles would keep her spirits high. And Elizabeth's spirits could not be higher as she contemplated all that had transpired that day.

~~*

The Wedding Ball at Netherfield

The summer day had cooled slightly and the setting sun promised an exquisite splashing of colours on the horizon. As the Bennets pulled up to Netherfield, Elizabeth thought about how much she missed Jane's calming presence already. The two of them had always done everything together, and now her husband would have that role.

She shook her head, reminding herself how happy she was for Jane, and she could not wait to see her, as well as Mr. Darcy.

They stepped in to an array of flowers everywhere, an abundance of candles glowing, and soft music coming from the ballroom.

They were greeted by Charles and Jane, and when Elizabeth came up to her, Jane wrapped her arms around her and whispered in her ear, "Do you think we could sneak away upstairs a little later? I want to show you a few of the wedding gifts that were given to me, and also to talk with you about something."

Elizabeth nodded. "You know I would love to. Come and find me when you are ready."

Elizabeth and her family walked into the ballroom and Elizabeth looked about her, but did not immediately see Mr. Darcy. When she finally saw him, he was speaking with several gentlemen. His glance happened her way and he sent a smile in her direction.

Elizabeth was content to see that he was making a concerted effort to be amiable with people in the neighbourhood.

Charles and Jane finally stepped into the ballroom, signalling it was time for the dancing to begin. Charles eagerly brought his new bride out to the dance floor as others joined them.

Darcy looked at Elizabeth, and suddenly recalled the last time they had danced together at Netherfield. Actually it was the only time they had ever danced together. It had not been good. He looked at Elizabeth who was in an animated discussion with Georgiana. As he started walking toward them, he was stopped in his movement by the appearance of Mr. Collins, who had, it seemed, come from nowhere to stand at Elizabeth's side.

He turned, frustrated, not wanting a confrontation with him in front of Elizabeth. Georgiana excused herself from Elizabeth and went to her brother, noticing his dilemma. He saw her come up and asked, "Would I be so fortunate as to dance the next dance with you Georgiana?"

"Are you sure it is me with whom you wish to dance?"

"There is someone else I would like to dance with, but right now you are the only one I would like to ask." He looked back at Elizabeth and said, "If I were to walk over to her now and ask her, it might cause a scene!"

Georgiana laughed. "Dance with me this one, and if he is still talking with her at the next, I fear I will again have to resort to some trickery to remove him!"

As they fell in line to dance, Darcy confronted her, "Georgiana, that was not very nice of you to make a fool of me today!"

"But I believe it did get you and Elizabeth talking. You two seem to be getting along very nicely now, whereas before, you barely tolerated each other." She smiled up at him, waiting for his affirmation of her successful scheme.

"Georgiana, I had planned all along to talk to Miss Bennet of my feelings."

"Yes, but when? You have had so many opportunities and were not taking any! I just helped things along."

"But how did you know I would even pull out my handkerchief at the wedding?"

"I could not be sure. However, as often as you used one at the rehearsal, I thought there was a pretty good chance you would. Besides, if you did not, I would have joined you and Elizabeth in the carriage after the wedding and asked to borrow one."

"So you had it all figured out."

She merely smiled.

He finally decided he would give in and agree that what she did certainly had an influence on the way things now appeared to be between him and Elizabeth. "But, I would not make it a habit of trying this form of match making on a regular basis. It will not always work!"

Georgiana let out an enthusiastic giggle. "I have no intention of doing any more of this. It is too wearisome! It is enough to see that it resulted well with my beloved brother and a very special lady."

As the dance ended, Darcy was grateful to see that Mr. Collins had moved on. Georgiana whispered, "You best take yourself to her side quickly before someone else gets there before you!"

Darcy walked over immediately, as Georgiana watched from the side.

"Miss Bennet, would you do me the honour of dancing the next with me?"

Elizabeth suddenly experienced a recollection of that first time she had danced with him. She smiled as she answered that she would be most honoured.

"And what causes you to smile in that way, may I inquire?"

"Just a small memory, Sir."

"Would it be of our first dance?"

"It would be of our only dance together, Sir."

They stood apart from each other, waiting for the music to begin. As the first notes were played, they eagerly stepped toward each other and grasped each other's hand. They beheld each other's eyes, letting their fingers linger, as they had to let go to proceed to the next movement.

When they came back together, Darcy began a conversation. "Miss Bennet, is it not your practice to sketch your partner's character while you dance?"

Elizabeth pursed her lips at his attempt to tease her. "Mr. Darcy, I fear it would take a lifetime to sketch your character!"

As they passed each other, Elizabeth suddenly realized what she had said. She knew from the warmth of her face, that when she turned again to face him, he would most likely notice her blush. As she turned, she kept her eyes down. If she were to meet his gaze, however, she would have seen a very pleasant smile, and if she could have read his thoughts, she would have heard, *Are you willing to give me a lifetime to do just that, Elizabeth?*

As they joined their hands together again, Darcy gave her hand a gentle squeeze. "I believe, Miss Bennet, the last time you tried to sketch my character, I was not in the best frame of mind for it to be sketched. Remember I had just heard your praiseworthy opinion of Mr. Wickham and condemning opinion of myself, coupled by the announcement by Sir William Lucas that a marriage was expected by almost everyone in Hertfordshire between your sister and Bingley, when I believed she did not love him."

"And, now, hopefully, you admit your feelings on the latter to be incorrect?"

"Yes, you know I do, and hopefully you admit your feelings on the former to be incorrect."

"I do, Sir."

The smile he gave her warmed her through.

They proceeded through a few more movements in silence. "Is it not also your practice to guide me through some conversation as we dance? Perhaps just a little would suffice."

Elizabeth laughed and said, "I do believe that I have come to know you well enough to know that you are perfectly capable of carrying on your own conversation, Mr. Darcy. So what shall we find to talk about?"

"I could say that since you have taken my only handkerchief for the evening, I find myself without one."

They turned reaching out for the partners next to them, and Elizabeth had to wait to respond.

When they came back together, Elizabeth was finally able to say, "Then I might say to you that since you have a room here at Netherfield, it would not be too much trouble to fetch another one."

Again the movement in the dance parted them. Darcy was smiling as he came back around to face her. "But maybe I would then say that I have a particular fondness for that very handkerchief you took from me."

"Took from you! Mr. Darcy, you gave it back to me, and besides, it is mine." How she enjoyed teasing him but wondered how far she should go with it.

Again their hands were joined. "If that is how you feel, Miss Bennet, you may keep it."

Just before the dance was to end, they had one last turn away from each other. While Elizabeth had her back to him, she quickly pulled out her handkerchief from a small pocket in her dress. As they one last time reached forward to grasp each other's hands, Darcy noticed a small bundle in his palm. When they parted to their prospective side of the line, he looked down and discovered her handkerchief back in his hand.

The last notes of the music played, and the partners bowed and curtseyed to each other. When Darcy walked toward her to take her hand again to lead her from the floor, he dangled the handkerchief in front of her. "Are you sure you are willing to part with this?" He stood next to her and enjoyed the rosy blush of her cheeks that the dance and their conversation afforded her.

She looked up at his face, and noticing the beads of moisture that lined his brow offered, "I believe you may have more use for it than myself at the present."

Throughout the rest of the evening, Darcy and Elizabeth danced two more together. He also enjoyed taking his sister out on the dance floor and gave her the opportunity to dance with him. Elizabeth also danced with Bingley as Darcy took her sister Jane as his partner.

When Darcy was on the dance floor with his sister, and Charles was dancing with his sister, Jane came up to Elizabeth.

"Are you free to come upstairs with me now?"

Elizabeth nodded, "Yes. I am looking forward to it."

The two ladies left the ballroom and proceeded to the staircase. The Bingleys were to spend their first night at Netherfield, in a guest room suite that was upstairs and at the furthest end of the west hall. It was perfect as it had dressing rooms on either side with adjoining doors to the suite. The doors to the dressing rooms themselves were across the hall from each other. Jane brought Elizabeth up, and entered into the door on the north side of the hall.

"This is beautiful, Jane. And this is merely the dressing room?"

"Yes, our suite is through this door." She walked over to open it, and they looked into a sizeable room with a large canopied bed. As both their eyes lit on the bed, Jane blushed violently.

Elizabeth raised her eyebrows at the splendour of the room. "It is very beautiful, Jane. Will this be your suite all the time?"

"It is too far out of the way, ours will be one down the hall and just to the left." Jane said, backing out of the room and closing the door. "Because this one is so secluded, we thought it would be best... for tonight." Jane found herself struggling with every word.

"And then you leave tomorrow morning for a two week tour of the country! How splendid that will be!"

"Yes," said Jane, grateful to have the subject changed. "Anyway, I wanted to show you what Charles' cousins gave me as a wedding gift. I believe you met them last night."

"Oh, yes, I believe I did." Elizabeth said, smiling.

Jane went over to a dresser and opened a drawer. She pulled out a beautiful silk nightdress that had an accompanying matching robe. "Is this not the most beautiful gown you have ever seen, Lizzy? Feel it!"

Elizabeth laughed and said, "I do believe it is, Jane." She reached over and felt it. "Quite exquisite!"

Jane pensively looked down at the ring on her finger. "Lizzy, did Mr. Darcy say anything to you today? Particularly about why he had your handkerchief?"

Elizabeth could not hide her smile. "Yes, Jane, he did. Apparently he has been carrying it around with him since we left Pemberley. He said it was his way of holding on to me."

"I am so glad he told you! When Charles told me earlier when we were in the carriage, I just felt that you had to know. I had hoped so much he would tell you himself! I would have had a hard time keeping it from you! So what happened?"

"Jane, nothing else happened. This is yours and Charles' day; not ours. But he did ask me if I would accept a call from him tomorrow."

"And?"

"And I said I would like that very much."

"Oh, Lizzy, I am so happy for you!"

"And I am happy for you! And so are many other people out there, so I think we should be getting back downstairs!"

The two sisters walked arm in arm down the long hallway, turning at the main hall that took them to the stairs. From there they could hear the voices of the people below, and both were anxious to get down to the very special men in their lives.

When the meal was announced, Darcy brought himself up next to Elizabeth. There was no designated seating, other than a special table set up for Charles and Jane, Mr. and Mrs. Bennet, and Charles' sisters and Mr. Hurst. Georgiana found her brother and Elizabeth and was most anxious to sit nearby so she could continue to watch this couple.

Darcy pulled out a chair for Elizabeth and seated himself next to her on her left. Georgiana walked around to the other side of the table and took a chair opposite her brother.

During the meal, Darcy would on occasion inadvertently bump Elizabeth with his right arm as he ate his meal. She did not make any attempt to move from him, and often their arms would rest on the table slightly touching the other. As Darcy tried to make calm, collected conversation with her, Georgiana watched with eager interest. Something definitely had happened between them, and she could not wait to find out. It gave her great satisfaction to know that her planted handkerchief had somehow managed to bring the two together!

At the end of the meal, servers brought pieces of cake out to the guests. As Elizabeth joyously dug into her piece and brought it to her mouth, she unknowingly left a little frosting on her lower lip. Darcy looked at her, and without thinking anything of propriety, took his little finger to it and wiped it off, bringing the guilty piece of frosting to his mouth to enjoy for himself.

His action brought a colouring to Elizabeth's cheeks, and Darcy suddenly felt embarrassed. He looked around to see who may have seen. He knew Georgiana would not have missed any of it. He saw that most people were otherwise engaged in conversation, but found himself staring into an all-knowing look of Mrs. Gardiner. He smiled hesitantly, unsure of what her reaction would be to such behaviour. She gave him a polite nod and then looked away.

He was a little concerned that she may have a little talking to Elizabeth about this. He decided he had better be on his best behaviour from now on. No more slips. He pulled himself straight up, and made sure nothing was touching the lovely lady sitting next to him.

As people finished eating, many began filtering back into the ballroom. There was more dancing, and as the evening progressed, people gradually began to leave. The number of guests remaining was thinning out, and Elizabeth could see the weariness on Jane's face. It was but a half hour before midnight when Charles and Jane announced to those few close family and friends that remained that they would be departing. They bid good night to all that were left, and that set in motion the remaining guests to take leave.

The Bennets were gathering up all they had brought with them when one of the servants came up to Elizabeth. "Miss Bennet, Mrs. Bingley requests your presence up in her dressing room. She would like you to bring up a cup of your special tea. Do you know what she means?"

Elizabeth laughed. "Oh yes, if you could help me find some things in your kitchen, I would be glad to prepare some for her."

The servant escorted her into the kitchen. On the way back, she found her mother and told her she was going up to see Jane. Her aunt was standing right there, and offered that she and her husband would remain and take her back with them, allowing the Bennets to take leave.

Elizabeth carried the cup of hot tea up the stairs and down the long, dark hall, turned, and continued down the hall that led to Jane's room. She felt awkward coming up here, almost as if she were trespassing. She determined to stay only long enough to give Jane the tea. When she reached the room she lightly tapped on the door, and said, "It is me, Jane."

"Come in, Lizzy."

Elizabeth walked in with the tea, and set it down in front of her. Jane had slipped on the silk nightdress and robe, and had let down her hair. Elizabeth could not contain her admiration for the beauty of her sister. She had never seen her look so beautiful; so glowing!

Jane took the tea and sipped it. "Thank you so much for bringing this to me. I know how much it helps calm you down. I feel as though I needed something."

Elizabeth smiled and was not sure what to say to her sister.

"Lizzy, do you remember all the talks we would have late at night… wondering about things… about the mystery of the wedding night?"

Elizabeth laughed. "Oh, yes!"

"I knew so little back then. But Lizzy, I fear I know no more tonight than I did then."

Elizabeth sat down and took her hands in hers. "Jane, you *do* know, however, that you have as your husband a man who loves you very dearly. I believe by tomorrow at this time, you shall know everything you need to know!" Elizabeth cocked her head at her and gave her a reassuring smile. "Do not worry, Jane. Just trust your feelings and trust your husband."

Jane blushed at her words.

"Now, I must leave. I believe you have a husband in there who will be most overtaken by how beautiful you are. And he is most likely very anxious to see you." She stood up and leaned over and kissed her on top of her head. "Good night, Mrs. Charles Bingley."

"Lizzy, we will be coming by tomorrow morning before we depart for our wedding journey. I shall see you then."

"Yes, Jane, I am looking forward to it."

Elizabeth slowly and quietly opened the door, and began backing out of the room. She did not want to make any noise, alerting Charles to the fact that she had been in there. As she was closing the door behind her, she heard a noise across the hall, and a familiar voice say, "Go to it then, man!"

Elizabeth's eyes widened it horror, as she realized it was Darcy. She turned to see if she could sneak back in the room. Just as he turned, he drew back startled when he saw her there, too.

"Miss Bennet!"

"Mr. Darcy."

Did she hear that blasted remark I made as I came through the door? He felt terribly ashamed of his last remark, the crudeness of it, and awkwardly came up to Elizabeth. *What do I say now?* "You were in with your sister?" *That was stupid, of course she was!*

Elizabeth felt the inopportunity of the moment, and fumbled for something to say. "I just brought... um... Jane some tea."

"Bingley asked me to bring him... something, as well." He looked up at the ceiling, wishing he could disappear.

"How is Mrs. Bingley doing?" *Oh great, another blunder!*

How do I answer that? That she is very nervous, but I fear not as nervous as I feel right now! "Fine."

The two walked down the rest of the hall, this time awkwardness prompting the silence and distance that separated the two.

As they came to the far corner of the hall and turned to head for the stairs, Darcy happened to look out the window that faced the east and saw a huge full moon, just rising in the sky. Being just on the horizon it appeared unusually large and was a light shade of orange. Its appearance was so stunning and so unexpected that he said, "Look at that!" and, taking Elizabeth's arm brought her over to the window.

As they came up to the window for a close look, Darcy stood behind her. Elizabeth was awestruck by the beauty of it. "It is beautiful!" she exclaimed.

Darcy, looked down at the moonlight playing off her curls, and echoed her, "Yes, beautiful."

Elizabeth's heart began pounding as she realized how close he was standing behind her. He brought his hands up to her shoulders and lightly rested them there; causing her to feel somewhat wobbly, yet at the same time their presence steadied her. She could hear the ticking of the large grandfather clock that was just down the hall from where they were standing, and felt her heart was beating just as loudly.

They stood watching in silence, as the moon slowly lifted in the sky. An occasional thin, wispy cloud passed over it, picking up a light tint of the now fading orange glow. As they watched it slowly rise, it began to lose its colour and apparent size, but they stood transfixed.

The quiet that permeated the hall was suddenly broken by the sound of the clock just down the hall from where they were standing. Its booming song rang out that it was striking the hour. Darcy unconsciously counted as the clock announced the hour. *One... two... three...* It continued on. *Ten... eleven... twelve.* Darcy stiffened, taking in a sharp breath.

He slowly lowered his head and Elizabeth felt the warmth of his breath near her ear, followed by a softly spoken voice, "Elizabeth, it is *tomorrow.*"

Elizabeth closed her eyes as she felt her world begin to spin. In a voice barely above a whisper, she asked, "Tomorrow?" however fully she believed herself to understand his meaning.

He lifted his right hand from her shoulder and picked up one of her curls again, causing her to arch her head toward it as she had done earlier, shivers of delight running through her and culminating at that point on her neck where his hand had lightly brushed up against it. This time, though, as her long, sleek neck was arched away from him, he slowly leaned down and kissed it. The unexpected touch of his lips on her neck suddenly drew all strength from her and in an instant she felt herself lose all equilibrium and fall back against him. Just as quickly, he reached around her waist to support her, and she struggled to regain some sense of strength and attempted to compose and right herself.

When he was confident that she was steady, he moved around her and stood between her and the window. The moonlight, which was now a full bright orb in the sky, was casting beams of light upon her face. Her eyes, though dark from the room, were reflecting the image of the moon deep within them.

He tried to control the quivering in his voice, "It is no longer Jane and Charles' wedding day."

Elizabeth looked toward him, but could not see him well as his face was turned away from the light. He slowly leaned down and gently placed a kiss on her cheek.

Darcy pulled away, steeling himself against the powerful longing to kiss her lips, when a noise at the end of the hall caught his attention. He looked back toward the hall, from which they had just come, and turned back to her.

"I think it would be best if we leave this part of the hall quickly." He resolutely, but gently, took her by the arm and they quickly proceeded down the length of the hallway that led to the stairs. He took her arm to escort her down, and she firmly grabbed the rail with her other hand.

They had taken but a few steps down, when Elizabeth momentarily stopped. Darcy, having taken two more steps down before coming to a stop himself, turned to see Elizabeth's flushed face looking down to him. He turned completely around to face her, and took a step back up, bringing him eye level to her. With much trepidation she stepped away from him up one step, but Darcy soon closed the gap again, bringing himself up to the step just below hers.

Darcy was again at eye level with her, and so close. Their eyes met and held. He slowly moved from admiring her eyes to her mouth. As she noticed this, she parted her lips slightly, as if knowing what was to come. Without much concern for who might see, he leaned over and captured her mouth with his, enveloping her in his embrace. He could feel her again go limp in his arms, and tightened his hold on her. After a few moments, he felt her hands come against his chest and she gently pulled herself away.

Her head went down on his shoulder, and she could hear his heavy, laboured breathing. She grabbed the stair rail again, and using it for support, she drew her head back.

Darcy breathed in deeply. "I beg you to forgive me, Miss Bennet, for my momentary lapse of judgment."

She took a few moments before looking back up at him, and with an unsuccessful attempt to disguise her trembling, said with a reassuring smile, "You have no need to apologize to me, Mr. Darcy, but I fear it would not be good to be discovered here together. I need a few moments; perhaps it would be best if you go down first, and then I shall come down after a few minutes."

He looked at her and smiled. "Do you think that I am in a better position to go down first?" He closed his eyes and breathed in a few deep breaths. "All right, Elizabeth, but do not wait too long. They are probably already wondering where the two of us are!" He picked up her hand and turned it over, gently kissing the inside of her palm. She swayed again, and marvelled at the swelling of emotion within her.

He turned and walked down the stairs, looking back up to her and smiling as he reached the turn. She stood still as she heard voices greet him downstairs. It was fairly quiet below as most people had likely departed. She took in some slow, deep breaths, smoothed her hair and felt her face. It was still fairly warm; she wondered how flushed she looked. She could only hope they had started extinguishing some of the candles and she could get outside quickly enough to escape anyone's notice.

When she came down moments later, her aunt and uncle were waiting and talking with Mr. Darcy. Mr. Hurst was asleep on a sofa, and Caroline eyed her suspiciously as she came down. She picked up her things, and came up to her aunt and uncle to let them know she was ready to leave.

Darcy escorted them outside to the waiting carriage. "Good night, Mr. and Mrs. Gardiner. Good night, Miss Bennet."

He stood back as he watched them enter the carriage. Mr. Gardiner, however, did not get in the cab with his wife and niece. "It is such a nice evening; I think I shall ride up on top with the driver."

Elizabeth watched in amazement as he did this, but soon realized they had most likely agreed to this ahead of time so her aunt could talk privately with her. Elizabeth turned and saw the very familiar all-knowing look on her aunt's face, reflected in the moonlight.

"Lizzy, I think we need to talk."

Chapter 20

Mrs. Gardiner compassionately took her niece's hand. "Lizzy, my dear, do you know what Mr. Darcy's intentions are toward you?"

Elizabeth pondered, in the darkness of the cab, how to respond. She knew that her aunt had a keen sense of observation and there was nothing she could say that would convince her otherwise, save the truth. But she wondered how much of the truth to tell.

She took in a deep breath and proceeded to share with her what her feelings toward him were. "It has been slow in coming, but I believe we share a mutual regard for each other."

"Has he told you as much?"

Elizabeth looked over at her. "Yes." She paused. "Dear Aunt, there is something that I never told anyone, except Jane. You knew that when I was at Kent visiting Charlotte, he came as well, visiting his aunt." She took in a deep breath. "While we were there…" She wondered at the wisdom in continuing, but in noticing her aunt's encouraging countenance, she decided to proceed. "While we were there, he offered me his hand in marriage, declaring his love for me."

"Heavens, Lizzy! Do you mean to tell me that you have been secretly engaged to him all this time?"

"No. No. We are not engaged. I turned him down."

"You turned…"

"Yes. You remember how we all thought him so proud and arrogant. And there were other things… I simply could *not* accept him."

"So my dear if that was the case, something has obviously prompted your feelings toward him to change. What brought this about?"

Elizabeth went on to tell her how, after she turned him down, he wrote her a letter to clarify some issues she had misunderstood. Then when Georgiana asked her to come to Pemberley and she heard the young lady talk so highly of her brother, in addition to spending a little time with him, gradually her feelings toward him began to change. And then, of course, there were the past few days.

Mrs. Gardiner patted her hand. "I would never have believed that he would have asked someone I knew, let alone a relation, to be his wife. Lizzy, I know what you thought of him before. I hope you fully comprehend what a good man he is. From what I have heard from acquaintances I still have in Lambton, he has always been highly regarded, but they have seen a notable difference in him even these past two months."

"I do believe him to be good, Aunt. It just took some rearranging of my perception of him; that is all. Tell me, Aunt, what *do* they say about him?"

"Recently he has taken to visiting folks in town with Miss Darcy. I even have on good authority, that he is in the process of helping start a school for the deaf in Derbyshire."

"Why he has not mentioned that to me at all!"

"I believe it could be because he does not want any credit for it."

"I had no idea."

"So, my dear, back to my original question, do you know what his intentions are?"

"He has asked to call tomorrow... I mean later today. It is possible he will make his intentions known then."

"Lizzy, I have observed the two of you together. I know that I am not your mother. I fear if your mother was aware of the little interactions I noticed between you two, she would behave in the most unrestrained manner to secure him as your husband."

"Oh, she would behave most abominably." Elizabeth laughed nervously. "I only hope she can contain herself when he comes later."

"I trust she will be faithful to herself, unfortunately. As much as I would like to be there, we will be leaving for home straightaway after services."

"I do wish you could be there to help calm the storm, if need be. By the way, Mr. Darcy paid you a compliment, Aunt."

"Did he?"

"Georgiana told him to watch other people as they responded to Mama, as he felt his reaction to her would not be most gracious. He told me that he found watching you calmly interact with her helped. He said you had a gift in dealing with her."

"Well, I have known her many years and I have come to know what sets her off and what calms her down. And Lizzy, I have known *you* for many years too. I do not doubt that he cares for you deeply. But do you love him?"

"I believe I do, Aunt. I believe I do."

~~*

When the sun first peeked over the horizon that morning, few in the Bennet household were ready to get up, after having such a busy day and long night. Elizabeth had not slept well; her heart not wanting to settle down throughout the night. At one point, early in the morning, she arose from her bed and walked to her window. She looked up at the full moon, high in the sky and smiled at the remembrance from the night before.

Now the sun was beckoning everyone to awaken, and she struggled to pull herself out of bed. She knew she had to get ready for services, but also at some point this morning, Jane and Charles would come by to bid their farewells as they left for their honeymoon. She sat at her dresser and brushed out her long, dark hair. With each long stroke, she recalled each word Darcy had said to her yesterday, each kiss he had bestowed on her.

After she had dressed, she came downstairs to get something to eat. She discovered that all but her two younger sisters were already in the dining room. "Good morning everyone," a glowing Elizabeth said.

"Good morning, Lizzy," her father spoke. He looked closely at her, not being able to recall when he had seen her look so content and at peace in at least several months.

Jane and Charles soon arrived and promptly were let in the house. Everyone greeted them with much enthusiasm. They could not stay long, but came in to take some tea with the Bennets and the Gardiners. Elizabeth noticed how happy Jane looked and she was glad.

As they all walked out, Jane came over and gave Elizabeth a hug. She had a very conspiratorial look in her eye as she pulled back from her and said, "It is so wonderful! I cannot wait until we can talk when we return!"

Elizabeth reacted with a start at Jane's words and looked at her in amazement. She narrowed her eyes as she contemplated what Jane could be referring to. *Certainly not.* Jane turned to join her husband in the carriage, and Elizabeth looked at her with utter surprise written across her face. The surprise was soon replaced with a smile as she lightly shook her head.

Later in the morning the whole Bennet clan attended church services. It had taken some delicate admonishing from Mrs. Gardiner, and some frantic flailing from Mrs. Bennet to get Kitty and Lydia up and ready in time, but it happened. As they arrived and met other church goers, Mrs. Bennet overflowed with raptures to everyone she met about how wonderful it was to have a married daughter, a son-in-law worth five thousand, and how lovely the wedding was, just in case that bit of information had escaped anyone's notice.

As they entered the church, Elizabeth made a quick survey to see if the Darcys were there, but she did not see them. They walked down toward the front of the church. With the Gardiners with them, the Bennets were barely able to squeeze into one pew.

Elizabeth would have preferred to sit further back so she could have seen people come in without having to look around. As the time for the service drew near, she concluded she would have to wait until afterwards to get the chance to see him.

The service began with a familiar song from the hymnal. In the midst of the song, she became aware of some latecomers moving into the pew behind them. A tap on her shoulder and she turned slightly to see Georgiana and her brother standing behind her, picking up the hymnal. Darcy looked over her shoulder to see what page number they were singing from. Although she knew the song by heart, suddenly she found herself scanning the page before her as his presence confounded her and she somehow could no longer recollect what the next words were.

The minister came up to the front and announced that they were blessed to have a visiting minister that morning who would share the message, a Reverend George Austen.

At the close of his sermon, he entered into a time of prayer, asking his daughter to come up and lead the congregation in a prayer she had written.

She began, *"Father of Heaven, whose goodness has brought us in safety this day, dispose our hearts in fervent prayer. Another day is now beginning, and added to those, for which we were before accountable. Teach us Almighty Father, to consider this solemn truth, as we should do, that we may feel the importance of every day, and every hour as it passes, and earnestly strive to make a better use of what thy goodness may yet bestow on us, than we have done of the time past.*

"Give us grace to endeavour after a truly Christian spirit to seek to attain that temper of forbearance and patience of which our blessed saviour has set us the highest example; and which, while it prepares us for the spiritual happiness of the life to come, will secure to us the best enjoyment of what this world can give. Incline us oh God! to think humbly of ourselves, to be severe only in the examination of our own conduct, to consider our fellow-creatures with kindness, and to judge of all they say and do with that charity which we would desire from them ourselves.

"We thank thee with all our hearts for every gracious dispensation, for all the blessings that have attended our lives, for every hour of safety, health and peace, of domestic comfort and innocent enjoyment. We feel that we have been blessed far beyond any thing that we have deserved; and though we cannot but pray for a continuance of all these mercies, we acknowledge our unworthiness of them and implore thee to pardon the presumption of our desires.

"Keep us, oh Heavenly Father, from evil this day. Bring us in safety to the beginning of another day and grant that we may rise again with every serious and religious feeling which now directs us.

"May thy mercy be extended over all mankind, bringing the ignorant to the knowledge of thy truth, awakening the impenitent, touching the hardened. Look with compassion upon the afflicted of every condition, assuage the pangs of disease, comfort the broken in spirit.

"More particularly do we pray for the safety and welfare of our own family and friends wheresoever dispersed, beseeching thee to avert from them all material and lasting evil of body or mind; and may we by the assistance of thy holy spirit so conduct ourselves on earth as to secure an eternity of happiness with each other in thy heavenly kingdom. Grant this most merciful Father, for the sake of our blessed saviour in whose holy name and words we further address thee." *

After the prayer, the congregation stood up to leave, touched by the words of this young lady, Jane Austen.

Darcy waited for Elizabeth to step out of the pew and then he stepped out behind her. As they walked out, they greeted the visiting minister, and Darcy watched as Georgiana walked over to talk with his daughter. Once outside, everyone gathered together and spoke. They parted to leave and Darcy remarked to Elizabeth that he would be over to see her directly, and he then walked over to join his sister.

After church, the Gardiners left directly to return to London. They all bid their farewells, and Mrs. Gardiner particularly singled Elizabeth out to hug her and give her some encouragement. "Lizzy, I will be thinking of you today, and will keep you in my prayers. I look forward to hearing from you soon."

Elizabeth wondered if she was making something bigger out of this day than it really was, yet if she were to think about it clearly, what happened between her and Darcy last night *was* significant. Suddenly everything between them had changed!

Elizabeth told her parents on the way home from church that Darcy was coming over to call on her. She had not told them earlier, as she did not want her mother behaving erratically around him any more than need be. But telling her now would give her time to calm down before his arrival. Her father took it in stride, but deep inside he was greatly hoping Darcy would seek him out later to have a talk with him. He was not blind to the change that had taken place between his favourite daughter and this man. He could tell she was quite taken by him. His only fear was that she might in some way get hurt.

When Darcy finally arrived, the ladies were seated in the drawing room. Mr. Bennet had been outside when he arrived, and greeted him, escorting him in. He then retreated to his study. Darcy came in and politely sat down with the ladies. Elizabeth watched her mother nervously shifting in her chair. She knew that some kind of embarrassing prattle was imminent. Darcy nervously looked about, trying to ascertain just how long he needed stay here to be proper, but wanting desperately to go out and walk with Elizabeth.

Finally, feeling she could contain herself no longer, her mother said, "Mr. Darcy, you do not know how much we have come to consider you and your sister a part of our family. We want you to know that anytime you come to visit your friend Bingley, you are welcome here as well."

"Thank you, ma'am," was his cordial reply. "May I extend the same invitation to you to visit Pemberley?"

"That is so kind and considerate of you, Sir. Ever since my daughters came home from their visit there and spoke so highly of it, I have so greatly desired to see it! I understand it is grand; simply grand!"

"Any time, ma'am."

Suddenly it appeared a light went off in her mother's head. "You know, it is such a beautiful day; such a pity to waste it indoors. You two ought to go out for a walk." As she said this, she literally pulled Elizabeth up from the chair she was in, and practically shooed them toward the door. Her brash behaviour heightened Elizabeth's anxiety. It was most apparent that she was conniving to get them alone, for the sole purpose, she was sure, to give him the opportunity to ask for her hand in marriage. Elizabeth was not even sure that was on his mind, and only hoped he would overlook any unseemliness on her mother's part.

But Darcy was all too willing to take her up on this, and although inwardly chided her mother for her behaviour, was grateful for it. The last thing he had wanted to do was to spend the day with Elizabeth as her mother and sisters looked over his shoulder.

When they stepped outdoors, Elizabeth sensed that Darcy relaxed considerably. She pursed her lips in amusement as she considered what an effort it must be for him to behave tolerably around her mother. They walked slowly down the lane and across to the walking path that led to Oakham Mount, keeping a proper degree of distance between them while they were still in view of the house.

When they reached the base of the mount, where the path began its gentle slope upwards, Darcy offered his arm to Elizabeth. This time when she took it, she wrapped her hand around his arm snugly, and brought her other hand over atop hers. Darcy, not to be outdone by Elizabeth, then brought his free hand over, covering both of hers with his. They walked in silence for awhile, occasionally noting some pleasing or unusual flower or tree, but mostly basking in the warmth of each other's presence.

Along the way, Darcy spoke of Georgiana. "Did you see how Georgiana spoke to the visiting reverend's daughter after services?"

"Yes, I did."

"She would have never done that two months ago. She would have been too shy. She really enjoyed talking to her. Apparently she is a writer. She encouraged Georgiana to keep writing in her journal, as that is what Miss Austen has always done."

Elizabeth smiled. "I think your sister is growing up."

"I think my sister has grown up a lot as a result of your help."

Elizabeth tried to protest, but Darcy reached over and gently covered her mouth with his fingers. "You gave her encouragement and practical advice. She took it, especially the advice to write in a journal. She writes in it all the time."

"She told you about that?" Elizabeth asked flustered.

"Yes, she did."

When they reached the summit, they walked over to the place they had rested a few days before. Elizabeth sat down on a large boulder, and Darcy squeezed next to her. He took both of her hands in his, and proceeded to nervously stroke her hands with his thumb. Elizabeth thought to herself that she liked this nervous habit of his, as long as he had her hand in his.

"Elizabeth, you know that for some time now, my feelings for you have been of the highest regard. In my previous attempt to secure your hand..."

Elizabeth interjected, "Oh, please, do not mention that! I do not want to be reminded of the terrible things I said!"

"No, it was I who said the most abhorrent things. I cannot believe I said some of those things in my offer of marriage. But I was very presumptuous and arrogant. I was not worthy of your hand in the least. Your refusal to my offer was the best thing that ever happened to me. It caused me to really look at myself. That was not always easy because I did not like what I saw. I knew you were right and I had to change, although I did not really know how."

He had been looking down at their hands, and now looked up at her. "Elizabeth, I still love you more than life itself. I would give anything to have your love in return." He paused, taking a deep breath. "Do I dare... would it be asking too much... can I even suppose... Elizabeth, I *do* ask you again, knowing full well that I am not worthy of such an exceptional woman. Would you consent to be my wife?" When he got the last of his words out, he held in the last of his breath, awaiting her answer.

She looked at him very sombrely. "The last time you offered your hand in marriage, I said I could not oblige you an acceptance. I still cannot."

Darcy started, the colour draining from his face. He started to draw his hand from hers.

Elizabeth responded by reaching out to retrieve it. "I could never marry a man out of obligation, no matter who he was. I shall only marry for love. Therefore, I will only accept your offer of marriage because I love you. I do love you with all my heart!"

Darcy looked at her, afraid he may have not understood her. "So, your answer is… yes?"

She nodded. "To know that you are still willing to ask for my hand when I have put you through so much, is very humbling indeed. I would be very happy… no, I would be eternally happy, to be your wife. Yes, I *do* most wholeheartedly accept."

Suddenly he felt the tension that had been building up inside of him recede. His mouth curved upwards into a smile that came from the depths of him.

He reached into his pocket and pulled out a ring. "This was my grandmother's ring. It was left to me to give to my intended." He opened Elizabeth's hand, and gently slid the ring onto her ring finger. "It seems to have been made just for you."

She smiled as she looked at her ring. "It is *so* beautiful!" She looked up from the ring into Darcy's face. She took her hand and slowly traced her fingers across his face, inducing him to bring his hand up to capture hers against his cheek. From there he brought it around to his lips and left impressions of kisses in it.

"You have made me the happiest of men. I love you, Lizbeth." He leaned toward her, anxious to seal their engagement with a proper kiss.

Elizabeth drew back, amused. "No one has ever called me that before!"

"Do you object to my calling you that?" he asked, feigning impatience.

"No, I like it. I have been called Elizabeth, Lizzy, Eliza, but never Lizbeth." She looked up into his eyes. "And what would you have me call you? Fitzwilliam?"

Darcy squeezed her hands, but drew back a little. "Anything but Fitzwilliam. I usually only get called Fitzwilliam when I am in trouble. Now, I know that I may often find myself in trouble with you, so you may just end up calling me that all the time anyway."

Elizabeth teased him and answered, "I shall have to think about this, Sir. The name I call my husband must reflect a certain love and respect, but also an affectionate friendliness." After a moment's pause, she said, "I think I shall call you Will."

"And that is a name that I am not often called. But I shall like you calling me that." He drew close to her again. "Now, where were we?"

He brought his hand up to her face again, stroking her cheek and her lips with his fingers. She closed her eyes as he leaned over and kissed her, wrapping his arms tightly around her.

Darcy pulled himself away, and running his fingers along her neck and into her hair said, "Do you think we could get married in, say, three weeks?"

Elizabeth was suddenly shocked out of her reverie. "Three weeks?"

"Charles and Jane have left and will be gone for two weeks. I would like to get married the week after they return."

Elizabeth suddenly realized that Jane left and she could not tell her of their engagement. "Oh, Jane! How I wish I could tell her. How I wish Jane knew!"

"She does."

Elizabeth looked at him, startled. "I told Charles this morning before they left that I was going to ask for your hand today. I wanted to ask him to stand up for me so he would not tarry in their return. Now, I do not want you to think I was being presumptuous again of your consent. I did tell him this would only happen if you accepted. I told him he could tell Jane, and she would most likely know in her heart whether or not you would agree to be my wife."

Suddenly Elizabeth started to laugh, laugh so hard that she could not speak. Darcy asked her, "What is so funny? Was it something I said?"

"No, nothing you said. It was something my sister said."

"What did she say?"

"Oh, I do not think I can tell you!" Elizabeth said between uncontrollable laughs.

"I may just have to hold you here until you tell me, Lizbeth." He wrapped his arms around her tightly.

"I really should not." Finally Elizabeth calmed down enough to speak. Darcy looked at her curiously, and she knew he would not relent until she told him.

"Jane came up to me this morning just before they left and she whispered in my ear, 'It is so wonderful! I cannot wait until we can talk when we return!' I was a little shocked that she would say something like that. She was obviously talking about the fact that you were going to propose. Apparently she was not talking about what *I* thought she was talking about!"

"And just what *did* you think she was referring to?"

Elizabeth blushed and found herself at a loss for words.

Darcy pulled her up against his chest, and quipped, "Perhaps you thought she was referring to breakfast at Netherfield? It is quite an experience!" He held her close for a few minutes, Elizabeth drowning in the strength of his chest and his manly scent and smiling at his little display of humour.

"So what do you say about marrying in three weeks?" he asked in her ear.

"Just three weeks?"

"Is that too soon for you?"

"No, not for me. But to plan a wedding, I do not know."

"It does not have to be elaborate. Jane and Charles' wedding was simple, yet very nice."

"Yes, really all I would need to have made was my dress. We could use much of the same things from Jane and Charles' wedding."

"Anything would make me happy. I think now, Lizbeth, that all that is left is for me to go talk with your father."

"And we can only hope that you can get in to see him without my mother noticing. I really would prefer to tell her after you have left."

"I thought you were convinced that I could handle your mother."

"Not when she becomes totally irrational and incoherent. And that is only when something good has happened."

"To be honest, when I met your father outside when I arrived, I asked him if I could meet with him when I returned from walking with you. He said he would watch for me and meet me outside."

"I am of the opinion that the two of you think alike!"

They turned to walk arm in arm back to the house. "Lizbeth, after I talk with your father and we settle the date, I will need to return to Pemberley for a short while."

Upon hearing these words, Elizabeth sighed. He continued, "I have a project I am working on that needs some immediate attention. I cannot stay on at Netherfield with Bingley away and his sisters there. Georgiana will stay and looks forward to visiting with you."

"I shall miss you, Will."

How those words touched his heart. "I shall miss you, too, Lizbeth. But, I shall have a little token of yours to keep close to my heart." He reached in his pocket and pulled out her handkerchief. "Unless you demand it back, again."

"No, you may keep it," she laughed.

"Earlier, when we talked of Georgiana and her journal...I have a confession to make regarding that."

"Please do not tell me you sneak in and read what she has written!"

"No, nothing like that. I began keeping one also." Elizabeth's eyes widened. "I do not use it for the same purposes as Georgiana, but it has helped me to see things in a different light, to make goals and take steps to reach those goals; to improve myself."

"I am impressed."

He turned and brought her chin up to look at him. "You do not know how much of everything that has transpired these last two months are a direct result of you. When Georgiana first told me you were at Pemberley when I awoke after my accident, I was still confused and hurt; my pride was completely destroyed. But I still loved you and that love moved me in ways I would never have imagined. And with all that you did for Georgiana, she, in turn, did for me, in opening my eyes to things." He leaned over and gently kissed her. "My dearest loveliest, Lizbeth!"

* The prayer is actually a prayer of Jane Austen's. Her father was a clergyman, and this was a prayer she wrote. I changed just a few of the words to make it appropriate for the setting in the story.

Epilogue

The two weeks went by quickly for Elizabeth as plans were quickly made for the wedding. She longed to see Darcy again, but was grateful to keep busy. She had immediately gone to see Charlotte after Darcy departed and told her that it would be best if she did not return to Hunsford with her husband, as things would only get worse with Lady Catherine once she heard of their upcoming marriage. Charlotte made an excuse to her husband that she would like to stay an additional three weeks, and sent him on his way. She agreed that if she had returned with him, he would most likely forbid her to return to attend their wedding if Lady Catherine forbade it.

When Jane and Charles returned, Elizabeth was grateful to have her support and help deflect her mother's excitable behaviour. She was most anxious for Darcy to return, and eagerly greeted him on Monday, the week of the wedding.

Plans went along smoothly and each day crept slowly toward the anticipated day. The last week had the added stress of final preparations, and Mrs. Bennet felt it severely. The Gardiners returned Wednesday, which helped Elizabeth in dealing with her mother.

Darcy had written to his relations, including Lady Catherine, but he did not hear back from her. He only assumed she would refuse to attend the wedding, sending a very loud statement to him of her disapproval. He was sent words of congratulations from Colonel Fitzwilliam's family, and he was grateful they were all able to take the time to come to the wedding.

There were two things that Darcy insisted on taking care of for the wedding. One was the flowers. When Elizabeth first walked into the church on her wedding day, the number of flowers and the scent that permeated the whole room overwhelmed her. He had ordered gardenias from all over the country and even from the continent. There were some that were still potted, others cut and in arrangements, and still elsewhere there were loose petals around.

The other thing he insisted on was where they would spend their first night. He was not about to spend it at Netherfield. He made arrangements at a nearby inn that had small separate bungalows. He picked out one in particular overlooking a small lake. From there they would travel across to the continent to France and visit places Elizabeth had only read about.

The day before the wedding, Elizabeth felt deluged with plans, decisions, details, and her mother. Darcy unexpectedly came by in the middle of the afternoon and asked if they could go out for one of their walks. They both knew where they would go and soon were up at Oakham Mount.

Darcy pulled out a package and presented it to her. "What is this?" she asked.

"It is my wedding gift to you."

"My wedding gift? You want me to open it now?"

"Yes, right now."

She slowly opened the box and first pulled out a folded handkerchief. She unfolded it, and found it to be very similar to her other one, but lacked the embroidered initials and flowers. "This must be to replace my other one?"

"Yes. But you will notice this one is missing something."

"Yes, my initials!"

"And what are your initials?"

"*EB*! You know that!"

"And what will they be tomorrow?"

Suddenly her eyes lit up. "*ED*," she said with a beaming smile.

"So it seems that you would need to embroider another one with your new initials."

"That was very sweet of you."

"There's something else in there."

She looked in the box, moving paper aside, and found a bottle. She pulled it out and looked at it. "Perfume!"

"Gardenia scent perfume."

"I have never had real perfume before."

"Well, then, there is something you must know." He took the bottle from her and opened it. Taking his ring finger, he put a drop of perfume on it and brought it up to her neck, lightly drawing it down. "You only need a little bit, and it will last a long time." He put another drop on, and brought it to her wrist. Putting the bottle down, he then nestled his head against her neck, breathing in the tantalizing scent.

"Lizbeth, you are, indeed, the fragrance of my life. I love you so much!"

Elizabeth wrapped her arms around him, answering, "I love you, too, Will. I love you too!"

The Wedding Day

Fitzwilliam Darcy stood at the front of the church, his mind giddy, his body restless, and his impatience displaying itself in more than one visible way. He shifted his weight from one foot to another; his hands either tightly gripped together or when separated, he rubbed his fingers raw. His breaths were deep, yet controlled. Despite all these things, his eyes remained set on the centre aisle at the back of the church, waiting for his first glimpse of the woman for whom he had so longingly, and for such a long time, awaited.

The church was full, but he could not bring himself to look out at the guests. To know that every eye was upon him was disconcerting. He knew that once his bride, Elizabeth Bennet, came up the aisle to join him at his side, she would garner everyone's notice and he could be more at ease, at least in that regard.

His younger sister, Georgiana, was seated in the front with his cousin, Col. Richard Fitzwilliam, and his family. He knew the Bennet family was in attendance to his right -- the three younger sisters and Mrs. Bennet. Charles was standing up for him; presently at his side. Jane was to stand up for Elizabeth.

Darcy inhaled the fragrance of the gardenias that filled the church. With the flower and fragrance being the favourite of both his mother and his beloved Elizabeth, he could have no other.

Darcy had grown oblivious to the music playing in the background, but suddenly it changed and he realized the moment was drawing near. He saw Jane Bingley step out into the centre aisle and begin her procession up to the front. Next to him, he heard the intake of breath from Charles and he knew, without glancing over at him, that a grin from ear to ear was most likely deeply embedded upon his friend's face.

Darcy took in some deliberate, deep breaths as he knew the moment was imminent. The sun was shining in through the back door and he was able to see two figures emerge. His heart pounded incessantly as he waited for his first glimpse of her. They were somewhat shadowed by the glare of the sun, but suddenly, as they took their initial steps inside the door, the white of Elizabeth's dress took on an ethereal glow and everything else around her disappeared.

Darcy gazed upon her as though she were the only other person in the church. She radiated with love and beauty. He had always been intoxicated by her beauty, but he was certain she had never looked more beautiful than she did this day.

As she slowly came toward him, escorted by her father, Darcy had to resist the urge to bridge the gap between them by striding out to meet her. He forced himself to wait patiently for her, as he continually had to learn to do since first becoming acquainted with her. But now his patience would pay off, in that within the next hour, she would become Mrs. Fitzwilliam Richard Darcy.

As Mr. Bennet handed his favourite daughter to the man who would be her husband, he leaned over and gave her a kiss. His heart was swelling with love and admiration for her and respect and esteem for his soon to be son-in-law. He could not ask for a finer man to marry his Lizzy, although he had not always held such favourable thoughts toward him.

Darcy reached out for his Elizabeth's arm and she smiled at him; a smile that seemed to reach to the depths of her. He returned one back in her direction as they turned to face Reverend Burbridge, who was to marry them. As Elizabeth took Darcy's arm, she treasured in her heart the fact that this man was soon to be her husband. Darcy was dizzy with rapture as the woman who had so captured his heart was finally to be his.

The End!

Kara Louise lives in Kansas with her husband.
They share their 10 acres with
an ever changing menagerie of animals.
They have one married son who also likes to write.

Other published books by Kara Louise

"Drive and Determination"

"Pemberley's Promise"

"Master Under Good Regulation"

and

"Assumed Obligation"

Visit her website,

www.ahhhs.net

where you will other stories

written by her and Australian author, Sharni.